WILD WOLVES

WILD WOLVES

WOLFPACKS OF SHADOW MOON ISLAND, BOOK ONE

By

GINNA MORAN

SUNNY PALMS PRESS

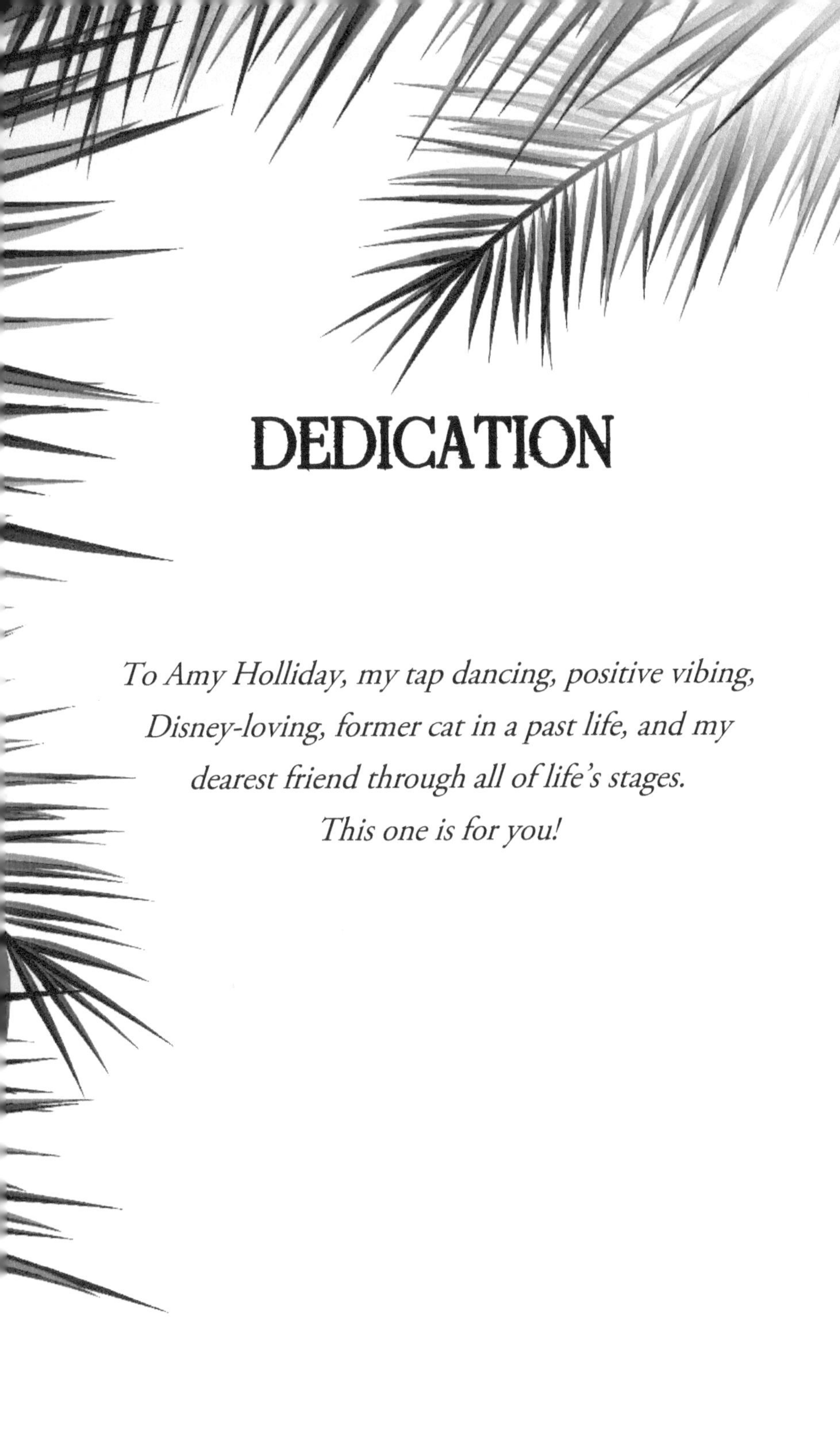

DEDICATION

*To Amy Holliday, my tap dancing, positive vibing,
Disney-loving, former cat in a past life, and my
dearest friend through all of life's stages.
This one is for you!*

CHAPTER 1

Eliana

CAPTURED

I CAN'T BREATHE. The bag tied over my head blocks out the world around me. Voices hum in my ear, mostly crying and praying. I don't know how long we've been bound in this place, but I think we're moving. My stomach flips and flops, reminding me of the time I went on a day cruise just off the coast of California. The water was rough then, and it feels like we rise and drop in the same way.

Fuck. I hope I don't get sick. If I get sick, I'll probably die. Drowned in my own disgusting body fluids.

"Shut the hell up. Screaming isn't going to do anything. We need to think. These fuckers haven't been here in at least an hour, according to my watch chime. If one of us can manage to get untied, we can free the rest. There's enough of us to fight back," the feminine voice whispers lowly, dragging my attention away from my rolling stomach.

"You don't think I've been trying? These chains can't be broken." The man beside me groans under his breath. His movements, bumping into me every couple of minutes, haven't helped my motion sickness. "I've been working on trying to loosen the screw of the anchor ring, but it's tight."

"Chains? I don't have chains. Who else doesn't have chains?" the woman asks, her voice sounding over the sudden silence falling through the air. "I swear if it's all of us wo—"

"Seriously? You're about to get up in arms about not having chains?" someone snaps.

"I'm sorry. I'm just so pissed. I shouldn't be here. They caught me off guard all because of a damn piece of gum stuck to my shoe." The woman stops talking, though I wish she didn't. She was surprised like me and attacked too. No one responds to her, letting her wallow in her thoughts.

That's when I hear it. The roar of the ocean. I was right. We're being relocated by water. But where to? Why? Shit. This can't be happening. I've heard of the stories of women getting kidnapped and trafficked. I always thought I was careful and aware. I've always had to be, but especially lately with my crappy luck.

It takes everything in me to keep my shit together.

The last thing I expected tonight was to have been attacked and kidnapped. And obviously, the same goes for everybody else here. I don't know how the bastards managed to snatch so many of us, but I hear at least ten different voices.

"Don't feel bad," a different man says, speaking up. "They caught me with a damn paper on my windshield. Like what the fuck?"

If only I had a chance to think about a paper on a windshield or gum on my shoe. I had a date with a new client who was supposed to help me get back on my feet. But I think I was set up. My captors jumped from a utility van so quickly and grabbed me from right outside the hotel I was meeting Joseph at. I thought it was finally my luck changing since he insisted that I call him by his first name on the phone instead of something else like the other potential clients I had spoken with.

I had no time to prepare or scream. My pepper spray was useless. So were all the self-defense moves I've been practicing since shit went bad with Mr. Beck last summer, and he...I can't think about it. I've never been so thankful to have a man underestimate how much fight I have in me. Not like it helped now. I guess I got too comfortable being alone. It's when I'm not that I've always worried.

"And to answer your question, I don't have chains either," the man murmurs, sounding like he comes from my right now that I focus.

"I do. Looks like you were wrong," another woman's voice says. "Maybe they gave us fighters something harder. They probably thought it was unnecessary if they managed to get you for gum and him for a damn paper on the windshield. I left that shit in place. They dragged me from my car at a light."

The first woman huffs. "Whatever. Normal people—"

"Shhh! They'll hear you. Now is not the fucking time to get angry that you don't have fucking chains. Be grateful." Metal clinks metal as the man to my left shakes his restraints.

I wish I didn't have this bag on my head. I desperately want to see what's going on and who these voices belong to.

"Don't—"

"I have chains and wasn't fighting," I say, cutting the woman off. I force my mouth to work, despite the roiling pain in my stomach. "I'm also restrained to the wall. I think they just used rope when they ran out of chains. What about everyone else? Are you guys in chains?" I don't know why I ask and interrupt, but it helps with my panic and anxiety arising from the others arguing.

A couple of yeses and two no's sound through the air, confirming my speculation. There's no strategy set in place to how we've been bound.

A deep groan hums close by. "This is pointless. We need to think about what we're going to do and how we are going to get the fuck out of this. It doesn't matter who was bound by what. We all need to stick together. They can't take on all of us."

"Stick together? Fuck that. I'm not sacrificing my damn self for you assholes," another man says. "You're a bunch of damn crybabies."

The world suddenly rises and falls again, and I screech at the sensation of my heart flying into my throat. I'm certain we're on a boat now. The motion and the sound of the waves coming through the air clue me into as much.

And I'm terrified. I knew I was being trafficked, but I still had hope until now. Why else would our captors bind us and relocate us somewhere like this? They're taking us to sell or something. I might've had a shitty life and made my living in unconventional ways, but at least I was in control. I had a say. I was in charge. But this?

Fuck my life.

No one will even miss me being gone. I haven't talked to my dad's sister since...I can't remember. I haven't managed to keep any sort of nine-to-five job at all in the last two years. And if my new client even thinks twice about me before moving on to someone else...it won't matter. I'll be dead by then.

"Fuck. I think we are getting close to shore," a man mutters, stealing my attention from my thoughts.

"We're on a boat?"

"Oh, God. Help us."

"Everyone, shut up."

"I don't want to die."

The voices mingle and sound through the air. I try not to pant, but my breaths are hard to come by as I hyperventilate. Fear clenches my body, and my chest tightens. The world lifts and drops again, and I can't stop myself from screaming. The bag sucks against my mouth, and I cough, my terror grabbing hold of me and refusing to let go. I rattle my chains and fight against the bindings. I will fight with my last breath. I'm not going to be a slave. I'd rather die than face this sort of life.

"Someone help her. She's freaking out." The voice sounds muffled as it reaches me.

"Hey, lady. What's your name? Tell us your name." The deep, velvety voice wraps around me, trying to break through the pounding in my head.

I still can't manage to calm down. I'm having a panic attack. I feel like I'm going to die at any second.

"Listen, we're going to be okay. We will stick together. Don't mind that one asshole. We can shove him to these monsters first if he doesn't want to stick by us." Something touches my leg. It's not a hand but another leg. The person tries to grab my attention with their body. "Do you feel that? I'm a runner. I'm strong as hell and can protect you."

Another man laughs in exasperation. "Are you gonna pick

my ass up too?"

"Depends on if you're hot. Do you put out? I make ass-holes like you work for it. Only ladies get things for free," the runner responds.

It's my turn to laugh. And with my sharp inhalation, I puff the fabric away from my mouth as I breathe out.

"Keep talking, you two. It's working." This man's voice comes out softly as if he's afraid to speak up.

"You like the idea of me being chivalrous to this pansy-ass, don't you? What's your name, lady? I'm Chase." The man nudges me with his body, the heat of his skin helping me overcome my panic attack.

I clear my throat. "Eliana."

Chase doesn't get the chance to respond as the world lifts and drops again. A couple of people scream, and I tense, bracing myself. Silence falls over us apart from the sound of the waves.

Someone whistles, the sharp noise stinging my ears. My heart smashes against my ribs, trying to throw itself out of me. I can't blame it. I kind of wish something like that could happen. I'm terrified. Whoever whistles is commanding some-one…no, something. A cool, wet nose touches my arm, and an animal steps right onto my lap. I cringe and recoil, my fear making me whimper. I think it's a dog. Maybe a guard dog of some sort.

"What? You're not going to fight? You're just gonna let

the big bad wolf tear your face off?" The deep voice startles me, and I feel teeth nip at the front of my shirt. "I expected more."

I gasp, afraid that I'm about to be mauled to death. "Please, don't do this."

A laugh cackles through the air, and a deep growl reverberates through my bones. The heavy paws of the dog shift, and something tugs at the head covering. I scream as it's ripped off, and I come face-to-face with a gray, black, and white canine...a wolf? Holy shit. I think it's a wolf. I can't be certain, but it's no dog.

The wolf bares its teeth at me, growling again. I struggle against my chains, despite it being pointless. I just can't sit still. I never expected this could possibly be how I'd die.

A shadow crosses over me as a man comes up behind the wolf. "What do you think? Is she a good one? You want to go on a hunt for this one?" A hunt? Fuck me.

Tears burn my eyes, threatening to spill onto my cheeks. I flick my gaze away from the wolf to look around. There are two other men standing in front of an elevator. We're not on a dingy, old vessel like I expected. And while this cell looks like a disgusting prison, the elevator gleams with metals and marble. This must be a luxury yacht. I've been on one with Mr. Beck before he thought I was more his property than anything else.

The wolf growls again. If I didn't know any better, I'd think it was responding to the man. Whether or not the guttural noise is a good response? I have no idea.

Bending down, the man shoves the wolf off me and onto who I think is Chase. But his head is still covered. Everyone's heads are. No one speaks or tries to move. No one threatens or fights. It's the only thing that keeps me complacent. If I act out, they might use me as an example, and that wolf looks ready to devour me on command.

"Listen up, Eliana. I'm going to unhook you from the wall. You're going to go with those nice gentlemen over there. You will strip out of your clothes and do as you're told. Do you understand? If you don't, this big boy will do it for you. And he's not gentle with his teeth, if you know what I mean." The man looks at the wolf and scratches his fingers between his ears.

My stomach flips, and I sniffle, the idea of being forced to undress in front of strangers is terrifying and humiliating. I can only think the worst. I'm being sold into sex slavery. I know it. Why else would he demand such a thing?

He grabs my chin, forcing me to look at him. "Did you hear me? I need you to answer when you're spoken to, Eliana."

It dawns on me that he knows my name. How the fuck does he know my name? This must not have been random. Maybe I've been stalked. Fuck.

I slowly nod my head. I can't find my voice to speak.

I expect him to yell, but he accepts the gestured answer and removes the chains. My wrists throb, and it hurts to move my arms, my shoulders aching from being in the same position for what feels like hours.

Extending his arm, he proffers his hand, and I have no choice but to take it. He drags me to my feet and studies me, the roll of the boat making it hard to stay composed. It also doesn't help that my body trembles.

And then he slaps me on the ass, pushing me toward the two silent, muscular men at the elevator.

Without another word to me, the man moves on to the next person. I don't get a chance to see what Chase looks like because one of the men on the elevator snatches my hands and yanks me onto it. Tears run down my cheeks, and my mouth quivers. Neither of them says anything as they hit the button to send the elevator to the deck.

I whisper a prayer, my whole body cold. I'm afraid to see where I am. I'm afraid of what happens next as the elevator door opens. Bright sunshine streaks across the posh yacht, and the salty sea breeze drifts around me. I automatically gulp in a deep breath, trying my best not to lose my shit.

"All right, Eliana. Strip. Everything must come off." The other man, the one not gripping my wrists, gets in front of me and gives me a once-over. "Don't be shy. I won't hurt you."

That's what they always fucking say in the movies. But I'm already hurt. I'm terrified, and I know that once my clothes come off…

I dart my gaze toward the side of the boat and spot an island not too far away. I'm a good enough swimmer that I know I can make it. I have to try. There's no fucking way I'm stripping down for these men and doing as I'm told. I need to escape.

Without thinking, I sprint toward the side of the boat and climb the rungs. One of the men shouts my name, but I ignore him. I nearly fall from the side of the boat but manage to launch myself a couple feet away. The world blurs around me. I brace myself to hit the water. It swallows me, and I kick my legs and stay under for as long as I can. I don't care which direction I swim as long as I get enough space between me and the boat. Maybe I'll have a fighting chance. I'll never know if I don't just do it.

My lungs burn, and my vision shadows. The salt irritates my eyes, but the water is clear enough to see somewhat as I swim. A shadow of a boat flies over me, and I panic, releasing the breath I'm holding. I have no choice but to kick toward the sunlight. I just need one breath. One breath and I can get farther away. Maybe they won't catch me. If I make it to the beach, I can run. I could hide and wait for them to give up.

Breaking through the surface, I gasp for breath and fling my hair out of my face, rubbing my arm across my eyes to clear my vision. I spin around and catch sight of the yacht a couple dozen feet away. The current grabs me, and I stay with it, using it to pull me along.

"There she is! Portside!" a masculine voice shouts over a megaphone.

I groan and splash my way in the direction of the shore. If I can get close enough, I can body surf and ride the waves to the sand.

Diving under, I freestyle swim, pushing my body to its limits. My shoulders ache, and tightness clutches my chest. It's hard to focus. I just want to escape. I have to escape.

Once again, I have to surface, my lungs aching to breathe. I spin underwater and look up at the glittering surface above, trying to catch sight of the small, motorized raft.

It can't be far away from me since I'm not a fast swimmer.

I spot it next to the yacht again. What the hell? They've given up on trying to get me. Instead, I watch as the man from the cell guides a couple prisoners onto the raft. They're all naked and some of them cry. I can't believe this is truly happening.

I don't wait long enough to see them step aboard the raft. Turning toward the island, I kick my arms and legs, swimming in even, consistent strokes. I do my best to save my energy. The moment I can touch the sandy bottom, I'm going to run for it.

The waves lift me up and drop me the closer I get to shore, and I manage to catch one and ride it until my knees hit the sand. White foam engulfs me, and I plant my palms on the sandy beach. My chest heaves with every breath I take. I can hardly see anything, the sun shining too brightly and reflecting off the glittering sand.

I whip my head around and try to figure out which

direction to head. My best bet is to enter the rainforest only two dozen feet away.

I don't know what kind of animals reside here, but I'm more terrified of the monsters on the yacht. I'll just stay near the beach but out of view. I just need somewhere to hide. I'm only one person. I can't imagine them wasting time doing whatever the fuck they plan to do.

A deep, guttural growl reverberates across my back, sending a shiver through me. I inhale a sharp breath and spin on the balls of my feet, watching as a wolf bounds from the waves, sopping wet. That can't be. This can't fucking be happening.

The sight of the aggressive animal kicks me into action, and I rush toward the trees and the first rock I see. I swivel and chuck it at the wolf, hitting it in the face. It yelps and skids across the sand, slowing down.

Bending over, I scoop up another smooth rock and yell, "Stay away! Get out of here!"

I never in my wildest dreams expected I would confront a wolf like this, but I don't know what else to do. I can't be weak. I can't allow it to see me as prey.

Jerking my arm back, I thrust my hand forward and chuck a rock at the wolf again. It launches from the sand to avoid my attack and heads toward the trees. I lose sight of it. Fear clutches me, and I spin and dart in the opposite direction.

Something heavy collides into me, not even letting me get more than six feet away from my spot. The wolf knocks me off my feet and lands on my chest, growling in my face. I swing out my arms, punching at the wolf. It jumps off me and rams its big head into my side, rolling me over.

I can't do anything as it locks its teeth to the back of my shirt and tears at my clothes. Another growl sounds through the air, and I struggle and try to shove the wolf off only to have another one lunge at me, snapping its teeth into my pant leg. I scream and fight, trying my best to get the beasts away from me, but I'm not strong enough. The wolves tear at my clothing, nipping at my skin, sending pain radiating through my body. But they don't maul me. They never sink their fangs into any of my limbs or make me bleed.

A whistle sounds over my shouts, and the wolves fall away, leaving me lying in the sand crying, my clothes now ripped to shreds and scattered in pieces around me. I've never been so exposed in my life.

"Eliana, what did I tell you?" The man from the yacht kicks sand at me as he approaches. "You just made it that much harder on yourself."

I don't have a chance to get up to run. The man links his fingers through my hair and yanks me from the ground. He snatches a bag from his hip and pulls it back over my head. The sunshine cuts away. He throws me onto his shoulder, and I flail, attempting to fight.

But it's no use. He's too strong.

My life might end here.

CHAPTER 2

Eliana

NAKED AND AFRAID

"PLEASE DON'T KILL us. I'll do whatever you want. Just don't hurt us." A guy's voice sounds over the crashing waves. I think I recognize it as one of the men imprisoned on the boat.

"Survival will depend on you," the man carrying me, who seems to be the leader, says as he flips me over his shoulder.

I screech as I hit my back to the ground. Hot sand scorches my bare skin. He nudges me until I shift into what I think might be the shade. At least I get one small mercy. The ground cools a bit, and I blink, my vision adjusting to the changing light. Digging my fingers into the sand, I clutch a handful and release it. I shouldn't be thinking about the fact that I'm going to have sand in all the unwanted places on my body, but I can't help it. There's only been one time I've been naked on the beach, and at least I had a blanket to help. This time? Not so much.

"What does that even mean? What are you guys planning? I don't understand." I recognize Chase's voice. "Why are we here?"

Linking my fingers to the bag over my head, I slowly pull it up, testing to see if anyone notices. I squint my eyes in the beaming sun. A dozen figures blur in my vision, and I flutter my lashes until I spot the group of naked prisoners standing in a circle. Three wolves sit by the sides of our captors like obedient pets. I've never seen one so close. The beasts are far bigger than I realized, the shoulders of at least one reaching the men's torsos. I lock my gaze with the man in the middle, the leader. He doesn't yell at me for removing the bag. All he does is slowly shake his head and turn his attention to one of the male prisoners.

So do I.

"Is this some kind of sick-fuck human trafficking thing?" The handsome prisoner flares his nostrils, darting his gaze from the man and around the circle, stopping on me. It's Chase. He still manages to remain even-toned despite everything.

Chase's question makes another guy groan and rub his free hand on the back of his neck, keeping covered the best he can. His palm can only hide so much. I shouldn't be gaping at everyone as I do. I already hate that they sneak glances at me, but it helps keep me from breaking down. I need to be clear-headed. More aware.

"That's one way to put it," the leader says. "We kidnapped you, yes. We plan to use you, sure. But what's the fun of giving anything away?"

Chase glowers, his muscles rippling in silent anger. Many people would react to that response, but again, Chase remains cool. He obviously doesn't want to risk things like I have, but I wasn't going to miss what could've been my only chance to escape, even if I failed.

"Fucking psycho," another familiar voice mutters. It was the guy that asked Chase to carry him. I don't know what I imagined him to look like, but it wasn't this. His black hair sticks up on one side like he's been lying on it. Stubble peppers his angular jaw, his features more rugged than Chase's clean-shaven look.

"What was that, boy?" One of the other captors grabs the man's shoulder. A wolf growls and circles. "Show some respect. You don't know shit, so keep your mouth shut."

"Easy now, Brent. He'll learn his place. Isn't that right, Adam? You're a smart guy." The leader smacks the prisoner, Adam, on the shoulder.

Adam's hazel eyes search around as if he might be planning to fight, but something keeps him frozen. Fear? Maybe. He doesn't respond either, tightening his mouth. Our eyes meet for a second, and we stare at each other in silence. Now I'm not the only one focusing on someone besides our captors.

"Now listen up. I'm going to take a quick look at you. You're all good-looking and fit. Your chances are above average," the leader continues.

I don't react as Adam drinks me in from his spot, refusing to look at the man looking him over. He remains still, not moving or shifting as I stare right back at him. Inappropriate? Probably. Do I care? I have bigger concerns than being a perv. Like remaining calm. It takes everything in me to do so. Adam's flexing muscles and the V of his hips help a bit. How handsome he is, too—actually, all the naked, imprisoned guys are buff as hell and cute. I don't think I've seen so many abs in a row. All eight guys cover their naked bodies with their hands, and the three other women sling one arm over their boobs while hiding their vaginas with their other hand. I do neither. I remain in my spot on the shaded sand, trying not to draw attention to me as the others try to plead for information.

Maybe if our captors are too focused on everyone else, I can try to escape again. Taking advantage of a situation has saved my ass more than once. And I'll keep trying. I don't like whatever the fuck happens now. I'm humiliated and exposed. Naked and afraid.

"See? That wasn't so bad, was it? I didn't touch any of you. We're not complete monsters around here." The leader strolls along the middle of our circle. "We're also not taking you anywhere else. This is it. You and this island. We will be back in a couple weeks to check on you. Use your smarts. Show us you have what it takes to survive."

"What? Survive? You're leaving for a couple of weeks? You can't do this! I have a life. You're crazy!" one of the women shouts. "People will look for me!"

The leader only shrugs. "I highly doubt it. You've all been carefully selected because of your lack of ties and connections in the civilized world. They don't need you anymore. Shadow Moon Island does. We need fresh blood."

I frown in confusion, opening and closing my mouth.

I don't get a chance to respond because one of the prisoners rushes forward, trying to tackle the leader. He dodges out of the way, tripping the guy, and one of the wolves pounces on him and snarls in his ear.

The leader smiles and crosses his arms. "That's what I'm talking about. It takes guts and courage. Bravery. Smarts. You all get that? Prove your damn worth and survive. May you be blessed by our lunar goddess. Good luck."

The other wolves growl, getting between the three men and the rest of us, allowing them to trudge through the trees and toward the beach. After a few minutes, the wolves dart away and disappear.

No one moves. We all remain in our spots, looking from one another for some sort of direction. I've never been so confused in my life. I was expecting something horrendous to occur. I was expecting to be murdered or raped. But this? We've just been abandoned on an island with nothing. Not even clothes. What the actual fuck?

From the various expressions, I'm not the only one with that thought.

One of the women drops to her knees, covering her face with her hands. Silent sobs grab hold of her, and she shakes as she cries. A man across from me does the same, but he turns his back to us and locks his fingers into his hair. He yells, his voice echoing through the air.

"We all need to keep it together. By the looks of the sun, we have a couple hours until nightfall. I don't know where we are, but it might get cold tonight. We need to split up and get shit together the best we can. We need shelter, freshwater, and food. We can also try to make a fire. I don't know how successful we'll be until we get a look around. Something needs to be done, though." This comes from a woman with hair darker than mine. Her brown eyes glass over with unshed tears as she manages to keep it together despite her voice cracking. "I'm Tiffany, by the way. Tell me who all of you guys are. It will help."

"Help? The only help will be is if we can figure out how to send out an SOS. We can't just wait for them to come back for us. There has to be planes or boats or satellites or...I don't know." The brunette man beside her fists his hands, scowling.

"Surviving the night comes first, don't you think?" A blond man with blue eyes and sun-kissed skin, looking exactly how I imagine a southern California surfer boy to look, whacks the man on the back of the head. "And if knowing my name will make any of you feel better, you can call me Tristan or Trist. I don't care. Hey you, works fine, too."

SOS guy purses his lips, pinching his nose. "Fucking fine. I'm Jack."

"Alicia," the crying woman mutters, her voice hoarse. She wipes the palm of her hand over her cheeks, swiping her bronze tresses away. Blond highlights add depth to her mess of curls, frizzing from the sticky humidity.

A clean-cut man with wavy black hair and black eyes says, "Evander."

One by one, each person says their name. There are fifteen of us altogether, and by the time a man with short auburn hair and bright green eyes tells us his name is Davian, I've already forgotten most of the other people's names.

Surfer boy Tristan bounces on the balls of his feet, fidgeting and shifting like he's incapable of staying still for more than a second. "Great, cool to meet you. Sort of. Obviously, those dickheads wanted to make this bullshit as uncomfortable as possible by giving us absolutely nothing, so I'm going to just put this out there to break the damn ice so we can hustle and get shit done..." Dropping his hands, he shows off his cock and flexes, keeping his eyes trained toward the trees. "Ladies, if you've never seen a dick, well, now you have. We can't afford to be modest until we get what we need, and my damn arm is getting tired."

The only blond woman laughs and throws her hands up. I think her name is Penelope. "Okay, yeah. You're right. Not like I haven't been streaking before, and I want to get this awkward shit over with." She motions to a couple of the guys. "I'll show you mine if you show me yours. We all know you've seen a woman—probably only in one of your pornos—but here I am. Now let me see. We're all adults, and it's not like we had a choice."

I sit up, not rushing to join in this weird-ass bonding moment.

The shaved guy—Ian, I think—whistles through his fingers. "Fuck, yeah! I'm over being scared and damn uncomfortable."

Tiffany grins and raises her arms over her head, laughing. "Damn straight. Those assholes leaving was a good thing." At least I can agree with her on that. She looks at two silent guys. "Right...Reggie? Hank?"

Davian bobs his head, grinning. He play-punches who I think is Hank. "We can do this, dudes. We can handle a few weeks here. You guys can be on my team." The auburn man with freckles—proving that the curtains match the drapes—

pumps his fist. His positivity helps ease the nerves inside me. "Once we get some damn water and shit, it'll be like paradise."

If he says so. As much as I want to believe him, I can't shake the tightness in my chest.

Twisting toward me, he extends his hand. "Come on, Eliana. You look like you could use a hand up. What you did on the yacht was fucking insane and awesome. I want you on our team. Would you prefer we be in charge of food, shelter, or water?"

I lick my dry lips, trying not to sound like a brain-dead zombie. "Water. Definitely water."

"Which of you men want to be on Team Food?" Tiffany asks, pointing around our group. "You guys are so lucky I'm a botanist."

Tristan raises his hand. "I fish for sport."

"Thank God. I don't want to eat like a rabbit." Ian moves past us to join Team Food.

"Since I'm in construction, I'll take charge of our shelter." Evander rubs his hands together. "Anyone else have some skills we can use?"

Penelope raises her hand. "I studied engineering. I can help you."

"All right, the rest of you split up. We can have equal teams. Everyone has to carry their weight even if they don't know how to do shit. I'm not looking to bond. I'm looking to survive." Jack joins the shelter group. He was who I nicknamed

Mr. SOS on the boat. I'm glad he doesn't choose our group because he'd be the one to shove me into danger to save himself.

Chase comes up to my side, joining Davian and me. Hank and Reggie stand off to the side, not saying much, waiting for someone to tell them what to do. Kind of like me. I'm not the leader type. I didn't have my shit together at home, and I don't now.

I fold my arms over my chest, trying my best not to think about the fact that I'm standing naked with four guys and about to head into the wilderness in search of water. In any other situation, this would be a hell no for me. But now? What choice do I have? At least if they try something disgusting, their weak points are all exposed. I'm not afraid to fight.

I stare in silence, watching as the other two groups disperse. Penelope's laughter echoes through the air, and I wish I could capture her carefree spirit. I don't want to be this scared still, but I can't help it.

Davian clears his throat. "Eliana, here. Take this. We don't know what kind of wildlife resides here." He stakes a long, straight stick into the ground. I hadn't even seen him break it from one of the trees.

His thoughtful gesture eases my nerves. I won't let my guard down yet, but his actions do help.

Chase looks around and finds another tree branch to break. "I'm not going to lie. I've already forgotten your two names."

The man to the right of me shrugs his shoulders. His brown eyes flick to mine, and he gives me a once-over like he can't help himself. "Hank."

"I'm Reggie," the other guy says, offering his hand out to Chase. "We should get moving. The place we'll most likely find a water source is inland. I don't know about you all, but I don't want to get stuck in that rainforest after dark."

All I can think about are all the things that can kill me as I head into the wilderness of this island. And now, I wish I would've chosen to be on a different team. I was just so thirsty that water was the first thing that came to my mind. Not snakes. Wild boars. Giant cats or something. Whatever else could be here.

As if Chase senses my sudden nerves, he reaches out and squeezes my shoulder. "We're going to be okay. I'm an experienced hiker. We have to be more concerned about the creatures we can't see than the ones that can attack us."

Great. I wasn't even thinking about spiders or venomous whatever that could be hiding everywhere. Man-eating ants. Disease-infected mosquitoes. Shit.

Instead of responding, all I do is tighten my hand around my stick and nod my head. Chase leads the way, and I stroll between him and Davian with the other two ending our line. At least Davian stays a couple feet behind me, so I don't have to think about his naked body getting too close to mine. It's bad enough that I have to trudge this forest with naked guys in the first place. I want to worry about the wild snakes hanging from trees and not the ones between their legs.

I swear. After we get our shit together, I'll figure out how to cover up. Leaves will be my new favorite fashion trend. Maybe I can even try making a grass skirt. I know I have bigger concerns, but thinking about the small discomforts of the situation helps ease the anxiety clenching my heart.

We hike deeper into the rainforest and away from the shore, the humidity leaving my scalp damp with sweat. Chase marks our way by using a stick to draw a line in the ground while occasionally stopping to scratch the trunks of several trees. I'm glad he thought of it because I don't think the rest of us would have. I can't even remember the last time I was outside of the city. The city park was about as naturey as I've gotten.

"So, what do you all do for a living?" Hank asks, keeping his voice low. I almost wish he didn't break the silence.

"Agriculture." Davian flicks his gaze to mine. "Don't tell Tiffany. She's already gotten on my nerves, and I don't want her ordering me around. I got enough of that before I tore my ex-boss a new one."

"That's fucking awesome," Hank speaks a bit louder.

I tense and look around. I can't shake the dread prickling down my back. I feel like we're being watched by a predator, and I'm afraid that any sort of noise will provoke them. Would it be wrong to push Hank toward whatever wild animal might attack since he would be the one drawing it to us? Maybe. But in this moment, I want to be selfish. I want to protect myself first. Any of them could overpower me and feed me to the beasts of the rainforest if they wanted to.

"I'm a scuba instructor, and I had been working on a day cruise whale watching boat, but it took some damage recently. It's the off-season, so...that's probably why these fuckers jumped me," Hank continues, answering his own question when the rest of us don't.

"Recently fired," Reggie murmurs.

Hank strolls up next to Reggie, and the two of them move in closer behind me. "Bummer. From where?"

"Doesn't matter. It was fucked up and not even my fault. But you know how it is with the big businesses. Always saving face." Reggie nearly growls with the words.

"What about you two?" Hank touches my shoulder, and I startle. I don't know if it's because of my nerves with the forest or what, but his touch sets me off.

I automatically take a few quick steps away and glare at him from over my shoulder.

Chase clears his throat, interrupting me before I snap. I don't really want to talk about how I haven't had reliable work for a while or what I've been doing to make money.

"I'm an MD. Family Medicine." Chase slows down and motions for me to step in front of him. I think he can tell I'm on the verge of another panic attack. I just want to find the water and get back to the beach.

Reggie claps his hands once and chuckles. "Well, there goes my theory. I was going to say they kidnapped all of us because we were out of work. Yet you're a doctor? Damn. I guess there always has to be one. Like the shows. Shitty luck that they targeted you."

"Who said I wasn't out of work? But that's none of your business. Now, be quiet. We need to listen for water. Save the small talk for later." Chase strolls up beside me, glancing at me in his peripheral vision. He stands close but not too close, almost protectively but cautious at the same time. It's hard to explain. It's also hard for me not to drag my gaze down the front of his body. I'm just so not used to being around naked people. But he doesn't look at me once. If he's truly a doctor, that's most likely why. It's probably why he also helped me in the middle of my panic attack on the yacht.

"Fuck. Just one question for Eliana, and I'll shut up. Are you out of work?" Hank comes up behind me, leaning over my shoulder, getting into my space.

I pick up my speed again while nodding my head. "Yeah. Can you please backup? You might be comfortable with your dick swinging around, but—"

The ground falls out from under me, and I screech as I tumble down a steep ravine. Davian yells my name, but I can't see where he is until I roll a couple times and land on my back.

The four men stare in shock at me from above.

My breath escapes my lungs. I wheeze in exasperation, my heart feeling as if it'll explode. I expect my whole body to scream in agony. I'm afraid I might've broken something, and I won't feel it until the adrenaline wears off. If that happens, I'm dead. I know it.

"Yo, Elle! Get up! Grab your stick. It's to your right!" Davian shouts the words from the top of the ravine. "There's something in the trees."

And then I hear the growl.

Holy fucking shit.

I'm about to be mauled to death.

CHAPTER 3

BEASTLY CLAIM

MINE.

The voice of my inner beast whispers through my mind as I see the breathtaking woman land on her back before me. I shouldn't confront her, but I can't seem to get my wolf and mind to comply. I've been ordered by my alpha not to interact with the humans. My pack and I are just supposed to ensure they stay where they belong. At least, until the full moon.

"Eliana! Run!" a masculine voice shouts. "The ground

evens out a bit over there. I'll help you up."

Just the thought of this woman, Eliana, leaving me to return to the group of the chosen angers my beast. A deep growl reverberates through my body as my hackles rise.

Eliana groans, shifting onto her side to look at me. Her golden eyes widen, and fear freezes her in place. It gives me the time I need to drink in the sight of her naked body. She is perfect, even down to the small scar on her hip. I can't help wondering how she got it. I want to get closer and inhale a breath of her scent. I crave to be able to pinpoint exactly where she is, even if she's not in my line of sight.

"Wait! Don't run. Move slowly." The words come from another man, toeing the edge of the hill leading into the ravine. He takes a cautious step as he contemplates coming down to test my power and claim my soul stakes on Eliana.

But he won't follow through. He's not worthy of protecting this beautiful human. He doesn't know the island like I do. I need to get her away, even if it's just for a couple minutes.

The man clears his throat. "Eliana..."

Snarling, I startle Eliana as I lunge toward her. I leap over her as she screams and rushes up the hill toward the four men. They scatter and run like the prey they are, setting my innate nature off. I'd chase them back to the beach if it didn't mean abandoning my beautiful human.

I just need to get them gone long enough for me to take Eliana somewhere they can't find her. I'm risking too much already in my sudden urge to reveal myself to her. But I'll do so in a way that she won't know the truth. I had planned to just drop the bag with the survival gear near their drop-off point for someone to find, but then I saw her. I've been following her since.

Mine.

I can't stop the raw need for such a claim on someone who may never be my she-wolf. My future mate. The alphas of the island's packs will fight it out for a female. There aren't many here. And fewer purebloods. Some of the alphas won't mate with a mutt. They'll wait until an allied pack has spawned a purer offspring and claim it. Other packs will hunt and kill off the female mutt because they know what is planned. They'd prefer never to have another pure bloodline apart from themselves again. They draw their strength from bringing humans here and finding who is strong enough for the gift of the lunar goddess.

If Eliana can survive the hunt and call of the moon, she'll be a mutt and considered the weakest of any packs, even lower than me, an infraborne. Even if she were strong enough to fight and defeat an alpha, another would just take his place. Females are not given such power here. Though, given the chance, I will worship my beautiful human.

"Get back!" The tallest man of the four swings a branch in my direction, trying to scare me off like that's even possible. I'm the predator and power on this island. One of my bites could end him.

I snarl and lunge, knocking the guy onto his back. He swings his fist and punches my snout, forcing me off him. Instead of fighting, I dodge out of the way and bound in the direction of the ravine again. We're far enough away that I can get Eliana out of their sight. I can have a moment with her.

So I take it.

I jump from the top of the steep hill and land in the dirt a few feet away from Eliana. She screams and crab walks, trying to get to her feet as quickly as possible. I bolt around her, snagging her hair in my teeth. She doesn't get a chance to fight back as I drag her deeper into the forest and away from her group.

"Fuck! Help! Someone help me!" Eliana's voice screeches through the forest, her fear stabbing into me. She carries an unexpected fight inside her I admire.

If only she wasn't so loud. She'll draw too much attention to us. It's the last thing I want. I'll be punished for disobeying my alpha's orders. Eliana doesn't need that. She needs me here and with her.

"Help!" she screams, throwing a fistful of dirt at me, sending it raining over my coat. She'll never settle with me in my lykoswulf—my moonborne—form.

I have to transform. I know I shouldn't. I really fucking know I shouldn't, but I don't want her to be afraid of me. Hearing the fear in her voice strikes me on a deep-seated level. I never expected my soul could feel such agony and torture.

She must know I won't hurt her.

I dart away from her and disappear into the trees. Lurking out of view, I wait for her to catch her breath and scramble to her feet. She spins around, looking for a weapon. Jumping up, she grabs onto the closest branch she can and manages to break it with the force of her body weight. I admire her sinewy muscles, flexing with her movements. She's so beautiful, even afraid, and I lose myself in the idea of turning her fear into relief at my closeness. I want it more than I realized. She shouldn't feel as if she must fight at just the sight of me.

If only I could spill my soul to her.

Closing my eyes, I tame my wolf, shifting into a man. I stretch my arms over my head and shake out my body. It's been a while since I've been on two legs. There's not much I need when I'm on the island. It's easier to be more animal in this setting.

Eliana whispers a prayer, my hearing picking up on the rasp of her voice. She's begging her God to protect her from me. She's begging for help from the divine.

Her focus is drawn toward her surroundings so much that she doesn't even realize she's a foot away from a creek. I brought her here for a reason. It's the main water source running through the island. It'll always flow and never dry, giving her what she needs to survive. If she follows it long enough, she will find the waterfalls. I wish I could take her there now, but I know I must be quick. The others will find her eventually, and I can't stay.

I carefully tread my way around the tree in her direction. I make noise by breaking a couple branches and dropping them, so I don't surprise her. I know she might already attack me, and I kind of hope for it. My beast wants nothing more than to feel the power I know burns just beneath the surface, waiting for her to accept that she's not some lost human in the wild. She's intended for more. For me. I know it with every fiber of my soul. It should be impossible. No infraborne takes a mate, yet here I am. The call to Eliana is as strong as the call of the full moon.

Mine. The thought refuses to leave me.

"Get out of here," Eliana growls, bracing herself for my wolf to arrive. She takes an automatic step back and lands in the creek. The cool water surprises her, and she jumps, her eyes turning away from me and giving me the chance to step out from my hiding place.

"I'll only be here for a minute. I'm sorry I scared you. I heard you fall and wanted to make sure you were okay." I offer her a smile, keeping my lips together as to not scare her by baring my teeth.

"There was a wolf. It went that way." She clutches her branch tighter but doesn't rush toward me for the protection she should feel she needs from me.

My jaw twitches and I hold my hands up. Her gaze darts down my body, stopping at my dick. Her lingering look sets me off with desire. She enjoys what she sees. I can smell the change of her scent. She might be afraid, but the carnal part of her recognizes me as a potential mate.

"Who the hell are you, anyway? You weren't with our group. Were you brought here before? Are there others?" She hisses her words, trying to keep quiet but unable to with her wild emotions.

I don't respond, ignoring her questions for the sole reason that she won't like the answers. I wasn't brought here. I was born here. And there are at least four other groups of humans around the island. It would take at least a day for the humans to cross paths. That is, if they were heading toward each other. The chances are slim but not impossible. The packs try to keep each group isolated for the duration of their survival test.

"Hello? Are you going to answer me? You're staring at me weirdly. Are you a...fuck, you're a murderer or something. I didn't even think about that. Uh..." She shifts on her feet, antsy the longer I stare at her. But I can't help myself. I could just look into her golden eyes forever. She is stunning.

I clear my throat. "I'm sorry. I can't help myself. It's just that you're breathtaking. I've never seen such beauty before me in my life."

She releases an exasperated, breathy laugh. "That's creepy. You don't just approach a woman in the forest and tell her she's pretty when you're both standing naked."

I can't help smiling. "Why not?"

She throws her hands up, unashamedly exposing her body with her annoyance. "Because it's just weird. Please, answer my questions. Are there others? Where did you come from? Tell me your name."

"It's Kellan. As for your other questions...I'm sorry. I don't have a lot of time. They might be watching, and your group draws near. I can hear them. You need to tell them to work on their quiet approach." I curl and uncurl my fingers, my body flexing. She darts her gaze down me again, taking an extra look at the desire arousing me.

"Who might be watching? Please, you have to help us if you know anything. Please. I'm scared. They just brought us from a boat and left us. I don't understand any of this." She takes a step forward, lowering the branch she's prepared to use as a weapon.

The gesture of trust strokes at my inner beast, and I cautiously close the space to her. She stops short, still keeping two feet between us.

"Kellan..." The sound of my name whispering from her pouty mouth drives me wild. It's no longer the other packs I'm worried about. It's me. I need to go. I've already spent far too long with her.

"I'm sorry, I can't say anything else. I have to go." Glancing over my shoulder, I peer in the direction I hear her group clomping. "But wait here for a minute. I have a bag of supplies. A knife, some fire starters, and a couple other things. It's the least I can do for you." I shuffle back, forcing myself to put space between us before I try to close it again. Her eyes capture mine, refusing to let me go. The sheen glossing over her beautiful gaze stabs deeply into me.

I hate how desperately she wants my help, and I can't give it to her to my full capability. Not yet. I can't get ahead of myself. My wolf might claim her, but the real test depends on the call of the moon.

She blinks a few times, clearing her tears before they spill. "You'll give me supplies?"

I nod my head. "I disagree with what they've done to you and the other humans. But I wish you well, Eliana. Try not to stray too far past this creek." I spin on my feet and tread toward the trees.

"Kellan, wait! You know my name!" Eliana shouts.

I pick up my pace until I'm out of sight. It hurts me to leave her, but I need to. If I stay any longer, I don't think my heart will allow me to stray even a foot from her.

I transform back into my wolf self and find where I left the bag of supplies. I carefully and quietly move through the trees, listening to her shout my name again and again. She only stops when I stand before her, holding the bag between my teeth as my wolf.

Fear crosses her expression, her eyebrows shooting up on her head, and then confusion twists her lips. I shouldn't have approached her like this. It'll only make things worse. But I couldn't help myself. My wolf wanted to be close to her one last time.

"He's one of them. That bastard. Fuck." She whispers the words so quietly that a normal human wouldn't hear them. But I do. Clutching the branch tighter, she guards her body the best she can from my beast. "You're his pet, aren't you, wolfie? That's why you haven't attacked."

Her mortal mind won't let her comprehend the possibility of anything other than me as a wolf being a pure animal and not a shifter. I don't understand why the concept is so hard on some, but she will learn soon enough.

I pad my way closer, and she shuffles back, stepping into the creek again. I drop the bag on the pebbly bank and whimper. She doesn't move. I'm pretty sure she's holding her breath. And then I hear the men from her group approaching, cutting a path clear through the wilderness.

It's the only reason I run.

But I won't go far.

Eliana will be mine.

CHAPTER 4

SURVIVAL INSTINCTS

I SHOULD TELL the others about the man in the forest. I was in such shock when Chase, Davian, Reggie, and Hank found me that I couldn't find my voice. I hate to admit it, but I cried. They probably think I'm the weakest link of our group. If this were some twisted reality show, I'd be banished from the island. If only. If I can't get myself to toughen up, they'll feed me to the wolves.

I'm better than this.

If I had my big girl panties, I'd tell myself to suck it up. Damn it. I'd take my granny panties right about now. Even my ugly period ones.

"So, you just found it?" Tiffany asks, plopping down on the leaves beside me. It's better than sitting in the sand on our bare asses. She stares at the side of my face and waits for me to look at her.

I twine my fingers together. "Yeah. It was by the creek."

"This has to be some sort of test." If only. She's not the only one skeptical.

Adam hollers in excitement, drawing our attention to him as the fire ignites. At least the man, Kellan, wasn't lying about the bag having everything we could use to help us survive at least the first night. But now I'm concerned about the wolves and about whatever lingers past the creek. He recommended not to go far. I don't even want to go back into the trees. I might just stay here in our makeshift shelter and teach myself how to make some clothes out of whatever is around.

"Super lucky for us. I'm already getting cold." Tiffany rubs her hands over her arms. "I mean, look at my damn nipples. They're so tight that they can probably cut glass."

I bare my teeth and cross my arms over my boobs. "Maybe try cutting some wood instead? It would be more useful for the fire." I don't know why I say it, but I couldn't think of another response to her. I'm pretty sure everyone's nipples are hard right now from the cool, crisp air. I don't even want to think about what the night will bring.

She cackles, her voice echoing through the air, drawing everyone's attention to us. "Shit, Eliana. I wasn't expecting that. I thought you'd blush. You seem...never mind."

"What? Modest?" I know it's not what she was going to say. A part of me wants to get angry, but maybe she's right. It's not that I'm modest. I'm just uncomfortable. Nervous. I feel exposed and weak despite knowing that we've managed this much already and can handle a night until we find something, anything, to protect our naked bodies from the elements.

"Hey, Tiff. Come on by the fire. I'll help you warm up," Ian interrupts. He offers his hand out to Tiffany.

I expect her to scowl and slap his hand away, but she laughs and lets him pull her to her feet. I guess we both got lucky that he chose now to hit on her and steal her away. I'm unsure about her, considering she already seems to have an opinion about me. Now, I wonder what the others think. Should I care? Probably not. But I do want them to like me enough that they won't turn against me if shit gets worse than it already is.

I take a moment to look at the others. Mostly everyone seems relaxed. They don't even care that the light fades by the second. Soon, we will only have the light of the fire. Just the fifteen of us in the dark on an island with who knows what. Fucking great.

"Hey, Eliana! You get the first bite since you found the

bag. I hope you like fish." Tristan waves something on a stick. I'm not usually one for seafood, but I'm starving. Just the sight of the offering sends my stomach growling.

"We have some bananas too." Adam holds up a bunch, showing off his find. "There's probably other tropical fruit around that we'll look for at first light. Alicia and Tiffany gathered some flowers as well, if you're feeling that kind of thing."

"*Edible* flowers," Tiffany corrects, rolling her eyes. "You might be surprised if you'd just try them. They make a good tea."

A shadow falls over me, and I tilt my head back, catching Evander's gaze. He holds a leaf as big as my head on his palm and offers it out. I automatically take it, keeping my eyes on him instead of his naked body, his chiseled muscles more defined by the glow of the firelight as twilight steals the sun.

"You look comfortable here, so I thought I'd bring you a little of everything." He twirls his finger at my bare leg. "That looks painful too. You doing okay?"

I shift my gaze to the scraped and bruised skin from my fall. "It's not so bad. It could've been worse."

"Like breaking something." Chase's smooth voice hums through the air, and I spot him kicking through the sand from where he'd been hunched next to the fire. He sits beside me and holds up the collapsible cup that was stored in the bag. "My grandmother was a holistic medical practitioner and she taught me a couple things. Banana trees are good for a lot of things. This will help with the pain. Drink it all."

"Yes, doctor," I say, bringing the cup to my mouth, watching him watch me.

"If bananas are that fucking fantastic, here, eat this next." Evander picks up the banana from the leaf on my lap.

I tip my head back and laugh. "You guys are treating me like I'm going to die. I really am okay. It's just some scrapes."

"That we don't want to get infected." Chase eyes me in his peripheral vision. I don't know why he worries about a stranger, maybe it's because of his oath as a doctor, but it makes me feel better.

"I suppose you're right. Thanks. It's been a while since I've had someone take care of me." My voice barely sounds out a whisper, but Chase hears the words and smiles at me.

"We have to change that. We're all we have right now, and we need to watch out for each other to survive this." Evander motions to the leaf on my lap with the food. "Now eat. Whoever finishes first gets dibs on our sleeping arrangements. I don't know about you, but it's going to be cold, and I'd rather not cuddle with one of those assholes."

I raise my eyebrows as a smile crosses my face. "You say that as if you plan to cuddle me."

"I thought I'd ask. Look at these arms. They'll keep you toasty." Evander flexes his muscles.

I tip my head back and laugh, the gesture effortless and like a breath of fresh air. I almost forgot what it was like to feel anything other than afraid. Maybe the others are right in treating this like a crazy-ass beach vacation instead of what it truly is.

"Looks like a no. I think she would prefer to cuddle with me instead. It's gonna take a lot more than a food offering. Try protecting her from a wild animal next." Davian kicks up sand in front of us, joining our small group. We haven't talked much since earlier, and I find myself meeting his green gaze.

"Rock-Paper-Scissors?" Chase asks, pounding his fist to his palm. "Though, the doctor might order Eliana to cuddle with me. I need to keep an eye on her all night long to make sure she's okay."

"What about me, doc? You promised to carry me around and be my protector. I even brought you payment in food." Adam fake pouts. He was the one joking with Chase on the yacht. I had blocked out most of that until now. "What do you say, Eliana? You can be the meat in our manwich. Extra warmth for you. You know, since nature is so fucking rough. It's cold enough that you won't have to worry about my midnight boner. The shrinkage will ensure that it turns into a damn innie."

My laughter rings through the air. I've never heard something so ridiculous in my life. They really are trying hard to make me feel comfortable yet also trying to distract me from my own dark thoughts. Or maybe they're trying to distract themselves. Either way, I like it. Things don't feel so frightening. I can ignore the darkness shrouding over everything. If we don't get a moon tonight, it'll feel as if we're in a void. I've always lived in the city. I have no idea what that kind of darkness of night feels like. I'm nervous, to say the least.

"That's a bit disconcerting, dude." Tristan flops down on the leaves in front of me, wiggling his fingers in a wave. "Just say the word, Eliana. I'll save you from these horn dogs. You know, they're more concerned about being cold. The babies. Can't handle a night on the beach."

I look at each of the guys now sitting around me. The voices of the others hum through the air as they laugh and eat near the fire.

"So, what do you say, Eliana? Do you want to bunk up with one of us tonight?" Evander clears his throat with the words.

This is the strangest thing that has ever happened to me. I don't think I've ever had so many guys want my attention, and I don't know if I should let my guard down to give it to them. I know we must work together to get through this, but I just don't know.

"You guys are serious." It's not a question.

Evander holds out his hand to me. "Let me show you the shelters, and then you can decide. You don't have to worry about anything with me. I'm just looking for company. You seem to be a lucky charm, how you survived the wolf and managed to find a survival pack."

"I forgot how badass it was that she jumped from the yacht and swam her way to shore. She's one tough babe." Davian gets to his feet and dusts the sand off his ass.

It feels like forever ago since I did that. I still can't believe that I got the nerve to do as much. Maybe he's right. I'm not giving myself enough credit. I've done plenty of things to survive in my past. Things are just a little bit wilder here. Feral.

I gather my bravery and accept Evander's offer to help me to my feet. He quickly checks me out, trying his best not to, but it's not easy ignoring the nudity of someone in front of you. I should know.

I can't stop myself from looking at him either. All of the guys here are toned and muscular, looking like they all hit the gym several times a week.

"That sounds like a plan. Show us your skills. I want to see what your fine ass came up with, you hunk of a man." Adam smacks Evander on the back with a laugh. He rubs his fist into his cropped hair next, and Evander spins and locks him in a choke hold until Adam calls mercy.

"Hey! Don't give them all the credit! He just did the heavy lifting. The design is all mine." Penelope points her finger. "And if you don't want to hang out with them, Eliana. You can join me. I don't know why these guys just assume we're camping co-ed. Obviously, the ladies' shelter is superior. They wouldn't appreciate it either."

I smile and shift on my feet, looking from the guys to her.

All the other women have been so flirty and friendly with the guys that I wasn't sure if I'd be welcome. It's nice that I am. "Girls' night on the beach? Hell yeah."

"Exactly! Make these fuckers work for attention. Since there's only so many of us to go around." Alicia sticks her tongue out, and the guy I recall being named Creed bows forward and clutches her feet in mock worship.

"Is that how it's going to be, huh?" Hank asks, speaking up from his place in front of the fire. "Then I'll wait it out. No point with the competition."

Tiffany pouts her bottom lip. "Aw, Hank. Come on. You can help Ian keep me warm."

Ian scowls while Hank grins. The guy is totally messing around. Hank knows exactly what he's doing, acting as if he's not as good as the other guys.

The bastard.

I don't get a chance to comment and point out the fact because Penelope grabs my hand and tugs me from the others.

I stroll next to Penelope, my nerves growing the farther we tread away from the fire. The shelters are only a dozen feet away, but it feels like a mile with how dark the world already becomes.

Penelope stops in front of a triangular shelter reminiscent of a teepee.

Straight branches are twined together at the top, and huge banana leaves cover the sides, creating a wall. It's big enough to fit at least four people, maybe five, and there are two others right along the tree line and away from the waves so that we shouldn't have to worry about a rising tide.

"Tiffany managed to find some citronella grass. It will help repel the mosquitoes." Penelope motions toward the grass floor of the shelter. "I don't know if you've heard from her about this, but she said the island foliage confuses her. She thought she could figure out where we might be in the world, but it's like this island has a mash-up of things that are native in different areas altogether."

I never even thought of that. "That's so weird. What do the others think?"

She shrugs. "They don't really care, because everything we have found we can use. I don't think it's just luck. I think it's more. I can't stop wondering what the purpose of all of this is. And the bag you found? That was really strange."

With the mention of the survival kit, I can't help thinking about the man in the woods, Kellan. I shift my gaze and look toward the tropical forest. It's too dark to see anything, but a cold feeling of dread washes over me. It's the same feeling of being watched like earlier.

Alicia squeals, startling me, and I nearly lose my soul as it tries to escape my body.

Then the howls start. Low and deep, growing louder and closer.

Grabbing my hand, Penelope drags me back toward the

others. Silence falls around our group, and Chase, Evander, and Adam close in around me. Davian grabs his makeshift weapon, a branch he carved into a point, and stands tall, staring at the forest.

"Fuck, did they sound like they're getting closer?" Evander mutters, keeping his voice low.

"Maybe they won't bother us if we just keep quiet and wait it out." Chase brushes his fingers against mine, and I automatically take his hand, my fear getting the best of me.

"We need to take shifts. Someone should be awake at all times. I think we need to all sleep together as well." Tiffany wrings her fingers, her hands shaking.

I nod my head. "I agree."

"Same," a couple of the others say in unison.

Our fear steals the good mood between everyone, and it doesn't seem like we will get it back tonight.

"Who wants to take the first shift with me? I don't think I'll be able to sleep at all." Evander digs his heels into the sand.

I raise my hand at the same time that Davian, Chase, and Adam do. Offering a small smile, Evander extends his hand to me. I link my fingers through his while I still hold Chase's hand. It should feel weirder than it does, but I just feel safe between them.

"Don't take your eyes off the trees," Alicia says, crossing her arms over her chest.

Creed drapes his arm over her shoulders. "We're going to

be fine. As long as we don't go into their territory or bother them, they'll leave us alone."

It's the best we can hope for.

This is going to be the longest night of my life.

I hope I survive it.

CHAPTER 5

ATTACK

RUN.

I jolt awake. The sharp, strangely familiar voice repeats the word in my mind. Sweat prickles over my body, and I realize that I have my palms pressed into Chase and Adam's bare chests. I feel as if I just got to sleep because of how nervous I was. I ended up taking the guys' offer to bunk together since Penelope and the women picked other teams to take watch. I can't blame them for feeling safer with someone other than me.

"Eliana? What is it?" Adam grabs my hand, squeezing my fingers to get my attention.

Was I really sleeping on my stomach with an arm over each of them? I now rest on my knees, still pressing them down with my weight. If panic didn't ignite inside me, making me gasp, I might fall flat to hide my boobs, hanging in the most unflattering way.

Run!

I don't respond to Adam and scramble to my feet, the command too powerful to ignore. He doesn't let go of my hand, getting up with me. I hit my head on the top of the shelter. It shakes under the force but thankfully doesn't collapse.

"Everyone up. We have to go. It's not safe." I keep my voice low, practically hissing the words. It squeaks with my nerves, cracking under the dryness of my throat.

I nudge Chase with my foot, getting him to wake up. He's a deep sleeper compared to Adam, unfazed by my commotion. But my kick? I get him hard enough in the hip that Chase snaps his eyes open and looks up at me. It's just light enough to know dawn approaches. I realize that he gets the perfect view of my vagina, and I can't stop the blush from crawling up my body. Sleep steals his professional doctor mentality away, and he gets a boner and licks his lips, wetting them.

"We have to go," I whisper again. "Now."

"What? Why?" He sits upright and peers around. Shoving his hand into Davian's back, he shakes him awake. "Hey, man.

Get up."

Evander groans and rubs his face and his eyes, hearing us. "What's going on?"

Adam motions to Tristan. "Get him up."

Run. The voice steals my attention again, but I know it's in my head because no one else reacts.

Run now! Go!

As if my feet take control of my willpower, I yank away from Adam and shift the banana leaves out of the way to step out of the shelter.

"Oh, no," I whisper, spotting our lookout group fast asleep near the smoking fire.

And then I see the wolf stalking toward them.

I don't get the chance to open my mouth to scream before a huge grey wolf launches from the sand and lands on top of Creed, sleeping next to Penelope. Creed hollers, trying to push the wolf off him, but it jerks down and bites his throat. My heart sinks into my stomach. I can't believe this is happening.

"Take Eliana. Head toward the water." Davian grabs my hand and places it into Adam's. "Tristan, go with them. Chase and Evander, grab anything you can. If there are too many, head toward the water."

A deep growl sounds from behind us, and I spot the familiar wolf from the forest. It's Kellan's pet. I know it. I recognize the wolf's strange blue eyes. The wolf stands in our way, kicking up sand as it lunges and retreats over and over again.

"Help!" Penelope screams, her voice striking me in the soul.

I can't help looking in her direction, only to see the wolf attack her next, grabbing her by the ankle and dragging her. A masculine voice shouts as another wolf attacks the other shelter. We're surrounded.

"Fuck!" Evander yells, swinging a stick at a wolf trying to sneak up on us. The wolf locks its jaws on the makeshift weapon, and Evander spins, tossing the beast toward the waves.

Penelope's shrieks vanish, and I jerk my attention back to where the fire no longer burns. I cover my mouth with my hand, my stomach twisting. This is not happening. I can't believe this is happening.

"We have to help them," I say, my voice shaking.

"No, we have to go. They'll come after us next." Tristan's words shock me. "You know damn well they'd abandon us. Come on, let's move. Stick together."

I'm torn between doing the right thing and the right thing for me. I wouldn't want someone to abandon me like that, but then again, I can't fight wild animals.

I can't even protect myself from humans. It's why I'm in this position.

"He's right. Maybe the wolves will give up. We can come back when they leave." Chase takes my hand and twines his fingers through mine. "We have to get past that wolf. I think he's too chicken to attack without the rest of his pack. He might just be waiting for them to finish. They're smart animals."

The fact that Kellan's pet wolf hasn't attacked confuses me. It attacked me in the forest. I wonder if he's been commanded or something. I don't think Kellan is a survivor here. He did mention that he was born here.

Just before I can nod my head to agree with Chase and Tristan, a long, low howl echoes through the air. It sounds as if it comes from the forest, but I can't tell how far away it is. It's not very close...I think.

Several wolves bark and howl in response, and I stiffen as five...no, six, dart from our shelters. They charge in our direction, and Davian scoops me up into his arms, using his height as a way to protect me to the best of his ability. My heart thrashes as the rest of our small group clutches onto their makeshift weapons.

I don't want to die.

I don't want to be mauled.

"I'll hold them back. Get to the water. Now!" Tristan shouts, rushing toward the wolves. He yells and swings the stick, trying to scare the wolves.

Davian kicks through the sand toward the waves, swinging his branch at Kellan's wolf as it tries to block us. He trips and sends us both into the ocean, and warm water engulfs me, dragging me into the surf a few feet. I let the wave carry me as I orient myself and manage to pop back to the surface, planting my feet into the sand. The waist-high water lifts me up and down, and I watch as Tristan continues to swing his weapon at the wolves surrounding him.

Another long, deep howl echoes over the thundering whitecaps around me, and the wolves spin and dart toward the trees. I can't believe they're leaving. Thank God. It's hard to grasp the concept of these wolves being anything other than wild, but with how they don't keep attacking until we're all dead? Are they trained? Was that howl an actual wolf or was it something else? Maybe the men that abandoned us here have a special wolf call.

Tristan shouts, swinging the branch back and forth even though the wolves vanish. A sob escapes my mouth, my mind and body seemingly reconnecting. Tristan might've wanted to sacrifice the others to save himself—ourselves—but he was also willing to sacrifice himself to save us. His actions leave me confused about my own moral standing. I never thought I'd agree to just abandoning people to save my own ass...well, abandoning people I haven't known long.

Damn, I'm messed up. How will this affect things moving forward? Will the others know and try to start shit? Will this divide us, or will they understand...if they're even still alive?

A low rumble steals my attention from the lifeless bodies in the sand. I can't see them clearly through my blurry gaze, my eyes stinging because of the saltwater. The familiar grey wolf paces back and forth, keeping its distance from us.

Whimpering, the wolf turns from vicious to pathetic. Fucking beast. It shouldn't be cute and scary.

Tristan straightens his shoulders and faces Kellan's pet, still lingering in the sand. The wolf tilts its head and looks at me, its blue eyes sparkling in the light of the early morning sun. I wish it didn't stare at me like I could be its possible next meal, licking its lips and releasing a bark. I startle, hopping back even more. And then the wolf dodges around Tristan and follows behind the rest of his pack now gone from sight.

A hand clamps onto my shoulder, pulling me around, and I meet Chase's gaze. His jaw twitches as he gives me a once-over, not checking me out but instead silently making sure I'm uninjured.

"Are you hurt?" he asks, confirming my suspicions. I've already learned to decipher his expressions, his ones of desire far sexier than his frown of concern.

I swipe my hand over my wet face, glad that the water disguises my tears. I'm so tired of crying, whether it's from fear or pain. "I don't think so. I mean, not any worse than yesterday."

Like he needs to assure himself I'm not lying, Chase clutches my hand and guides me to shallower water where the waves glide around our ankles instead of crashing into our backs. I suck in my bottom lip and spin around slowly. My heart thuds under his scrutiny, the sensation of his gaze sending tingles blooming over me.

"No! Oh, God! No!" Alicia's voice rips through the air as

she screams.

It knocks the sense into both me and Chase, and he straightens upright, locking his arms around me. If I didn't practically climb him, he'd probably throw me over his shoulder and dive back into the water.

"They're dead! I told you, Hank! We should've helped!" Alicia yells, releasing a sob.

"The wolves would've killed us too!" Hank's masculine voice snaps at me even with the distance, and I cringe. "You should thank me. I could've left you there."

"He's right. It was their fault for falling asleep during their watch. They could've gotten us killed." Tiffany hops down from a branch in one of the tangled trees. She spins around, grabbing onto one of the forgotten makeshift stakes.

"We could've at least tried." Alicia comes into view, her body scraped and bleeding. She must've climbed the trees too. "What if it was one of you?"

Tiffany steps closer to Alicia. "We wouldn't have fallen asleep."

A whistle cuts their argument off, the sound loud enough to hurt my ears. "Is the doctor alive? Jack is still breathing." I recognize Reggie's voice.

Chase hesitates, and the others look at him. I don't know if it's because he's afraid that the pack of wolves could come back or what, but he isn't quick to respond to the rest of our group on the beach. I can't really blame him. Just the sight of the blood on the sand twists my stomach.

"You don't have to be the doctor now, Chase." Davian tightens his jaw. "I don't even know how much you could do. Look at the amount of blood. No one could survive losing that much."

"No, it's fine. I'll do what I can. I was just...maybe stay here." Chase tries to let go of my hand, but my fingers tighten more. It's as if my body refuses to let him go.

He gives up trying and tugs me along through the waves. The others follow us, and we stay together, guarded, as we head to the aftermath. Bloody paw prints decorate the sand like spooky art intended for fall. I hop and step onto the clean spots while Chase kicks through, smearing away the blood the best he can.

My body cools as I search around the camp. Everything is ruined. The shelters lie in shambles, covered in even more blood. I've never seen something so horrendous in my life. Chase lifts me up, carrying me over...ugh.

No. Fuck.

I try not to think about the fact that Creed's body lies in pieces, torn apart like the prey he became. I keep my gaze toward the trees. These vicious wolves are on top here. I thought it was starvation or dehydration I would have to survive and not the wild monstrous wolves' unquenchable taste for blood.

"Fuck. This is not how I want to go." Evander steps up on my other side and brushes his shoulder to mine.

"Same, dude," Tristan mutters.

"We need better weapons. Higher shelter. Protection. Traps. Anything to give us a chance." Adam stays behind me out of view. "Maybe we can make platforms or something. Like hunters."

I accidentally dart my eyes to the sand, realizing that my foot sinks into a muddy pool of blood too heavy to absorb into the sand. I gag, nearly losing my dinner from last night, and Adam surprises me by spinning me around and scooping me up.

Our eyes meet, and his hazel eyes shift back and forth as he studies me, carrying me to the water. His chest rises and falls against mine, his muscles cording with his tenseness. The others continue to argue about what to do. I don't even care at this point. I just want the blood off me and the memory erased from my mind.

Adam sets me on my feet, letting the tide wash away the blood. Neither of us comments on the fact that my boobs were just pressed against his hard chest or how we're the only ones not trying to take charge. "There's nothing any of us can do until we come to an agreement. Why don't we see if we can find anything useful? I can't stand around and argue about pointless bullshit."

I bob my head, my tongue sticking to the roof of my mouth. Adam guides me back to the dry sand, keeping close as he tries to shield my view. His silent attempt to protect me from the aftermath hits me hard in a good way.

"We're going to gather more shit and do something useful. I suggest you guys salvage what you can here." Adam scoops up the empty supply bag. "Maybe we can find another one of these."

"Wait, I want to help. You're right, Adam. We need to act instead of fight." Alicia's voice shakes with her comment. I don't look at her. I can't. Behind her lies the bodies of several of our group. Including Penelope. My heart hurts remembering her screams for help and how no one even tried. Survival of the cowards is something I never thought about, but I guess bravery can ensure someone's death—at least on this island.

Tears well in my eyes, and I try my best not to cry. This is so unfair. The men who put us through this are fucking monsters. We shouldn't have to be in such a position to pick ourselves first, but here we are.

"If it's okay," Alicia adds when neither of us responds to her. I think Adam waits for me while I wait for him. Bloody feet step up beside mine, and I finally get myself to look at Alicia. Tiffany joins her, crossing her arms over her boobs. Ian falls behind them, keeping close and carrying a large branch.

"Yeah, sure," I manage to say.

Adam squeezes my hand. "As long as you don't trip us to save yourselves. Don't think I won't pull your asses down with me."

Tiffany scoffs, her eyebrows arching. "Don't act like—"

"Hey! See if you guys can get some more dry wood for the fire and fresh water. I need to try to clean Jack's wounds." Chase calls, cutting off Tiffany. His voice fades on the cool morning breeze. He points at Tristan and Evander. "One of you try to ignite the smoldering branches into a fire again. We need it."

"I thought I saw some fallen palm fronds not far down the beach. Why don't you guys grab them?" Adam asks the others, keeping his tone even. He obviously doesn't want Tiffany coming with us and gives them a task they can't really refuse. He turns to me. "I know you don't want to go back into the forest, but can you help me find the creek again?"

I lick my dry lips, tasting ocean salt on my mouth. It takes everything in me to nod my head, but I would want someone to do the same for me.

Just because we were attacked by wild animals and monstrous men left us here doesn't mean I have to act like them. We can still be civil and help each other.

"I will protect you, Eliana. I promise. We're going to survive this." Adam holds out his hand to me.

If only I believed him.

If only I didn't feel as if my life was almost over.

"Watch your step. I think this is where I ate shit and fell. Keep your eyes open for a grey wolf with freaky blue eyes. The one from the beach. It was the one that attacked me here too." I release a breath and look around the forest. Nothing has changed since I was here. I can even see the slide lines on the ground where I toppled into the ravine.

"It doesn't look as steep over there." Adam points to the right. "See how the trees begin to level out and straighten instead of curve? That's what we're looking for."

"You should've been the one helping to look for water." I smirk at him, trying not to think about why we're back here so soon. "You seem like you know what you're doing."

He shrugs. "My dad was a prepper. He thought the world was going to end, so we did a lot of camping and survivalist stuff. Who fucking knew that it would come in handy for me? And so, you know, I had planned to join whatever group you were on, but Tiffany kind of forced me into helping out with food."

"Davian avoided her too. Did you know he was in agriculture? I bet the guy can farm and shit." I let Adam guide me toward the level ground, leading to the creek shore.

"Already close to Davian, huh? I thought it would be Chase I'd have to worry about." He raises his eyebrows and stares at me in his peripheral vision.

"What?" I laugh in surprise. I knew they were all flirty, but this might be a bit ridiculous to think about right now. "I hope you guys aren't competing. That would be absurd. We're stranded on a damn island."

His smile widens, his face even more handsome with the gesture. I don't have to read his mind to know that he's only semi-serious. He's gauging my reaction. "Depends. Are the others my competition? Do I have a—"

Adam stumbles, his grip on me so tight that he pulls me with him, and together we trip. I land on my knees beside him, and something moves beneath me. I screech as fingers lock around my calf. Adam thrashes and kicks his leg, knocking whoever is beneath us away.

"Help...me." The strange, guttural voice sends ice down my back, and I scramble to get to my feet. It doesn't sound human—or at least, not like any human I've ever heard. "Help."

"Fuck, Eliana. Don't look. Turn away." Adam's desperation scares me even more. He waves his hand, shooing me, trying to get me to listen. My feet refuse to move. My fear wants me to throw myself at Adam for protection, but he holds his palm up. "Please. Just step back and look away. Don't look down."

Why did he have to say that? My rebellious eyes flick toward the ground. I gasp and cover my mouth, finally spinning away. I can't even process what I saw.

"Help," the creature—monster, weird-ass thing, whatever the hell it is—says again, groaning. "Adam."

Adam huffs and swears. "This can't fucking be real. I

mean, what the fuck? What happened to you, Freddy?" He knows him. I *know* him. Freddy is from our group. But that thing? No. Adam's right. This can't be real.

I look again, cringing as I force myself to try to pick out the familiar features of the man who was fine last night.

It must mean...I don't even know. Something in the food? The water? If that's the case—

"Help..." Freddy groans again. His words turn incoherent, and it sounds as if he lets out a deep cough.

"What the—shit! Shit!" Adam places his hand over my eyes, stopping me from looking again. It must be bad. "We have to go. This place is fucked up. Shit. Come on. We're tripping or something."

I snatch his hand and pull it away from my eyes, jerking my attention to where Freddy grunts and grumbles. And holy shit. Adam is right. I don't know what's going on but Freddy...he's not Freddy anymore. I don't know what he is.

His bloody body cracks and shifts, his back arching. His mouth opens inhumanly wide, and sharp fangs cut through his gums.

His skin breaks apart, and strange fur sprouts across his body in small patches.

Freddy screams, pain lacing his voice.

"What do we do?" I step a few feet away, pulling Adam with me. "Fuck. Let's go back to the others. Maybe Chas—"

A deep rumbling noise escapes Freddy's elongated mouth.

He stretches his curled fingers out. "Kill you. Run."

My body cools with his words.

I don't hesitate heeding his warning.

Grabbing Adam's hand, I drag him with me.

We run.

CHAPTER 6

CURSED

MY HEARTBEAT POUNDS in my ears. I try to ignore the pain as my feet crunch every stick and rock in my path. I hate being barefooted, and this cements the thought. I'm afraid to even look at the damage I withstand running in the wilderness of this godforsaken island. Freddy's warning repeats over and over again. I thought we'd be running from something else, but the terrifying noises echoing behind us come from him in his monstrous, mutated form.

A snarl sends goosebumps over my skin. I jerk my head and look behind us, catching sight of the familiar grey wolf with the blue eyes. I expect it to chase us, but it turns and jumps on top of Freddy, burying its teeth in Freddy's monstrous, cocked neck. He thrashes and bites the air, his fangs glistening even without the sun shining high overhead. It's dim in this part of the forest. The thick trees above us only allow a smattering of sunbeams to pepper the ground like starbursts.

"You're slowing down. Hustle, Eliana." Adam yanks me with him, heading toward the path we've broken that should take us back to the beach.

A whistle rings over my gasping breath, and a tall, muscular figure steps from the trees. My heart skips a beat at the sight of Kellan. I wasn't sure he'd be back or why he comes now. Maybe to call his pet off.

I nearly crash into Adam as he cuts me off, blocking me from Kellan. I automatically whip my head to look behind me, more concerned about the monster Freddy turns into and the wolf. Neither sneaks up on us. The wolf no longer snarls by Freddy. Shit. Where the fuck is...oh, God. Freddy's contorted body lies motionless on the ground. He's dead.

"Stay the hell back," Adam snaps, fisting his hands.

"I'm not going to hurt you, but someone else might. Come this way. I'll help you up. You need to be quiet. They're spreading out for one more sweep. If they catch you, you're as good as dead." Kellan waved his hand at me. "You could end up like the unworthy one."

Adam halts and tries to push me behind him. "Who the fuck—"

I dodge around him and head toward Kellan, my fear ignited by the collection of animal noises growing in volume. "It's okay, Adam. He won't hurt us. I've met him."

If snarls didn't bounce off the trees in a discordant song, Adam might argue with me. Instead, he rushes beside me and follows Kellan's instruction, pushing me up into the tree. Kellan helps Adam next, and the two of us sit on the highest branch we can before they thin out and grow too weak to support our weight.

"Don't worry about your group. They are being guarded. It's who lurks in the forest you must be worried about until we get them off our territory. You wandered too far upstream, Eliana. Next time, go the opposite direction, but don't pass the moon boulder. You'll know what I mean when you see it. Now, be quiet until I return. Not a sound. The unworthy one already drew enough attention as it is." Kellan gives me an intense look and then spins and runs away out of view, not waiting for me to reply.

So many questions flit through my mind. Like what is a moon boulder? Whose territory? Are we on someone's property and not an actual deserted island? And the others? Jesus. He's been watching us. I know he has. Whatever is going on here isn't good. It's lethal. Brutal. And I'm not so sure any of us are going to survive, even if we manage to keep food and water and shelter. There are far worse things on this island.

"Come here. I'll stabilize us. Just hold onto me," Adam whispers, wrapping his arm around my waist.

I bob my head and tuck my body into his side, trying not to think about the drop down to the ground below. Climbing up wasn't a problem, but now that I'm here, perched on a branch that scratches my ass, clinging to Adam...fuck. How are we getting down? What if I fall?

I inhale slow, deep breaths, trying to keep my body from trembling. I expect Adam to say something, but he remains silent. It's harder than I realized it would be. I fidget, wiggling my toes and fingers. If I shift too much, the branch will creak and give us away. Stupid anxiety. The bitch needs to leave me alone. I want nothing more than to distract myself by speaking what's on my mind to Adam. I can tell he's now suspicious because I said I knew Kellan, and he needs to know it's nothing like he could think.

Hours feel like they pass, and I listen to the sounds of the forest. Not a single wolf howls, and thankfully, I don't hear any human screams. Adam gently rubs his hand up and down my side, the sensation helping to keep me calm. Maybe it helps him stay calm as well. As worried as I am about what goes on in his head, the small gesture eases my nerves a bit. He wouldn't be silently affectionate if he already distrusts me. I have hope that he'll hear me out and let me speak without jumping to conclusions.

I snuggle closer, breathing in the scent of Adam's skin. He smells of citronella and seawater, the fragrance strangely comforting. The heat of his body combats the cool shade blocking the sun, and I meet his hazel eyes. He studies my face, his eyes drinking me in, shifting to glance at my mouth. My anxiety shifts into something lighter yet more intense. His attraction to me is more obvious than ever as we stare at each other in silence. It's not uncomfortable or awkward, but more as if we need this time to familiarize ourselves with each other. We have to survive this together after all.

Branches snap below us, and I hold my breath, digging my fingers into Adam's bare hip. His muscles ripple as he flexes in anticipation. If I can hear his heart, others might. I hate this. I hate how vulnerable I feel. How shitty this situation is.

"Eliana, it's me." Kellan steps into view below. "Jump and I'll catch you."

Adam stops me, tightening his arms. Leaning in, he whispers, "I'll go first and make sure it's really safe."

I slowly nod my head. I trust Adam more than I do Kellan. Even though Kellan gave me a bag of supplies, he still seems to be part of this mess. He doesn't have to worry about wolves or dying. He's just...I don't even know.

Kellan realizes that I'm not going to just throw myself from the spot and trust that he'll catch me. He crosses his arms over his chest, never taking his eyes off me. So I return the favor. As Adam shifts around me and lowers himself to dangle from the branch, I lock my eyes on Kellan, silently making myself clear that I'm not going to comply just because he acts like he's helping. Raising an eyebrow, he refuses to release me from our staring contest even with Adam dropping to his feet.

I refuse to break first, memorizing him as if my life depends on knowing every detail of his body. He's handsome in a wild way, his hair a mess of wavy strands and his face scruffy with at least a week-old beard. And his eyes? They're still the most mesmerizing color I've ever seen. The blue is nearly ethereal, glowing in the shadows as if something lights them from within. It's in this moment I realize something. No, it can't be. There's no way that his eyes match his pet wolf's. Right? I'll have to see them side-by-side...which I never have.

I push the thought away as Adam extends his arms out to me, wiggling his fingers. I gather the courage to abandon the branch. I carefully lower myself, trying not to think about the fact that both men get a personal view of my vagina and ass as I squat to dangle from the branch. I place my feet on the one below and use the side of the trunk to steady myself. Being naked and unfamiliar with someone is awkward as hell. This is relationship-status closeness. Maybe medical professional or waxer. Regardless, I'd prefer not to give a sexy man this view unless we're going to sleep together, and I've had time to prepare.

"You can just jump from there. I'll catch you." Adam

stands below me, his flexing form daring Kellan to try to intervene.

I tip my chin to my chest and look at both of them. Adam stares into my eyes, his gaze unwavering. Kellan, on the other hand, blatantly memorizes every inch of me, his attraction clear with the arousal of his body. Tingles burst through me, my excitement over his reaction surprising me. I never thought I'd like being stared at in such a way.

"Whenever you're ready," Adam adds, because I'm not quick to move.

The longer I hang like this, the harder it is for me to let go. I just need to fucking do it. I really wish I had my big girl panties. Any panties at all, actually. I shouldn't be thinking about Kellan liking the way I look. I shouldn't want anything to do with him, especially with Adam here.

Sucking in a deep breath, I release the branch. The world rushes around me, and my stomach flies to my throat, but I don't get sick or anything. It reminds me of why I hate rollercoasters. I hate the sensation of my body trying to rearrange itself.

The fall only lasts a second, so quickly that I can't make a sound, and Adam catches me, lowering me to the ground until my feet touch the cool dirt. He hugs me close, wrapping his arms around me, and I sink against him.

"See, you can trust me for anything," he murmurs, combing my hair behind my ear.

His words dig at me, the real meaning clearer than the ocean around the island. He wants me to know that I can tell him anything, especially regarding Kellan. Maybe that I shouldn't trust the man either. How I know? It's just a hunch.

I touch my hand to his shoulder. "I know. Thanks for that."

Clearing his throat, Kellan steps into my personal space. His confidence and bravado shock me. He acts like this whole situation is normal and like we're close friends. I frown at him, resisting the urge to step back. Another part of me wants to throw away my good senses and step closer instead. He hovers within my reach and close enough for me to catch a hint of his scent—like woods and musk and something more floral. Lavender, perhaps.

"I'll walk you back to your camp if you'd like, Eliana. You'll be safe with me." Kellan reaches out and grazes his fingers over my arm, ignoring Adam completely.

I inhale a soft breath, the strange shock of his touch sending a jolt of electricity through me. I gape at him, my mouth hanging open. I still have so many questions.

Adam slides his fingers through mine and tugs me closer to him protectively. "I think we're good, man. I remember the way back."

I automatically let him tuck me under his arm. Kellan scowls, his face transforming from soft to intimidating and hard in a split second. I swear that I spot a flash of gold crossing his irises.

Kellan flares his nostrils. "Eliana, he's already put you in danger. I will ensure nothing and nobody comes after you. It would be my plea—"

"Do you think we're stupid? There's no fucking way we'll ever be safe with you. You work with the fuckers who left us here, don't you?" Adam twists and grabs a tree branch, breaking it off one-handed.

Kellan doesn't step back or anything. His features remain sharp as he gives Adam a long look. He's trying to determine if he's a real threat or not. And with the way he crosses his arms, I can see that he doesn't believe he is.

"If you weren't stupid, you wouldn't have brought her here. And no, I don't work for anyone." Kellan's jaw twitches as he says the words, his blue eyes capturing mine all over again. He doesn't give Adam any attention despite speaking to him. "I was only trying to help Eliana. She deserves protection and respect. If you truly knew how special a female is, then you'd agree to let me escort you. But obviously, you were going to take your position of power for granted. Just like you probably have done with women all your life."

I frown and shift my gaze. That's kind of fucking weird of him to say.

Adam puffs out his chest, tightening his fingers around mine, and then he tugs me along. He doesn't respond to Kellan and guides me to where Chase had marked the trees to indicate where we need to go.

"Eliana," Kellan says, his voice echoing through the forest. "You don't have to obey him. You don't belong to him."

I can't help myself and turn to look at him from over my shoulder.

"I know you want answers, and it's almost time that I can give them to you. You have to trust me. I'll protect you." Kellan meanders behind us, following at a distance.

Trust him? No. His comment secures my guard in place. He has answers and doesn't want to share them. Shaking my head, I call, "I'm good with Adam. We can handle ourselves."

"I hope so, my love. Only the strong will be selected, so stay safe and remember what I said about the creek." Kellan offers me a soft smile. "I'll be around."

Adam tugs me faster, practically forcing me to sprint to keep up with him. I gaze at the ground in front of me, focusing on my footing to ensure I don't fall. Looking over my shoulder again, I try to glimpse one last look at Kellan, but he's gone.

And then I see the wolf. The bright blue eyes.

I can tell something is massively strange about this place, and I think it has to do with the wolves. There is no other explanation.

If only Kellan would offer me the answers now.

A part of me is afraid to find out.

I know I won't like the truth.

I just hope that the truth helps me survive. Because right

now, after everything, I'm not sure any of us are ever going to make it out of this alive. Not with the way things are going.

Now that my fear of dying subsides, everything crashes over me in a rush of despair. People are dead. Penelope and Creed never deserved that kind of end. It makes me sick to think about it. And Jack? Oh, no. It's been hours. We were supposed to bring the water.

I lick my lips. "We forgot the water. We have to go back."

Adam scrubs his face as if he's fighting with himself about what we should do. If we go back to the creek, we risk whatever danger lies in the forest. It might even be pointless after so much time has passed. Jack could be dead. But then, what if he's not? What if he dies because we don't bring the water?

"I can go get the water and you can go see how things are. I don't mind." If only I actually believed myself. I don't really want to go back to the creek alone.

"No, we're not separating. I don't like the way that fucker looked at you. He's obviously been watching and stalking. I wish you would've told us, Eliana. Had we known…never mind. There's no point in getting caught up with this shit. Let's just hurry. We'll get what we can, and then we need to think about another water source. I can build something for when it rains. My dad was a bit paranoid about world-ending shit and taught me a few things." Adam scrubs the back of his head, messing with his black hair. I can tell that me keeping Kellan a secret bothers him, but I don't think I would go back and change things. It's hard to explain. I know what people are capable of when they're desperate. I've done things that I never imagined I would to keep a roof over my head, especially after my parents died.

Damn. I haven't thought about them in a while. It always hurts too much.

"Hey! Eliana. Adam! Where the fuck have you been? We thought the wolves got you. We've been looking everywhere." Evander stakes his makeshift weapon into the ground, his eyes darting over me as if he expects to see me beat up and wounded. "We went to the creek and you weren't there, but we think we found Freddy. You need to hurry and see this bullshit. It's insane."

My heart seizes, skipping a beat at his words. With the thought of Freddy, I envision his weird form in the woods and how his body contorted, breaking and changing. I remember how the blue-eyed wolf went after him and sank its fangs into his throat.

"You found them." Chase strides up behind Evander and dodges past him, jogging in my direction.

The way his body flexes and moves with each of his steps draws my mind away from the disgusting image of Freddy imprinted on my brain. What is wrong with me? Is this whole situation going to make me constantly refocus my mind on more pleasant things? Maybe that's what I should do. I need something, anything, to get my mind away from the fact that

I could die at any moment.

I automatically open my arms for Chase, and he engulfs me in a hug.

It should be weird with the two of us naked, but all I feel right now is safe. I feel cared about. I never expected to be over-whelmed by such a foreign emotion. Adam confirmed that he wasn't the only one attracted to me, but this proves it.

"Are you hurt? Where have you been? I was so fucking scared." Chase buries his face into the crook of my neck. "We've already lost so many people. I didn't want to lose you guys either."

I purse my lips together at his words. I might've been overthinking things.

"I'm glad to hear that you fucking care about me, doc." Adam surprise hugs Chase from behind, leaning in until his face is close to mine. "Your chivalrous ways get me right in the nuts. Want to see? Don't forget you promised to protect me too."

Chase barks a laugh, his voice vibrating across my skin. His amusement with Adam's teasing eases the dread trying to keep me down. "It's more about losing your skills, asshole. Hate to break it to you, but my boner is for what you bring to the group, not you."

"Careful, doc. I know first aid. Don't think you're price-less around here." Evander scrubs his fist into Chase's hair.

I can't stop smiling at their banter. If I didn't know for a fact that we were all strangers before we ended up on that yacht, I'd have thought they were friends.

"And what about me? I haven't really proved anything except that I'm good at getting into trouble and crying." I don't know why I say it. Maybe because it's true. I'm not some badass who knows how to survive in the wild. I only know how to survive on the streets. I know how to protect myself to the best of my ability.

Trusting anyone has been hard for me...even now. A part of me wants to trust this group. Another part of me knows better. If they turn against me—I can't think like that.

Chase tips his head back and meets my eyes. "Give yourself some credit, Eliana. I'm pretty fucking sure Davian might've cried more than you."

Adam groans. "So have I. This bullshit is scary as fuck. The fact that you kept it together when we were up that tree was the only reason I wasn't a sobbing bastard." He's full of it, but I let him try to make me feel better.

I laugh, shaking my head. "I guess that's true. You were shaking harder than my favorite vibrator."

The three of them gawk at me, stunned by my comment. Chase breaks first, whipping his head back with a roar of a laugh.

"Fuck, Eliana. Don't look at me. You just slapped that image into my brain, and now I have a fucking boner. Not cool when I can't hide this shit." Adam pulls away from me. Instead of trying to cover himself, he flicks his hands at his dick, pointing it out.

"I'm going to slap something else if you don't point that thing away from me." I pretend to swat my hand at him, making him jump back.

Chase and Evander grab onto Adam, locking him in place. He surprises me by standing tall, refusing to fight against them. A sexy smile curls his lips, matching the ones crossing on the other two's mouths. They all silently dare me to stay good to my threat.

"Do what you feel you gotta do, little badass," Adam says, swinging his hips just enough to wave his hard-on at me.

"It sounds like you want me to whack your cock." I raise an eyebrow. "Is that your kink? You like it rough?"

Adam swears under his breath, finally reacting to Chase and Evander restraining him. And now I know why. It's a damn boner brigade. Adam's no longer alone with his cock salute to my teasing words about my vibrator.

"Are you guys kidding me?" I clap my hands with a laugh, bending over to clutch my knees. I shouldn't find this so funny, not in a time like this, but it feels like for the first time since arriving here, I can breathe.

"You can't hold something so uncontrollable against us," Chase says, still smiling. "It's a natural reaction."

I spin on my feet, my body heating up the longer I stare at them. "Whatever you say, doctor. Why don't the three of you do what you have to do and meet me back at camp?"

"You irresistible tease," Evander practically purrs. "You're planning on torturing us until we get off this fucking island, aren't you?"

I bat my eyelashes at him. "Maybe. Gotta have something to do to pass the time between all the deadly shit." At least, in the moments when we're not fighting for our lives. I don't say the thoughts out loud.

"Only *something*, little badass? Is that all I am to you? I thought we had a connection up in that tree." Adam wags his eyebrows at me. "Even the douche fuckhead knew it. He was go—"

"Who the hell are you talking about?" Evander asks, his body tensing.

I frown. The three of them distracted me. I hadn't even thought about telling them about Kellan yet.

"Some bastard helped us. He's one of them," Adam responds, not mentioning that Kellan met me first. "There is some weird shit happening on this island, and—"

"Chase! Chase, come quick! It's Jack!" Tiffany's voice rings through the air. "Something's happening."

Rushing toward me, Chase grabs my hand, yanking me with him. Evander and Adam jog behind us, and I kick up sand. We run the rest of the way to our camp, and I spot something on the ground by the trees. Ew, no. What the fuck?

Not again.

Fuck, please. Not again.

I turn my back on the beastly creature and cover my face. Why is this happening? Who is it now? I scream in anger, swearing at the island. At the situation.

A soft howl groans from a distance. And then I hear a familiar voice swirling through my mind.

"Eliana, I'll come for you tonight." It's Kellan.

But how?

A hand grabs my shoulder, spinning me around. Adam looks into my eyes. "Hey, take a breath. That's Freddy's body. They brought him back to bury him with the others. He's dead, remember? He won't hurt you."

I squeeze my eyes shut, trying to push Kellan's voice away along with the image of Freddy in his strange monstrous form.

"Don't tell anyone," Kellan's voice whispers, still tangling with my rushing thoughts, trying to draw my focus from Adam. "Please, trust me. You can't know yet. It's not time."

Time for what? I'm so confused.

"Fuck, restrain him!" Chase yells, dragging my attention back to our group.

I watch in horror as Jack bucks his body in the sand. His bones crunch and snap, the sound grating on my nerves.

It's happening again.

He's changing like Freddy had in the forest. Cocking his head, Jack glowers at me, his mouth contorting.

He snarls.

CHAPTER 7

Chase

MERCY

I'VE NEVER SEEN anything like this. My mind can't wrap around the fact that Jack's body cracks and splits apart as if something inside him tries to break free. Davian and Tristan pin his shoulders, and I use my weight to keep his legs restrained.

Guttural, wet sounds escape his monstrous mouth, and he yells in pain.

"He's dying." Eliana's words hum in my ears, the

statement sounding as if she knows for certain. "Adam, it was like this with Freddy."

"A wolf mauled him and ripped his throat out," Adam responds, keeping Eliana close within reach.

Their conversation is the only thing keeping me from letting Jack overpower us. He's strong as hell. More so than before. This is impossible. Physically impossible. It's as if Jack evolves from the human species to something else altogether.

"It was putting Freddy out of his misery. He was sick or something." Eliana steps closer, her movements distracting me. "We have to do the same. It's the most humane thing. We can't risk him hurting us either. He's not thinking the same."

"You better not be implying what I think you are," Alicia snaps, interjecting herself into Eliana and Adam's conversation. "If Jack is sick, Chase can heal him. It's his job."

I grind my teeth and press harder into Jack. "I'm a doctor not a fucking miracle worker. I have nothing to go on. No tests. Medication. Nothing." The last thing I need is for the others to believe I can work magic. I'm a man of science, and I know my limitations. This is one of them.

"He's not Jack anymore," Eliana says, standing up to Alicia. "And Chase is right. What exactly do you think he can do? Look at that thing. We can't let him stay like that."

It's clear on Eliana's face that she is implying a mercy kill. Seeing and hearing Jack in agony as his body breaks and destroys itself gets to me as well. I'm a man of compassion and mercy. It's why I lost my medical license and practice. I gave someone the humane death they asked for.

"You're crazy!" Alicia throws her arms up. "We can't do this."

"We aren't doing this," Tiffany says, speaking up. "Both of you shut up and let Chase work. He'll figure this out."

She's going to be disappointed when she realizes I agree with Eliana. It is in Jack's best interest not to remain in this state until his body destroys itself completely. I won't tell anyone, though. I don't want to fight them. They're too emotional to understand. Not only is Jack a threat, but he could be contagious. We don't know what we're dealing with and only that we're dealing with something dangerous.

"Chase, what do you need, man?" Adam asks, planting himself between Eliana and the other two women.

"Space. Get them back." I crack my neck and think things over once more just to be certain. I never imagined I'd be in this position again or how easy the decision is. I plan to show Jack compassion and mercy. This time, it won't only be for my patient. It'll be for us. I can't trust that whatever mutates Jack won't spread.

The others around me argue over what to do, so I take matters into my own hands. I don't need to wait for them. Jack changes rapidly until he writhes in a grotesque half-human state. Reaching for the hunting knife sitting with the few supplies we have left from the survival bag, I grip it in my fist and prepare to end Jack's life as swiftly and as painlessly as I possibly can.

I just need to get him into the right position. I would much prefer a different method, but this is the only one I know of with what I have. This might change everything. They're going to know what kind of doctor and man I truly am. I don't see another way. I need to protect us. I need to ensure Jack finds peace from this suffering. This is no way for him to live. He's already dying. His wounds were bad and he lost too much blood.

I tighten my jaw and look at Davian and Tristan. "I need you to help sit him up. Tristan, come pin his legs down. I need to reposition myself. Watch out for his hands and teeth. I don't know what the hell is happening to him, but if he's contagious..." I let my words trail off, allowing them to fill in the blanks with their own imagination.

Alicia and Eliana continue to argue, and Evander gets between the two of them next. Adam looks ready to do something crazy to get Alicia to back up. I already know that dude likes Eliana, and I don't know how I feel about it. Well, I'm jealous that she shows anybody else even an ounce of attention, but I can't exactly blame her. She doesn't belong to me. It's just...

Jack growls, sounding like an animal, and he gnashes his teeth, trying to bite. It kicks me into action, stealing my attention from Eliana. I scramble to my knees and crawl around Tristan, taking his place. I don't even wait for him to pin Jack's legs. I have to do this now and quickly.

Grazing my fingers over the back of Jack's head, I feel my way to the base of his skull. I have to get this right. If I miss even by a little, he'll just lose control of his body and not die. I want to end his life while I destroy his nervous system.

"I'm sorry, Jack. This is the only way to stop your suffering. I hope you understand," I murmur, praying nobody hears me before I adjust my hand.

"Chase, what are you doing?" Davian asks, his voice lowering. He must've heard me.

"What I have to do." I don't give him a chance to speak up or try to stop me. Aiming the hunting blade, I jam it into the base of Jack's skull, severing his spinal cord and ending his life.

He doesn't even make a sound as his monstrous form collapses, going to limp in my arms. Utter silence hangs in the air, and I realize that everyone stares at me as I pull the blade from Jack's body.

"Chase! Are you fucking kidding me? You killed him!" Alicia shouts, wringing her hands together. "You bastard!"

She charges me, but Eliana rushes her, shoving her hard enough to send her sprawling across the sand. Fisting his hand, Ian tries to grab onto Eliana, and Evander swings his arm and punches him in the face.

"Davian, take Chase and get out of here. I'll come to find you when things cool off." Evander points at me. "We're going to have a fucking talk. You got it?"

Alicia places her hands on her hips. "I want to talk now. What he did—"

"He did the most humane thing. You don't understand what's going on here. You haven't seen what I've seen." Eliana shifts in the sand, her sudden protectiveness hot as fuck.

"Enough! Everyone needs to chill out!" Tristan yells. He turns to me. "You and Eliana go take a stroll." Pointing at Alicia next, he adds, "Pick someone and head in the opposite direction. Stay on the beach. The rest of us are going to fucking clean up and bury these bodies. We can't have them near our camp. It could attract more animals."

"How is this even fair? They should be the ones to handle it." Tiffany speaks up, her lips curling in disgust.

Ian grabs her arm. "You won't have to do any of that. Come on. Let them work it out."

I inhale a deep breath and push to my feet. I only allow Davian to take the knife from me because I don't want to fight him. All I wanted to do was take Jack's pain away and protect us, and that's what I did. I don't regret it.

Eliana trudges her way toward me and holds her hand out. "Let's go see if we can find some more supplies. They're right. We need to take a break from this bullshit."

I let Eliana help me to my feet, and she closes her eyes and inhales a deep breath. This wasn't how I imagined the day to turn out. I was scared as fuck when Adam and Eliana didn't return right away and then relieved when they showed up. I thought I'd spend the rest of the day staying close to her but not because I ended someone's life.

Neither of us speaks as we stroll along the shore, heading who knows where. Eliana swings our hands between us, and I stare at her as she searches our surroundings.

"I'm sorry, Eliana," I say, breaking the silence.

She squeezes my fingers. "You don't have to apologize. I just hope that you didn't do that because of me. I would've done it if that were the case. You're a doctor, for Christ's sake. You save people."

I scrub my freehand on the back of my neck, the warm sunshine heating me up despite the crisp breeze blowing in from the sea. "I chose to do it. You didn't influence my decision. I might be a doctor...at least, I used to be before my license was suspended. But I'm also a man who believes in mercy when asked for it. This was one of those circumstances. I saw whatever the fuck happened to Freddy was happening to Jack. He was in a lot of pain, and he was suffering. There was nothing else we could've done, especially with his injuries."

She remains quiet, thinking over my words. I turn my gaze toward the waves, watching the foam crawl toward us only to be dragged back out. There is no other land on the horizon. This island is isolated from the rest of the world. I haven't seen a plane or a boat or anything like that either.

"What do you think the others are going to do?" Her soft

voice draws my attention back to her, and she glides her tongue over her bottom lip before she sucks it into her mouth. "I wonder if we should separate from them. I have a feeling they're going to act as if we're savages or something."

She might be right. I don't know anyone well enough to make an educated guess about what they would do.

"Whatever happens, I won't let anybody hurt you. We need to stick together. I know we don't know each other well, but I feel that we see things the same way." I can't resist reaching up and combing my fingers through her dark tresses, pushing them behind her ear. "What do you say?"

"I'm here now, aren't I?" Eliana shifts on her feet, reaching out to press her hand over mine. "You did the right thing. I'm glad you did it. If that were me..." She lets her voice fade.

"Same for me. If that ever happened, do what you have to do." I study her brown eyes, the bright sunlight bringing out flecks of gold in their depths.

She laughs, the sound sexy and breathless. "This is all so crazy. I can't believe we're making a mercy pact."

"Should we seal it with a kiss?" My question could ruin everything, but there's something about the new lightness in her voice untainted by what happens around us that I want to test. Like she said, she is here with me and not them.

She keeps her undivided attention on me despite hearing the others yelling at each other in the distance. Without a word, she stands up on her tiptoes, closing the space to me. I lean in and lock my lips to hers, feeling the softness of her pouty mouth against mine. The saltiness of her kiss reminds me of the seawater yet there's still a hint of sweetness from the fruit she seems to favor over anything else.

I don't get carried away, knowing that if I do, she will feel exactly what she does to me. Being so close to her beautiful, naked body fills me with so much lust that I imagine picking her up and pressing her back against the palm tree to fuck her how I want.

She moans, deepening her kiss and traveling her hands up my chest and to my shoulders.

Fuck. I'm going to regret this. Pulling away, I force myself to take a step back before she feels my cock against her body.

"If you keep kissing me like that, I'm going to want more," I murmur, grazing my fingers over her jaw. "I could really use that kind of distraction. And you are just so...it's hard to explain, Eliana. You're gorgeous and empathetic. Smart. You hold your ground, and I respect your ability to get shit done."

A smile lights her face. "You're not making denying you easy." Gliding her hand over my shoulder, she explores by bicep, working her way down until she shifts her fingers to my side.

I hold still under her touch, savoring the sensation of her body so close to mine. My nuts throb in anticipation, and I prepare myself to take this wherever she leads. Stretching closer again, she kisses me while pressing her tits flush against my chest. And fuck. It's been a while since I've had a woman in my arms. No one wants a man with a possible record hanging over his head. They usually don't go for my type of compassion either. But Eliana? This fucking island? It gets to me.

"Eliana," I murmur, trying to break away from her mouth. "If you don't want to fuck, we need to stop."

Her fingers wrap around my cock, stroking me in a way that weakens my knees. That was not what I was expecting, and I moan deep in my throat, picking her up with one hand to carry her toward the tree line. I prop her back against a tall palm tree, keeping us upright because fuck the sand, and she adjusts herself, aligning our bodies, letting me rub my tip to her wetness.

"Are you sure?" I ask, breaking from her mouth to kiss down her throat. "We don't have protection."

"I have an IUD," she says, stretching her neck, silently begging for more. "Now fuck me. We need something good to happen today."

She's not wrong. This moment with her will ensure I forget the day, even for a little while. Her warm pussy already feels so incredible, her lips welcoming me in as I tease her, not giving her more than an inch. I want to savor her and let her feel every inch of me. I want her to ask for more quicker. I want her shaking until I thrust hard and deep into her.

I kiss her more desperately, rocking slowly. She moans and nips my bottom lip, squirming like crazy. She slides her hand down my abs, rubbing her clit for a moment before trying to get me to slide all the way in as her body drips in hot, sexy excitement.

"Eliana, don't." The sharp tone of an unfamiliar voice snaps through the air, startling both of us. I nearly lose my hold and push into her. I can't concentrate on protecting her with my cock dying to feel more.

"What the hell!" I shout, slipping out of her. "Stay the fuck back."

I pull away from Eliana, spinning her around to set her on her feet. A man stands within the trees, the shade and thick vegetation obscuring his face, but I don't recognize him. How does he know Eliana's name? Why is he creeping around? I'm pissed. Furious. Fucking voyeur.

Muscles rippling across the asshole's body. He ignores me, stepping over a fallen trunk. "We don't know if he's worthy of you," the fucker continues, striding closer. "You can't be with him."

"Kellan!" Eliana screeches, digging her nails into my shoulders. "Seriously? You're stalking me?"

Rage burns through me at her comment. She knows him, but it doesn't sound good. Stalking? Commanding she can't be with me? What? I curl my hands into fists. I'll kill him before he tries anything. Not only did this asshole cock-block me, but he also now tries to get within reach of Eliana.

I swing my arm, putting my whole body into the punch.

Stumbling, I hit air. The bastard quickly dodges out of my way. He releases a deep, throaty noise—primal and possessive, almost like he is warning me.

I refuse to let him intimidate me. "Stay back and leave us alone. I mean it."

"Eliana—"

I prepare to tackle him, he is ignoring me completely, not helping my annoyance. Locking her fingers around me, Eliana tugs me back. I automatically step back without resisting. I don't know who the fuck this guy is, but Eliana cares enough about me to intervene.

Eliana rests her hands on my shoulders, pressing against my back. "Please, Chase. He's dangerous. I don't want you getting hurt." Sliding around me, she moves close to my side, letting me sling my arm across her lower back to squeeze her hip. She points at the guy—Kellan—pursing her lips. "You need to listen to Chase and leave. I don't want to talk to you unless you're ready to give me answers. And try to tell me what and who I can do again and see what happens. That's none of your damn business."

It takes everything in me not to look her in the eyes. I can't take my eyes away from the threat, but I want to study her expression and get a clearer idea of what or who I'm dealing with. She obviously knows him. But how?

And what does she mean about answers?

The guy continues ignoring me, locking his gaze on

Eliana. "I told you—"

Anger crashes over me, and I charge forward. I plow into the guy, knocking him off his feet. Swinging my arm, I punch him in the face, catching him off guard this time. Except he doesn't fight back, remaining calm. It pisses me off even more, and I take another swing at him.

"You know what's going on here! You better tell us before I beat the shit out of you, you asshole!" I grab a fistful of his hair, tipping his head back.

Again, he doesn't respond or react.

I jerk my arm, preparing to jab my fist into his nose, but Eliana locks her hand around my wrist, stopping me. She's stronger than she looks. Yanking back, she knocks me off of the man. I scramble to my feet and prepare to fight against his counterattack. He doesn't move from the ground. He just lays there, resting on his elbows.

"Chase, you need to calm down. He's with them. He's part of this, and I don't want you to risk your life. We don't know what they're capable of." Eliana wraps her arms around me from behind and tugs me back, adding more space between us and the bastard on the ground.

I release a heavy breath and shake out my bleeding fist. "We need to do what it takes to get answers."

She steps around me and faces me, leaving her back exposed. I train my gaze on the guy instead of her. I just want to pick her up and keep her safe. I want to clobber that bastard until he tells us everything.

"Let me handle it. He helped me on the first day when the wolf attacked and I found the creek. He's the one who gave me the backpack." Eliana presses her palm against my chest. "He helped Adam and me the last time too. He made sure that the others with him didn't find us."

"He could be setting us up. You can't trust him," I argue, flicking my eyes from Eliana to the guy.

"I don't trust him. But I don't want you risking your life by trying to beat the answers out of him. So, please. Let me handle this." Eliana runs her fingers up my chest and to my neck. Stretching up, she brushes her lips to mine, waiting for me to relax.

The guy burns me a glare, watching Eliana kiss me from his spot on the ground. His muscles ripple, and he digs his fingers into the sand. Watching her with me gets to him. He looks ready to jump up at any second now to finally fight me. I almost want him to. I kiss Eliana deeper, sliding my hand around her lower back to pull her even closer to test his resolve.

Something strange flashes in his eyes. It's as if the sun reflects at me, but he sits in the shade. Something's wrong with him. He's part of this mess, and I know whatever he's involved in might be the end of me.

"Please, Chase," Eliana murmurs against my lips. "I need to handle this. He won't hurt me. I know he won't. But you? Just please."

I have no right to deny her. I don't even know why she asks me. I don't control her. The fact that she does ask me awakens something inside me. My respect for her grows even more. My attraction does too.

Slowly, I nod my head. "Okay. I'll let you handle this. But I want to know everything."

"No secrets. Not anymore. We're in this together." She offers me a reassuring smile, though her eyes don't light up with it.

"No secrets," I repeat.

I turn my gaze away from Eliana to look at the asshole. My heart sinks into my stomach. He's gone. The fucker got away, and I missed it.

Eliana sighs and takes my hand. "He'll be back. I know he will be. Let's just find somewhere to wait out the day until Adam comes for us."

I let her guide me away from the tree line until we reach the waves. I never thought I'd be standing naked with a beautiful woman on a beach in a tropical paradise but here I am.

Eliana dips her toe into the lapping wave. "I still can't believe any of this. I never thought I'd be used to just strolling around butt-ass naked like this. My modesty is gone."

I chuckle, trying my best not to turn to search the trees again. "I'm used to seeing naked people. But being naked...at least, I can see what the competition is. Well, what the competition was."

Her smile falters, and I regret my words immediately. I shouldn't have assumed that just because we kissed and started to fuck that would mean we were together or anything.

She crinkles her nose. "Chase...I think you're sexy, funny, caring—"

I shake my head, laughing with my nerves. Damn it. I hate this type of speech. "Ending this already, huh? You didn't even give me a chance to show you a good time."

She blinks her eyes a few times, her face deepening in color and not from the sun. "We can still have a good time. It's just...with this whole situation, I think it's best if we keep things casual. I hope you understand."

I do understand, but it doesn't mean that I have to like it. It makes me wonder a bit. I know that she spent a couple hours alone with Adam. Who's to say they didn't do anything? Not that it matters.

At least, it shouldn't matter.

I force myself to nod. "Yeah. I get it. I didn't mean to assume anything. Why don't we—"

Eliana cuts me off with another kiss, her mouth molding to mine as she glides her tongue between my lips. I moan at the sensation, my body hardening once again. My cock throbs with need. I wonder if she plans to distract me like we had intended. I crave it.

A whistle sounds over the hum of the ocean, drawing our attention away from each other. I glower at the sand and then look to see part of our group kicking their way in our direction.

"Oh, no," Eliana whispers. "Are they carrying supplies?"

Squinting my eyes, I spot what she does. Tristan, Adam, Evander, and Davian look as if they are leaving the camp we had built. No one else is with them either.

I link my hand with Eliana's and pull her away from the water. "What's going on?" I ask, shouting the words.

"We're splitting up temporarily," Evander says, striding ahead of the others. "The others are going to need more time to cool off. We can discuss it more later. We need to get shit together for a new camp tonight."

I side-glance Eliana. "They must've decided I'm too much of a monster to have around."

She exhales a long breath. "They're going to realize they need a monster on their side if they're going to survive this. I'm sure they'll see."

If only that didn't have to be the case. But Eliana is right. This island seems to devour the weak. I'll do whatever it takes to be strong.

CHAPTER 8

Eliana

DIFFICULT DECISIONS

I REST MY head on Davian's shoulder, using him to keep upright. It's been three nights since we split off from the others, and we're all getting restless. I considered going back to our old shelter to see if we could work things out, but Chase and Evander asked me not to. They don't think the risk is worth it. I think they're just stubborn and want to make a point. I can't really blame them.

"Are you still hungry, Elle? There's enough light for me to

get a couple pieces of fruit for you." Davian meets my gaze. "I wouldn't mind. I'm bored as fuck and need to stretch."

I open my mouth to offer to go with him, but Evander grumbles something indecipherable under his breath and nudges Chase, pointing down the beach.

"Maybe stick around for a couple more minutes. That psycho is walking with a purpose." Tristan grabs his stick from the sand beside him.

He's talking about Alicia as she leads her group, carrying her own makeshift spear. They look rough, their bodies scraped and bruised up. Even from here, I can see the mosquito bites clustered across their limbs.

"Let's just hear them out, okay? I don't want to start shit if we don't have to." Adam gets to his feet and dusts the sand off his ass. He's already more tanned from sitting in the sun. Only Davian keeps to the shade of the tree beside me, his fair skin tinged pink with a sunburn.

My skin is super dry from the salt and the sand, but I try not to think about it. I've grown used to being uncomfortable. It could be worse. I could be in pain. I could be dead.

"Hey, if you're here for any other reason than to make amends with us, turn your asses around and go back to your camp." Evander takes the spear from Tristan. We each have one, but I know he wants to make it look as if we don't. "We don't want trouble."

None of us trust them. We've just grown to trust each

other. Because Tristan, Davian, Adam, and Evander chose us. Well, technically, they chose Chase. He's the one that group is truly pissed off at even though it was me who mentioned a mercy killing to begin with.

"Relax, hot-head. We're not here to fight. We're here to discuss the situation now that we've had time to think." Tiffany strides up next to Alicia and locks her arm with hers. It looks like they might've become best friends in the last couple days. I don't know why, but I'm a bit jealous. A bit sad too. It reminds me that Penelope died. I saw myself being her friend.

I hate that the thought crosses my mind, but a part of me wishes it was one of them instead of her. Am I fucked up? Maybe. At least I'm honest with myself.

"What situation? There isn't a situation. You guys need to accept that this isn't the world we left. This island is going to kill us if we don't take care of ourselves first." Tristan clenches his fingers into fists, his composure faltering. He might not want to start trouble, but he'll fight back if he has to.

Adam grabs his shoulder, ensuring he doesn't swing his spear or something. "He's right. You didn't see everything we did."

"Like hell, we didn't. We were almost mauled by wolves." Alicia places her hands on her hips. She scowls and looks at Chase. If she could murder him with her eyes...I'd tackle her. Just the way she looks at him infuriates me.

"Exactly our point. Whatever attacked us weren't normal

wolves. You saw Jack. He was infected by something. His body was evolving in a way I've never seen." Chase crosses his arms over his broad chest. "Freddy, too. If you can't accept that, then you're misguided."

I admire how hot he looks, standing his ground. I find myself gravitating toward him until I reach his side and clasp his hand. Ian and Hank both scowl. Alicia and Tiffany flick their gaze over me as if I'm some sort of monstrous trash. Maybe that's how they feel about me now. Because I stand beside Chase in our views. He doesn't deserve to be treated like this. He was helping. I don't care what they think. They aren't any better than us. They didn't rush to help save them either.

"You should've let us talk about it. You didn't know that for sure. You could've just killed him for no reason." This comes from Reggie, his voice rising in pitch.

Chase shrugs his shoulders. "Sometimes we have to make decisions for others because you guys can't think clearly. I don't know why you can't grasp the fact that Jack was already dying and whatever was happening to his body was only torturing him until the end. His wounds were too damn severe. If that was me, I'd expect you to do the same."

"Yeah, man. I agree. I don't want to be that bullshit. You could hear his bones snapping." Adam comes to my other side and laces his fingers through mine. It should feel weirder than it does, but all I feel is protected and safe between them.

Alicia tightens her hold on her spear and lifts it, pointing it at me. "This is all your doing. You're the one who suggested it in the first place."

Tristan gets in front of me. "Back up."

"Do you think I'm going to hurt her or something? I'm not the one who is a psychopath. So don't act as if I am one." Alicia leers, her face twisting with her outrage. "And you know what? We did come to try to amend things. We don't think all of you should be banished. Only Chase. We can't stay around someone we don't trust."

"Feeling's mutual," Chase mutters lowly.

"I'm starting to feel the same about Eliana," Reggie says, shifting his jaw as he tightens his mouth. He whips his gaze down my body and back up.

"We're not abandoning either of them. So just go back to your damn shelter. We don't need you or want you around. We obviously can't agree on how to deal with the situation. Might as well just do our own thing." Evander growls with his words.

"That's probably the only reason why they came," Tristan says, stabbing his spear into the ground. "They need us. We have the skills they don't. I doubt any of them are going to successfully spear a fish. They probably can't get their shelters to stay up either."

"Or fucking fight off a wolf," Adam adds.

"Or, you know, do a little first aid." Davian smirks, and I can't help my mouth as it mirrors his. Because they're all right.

I bet the only reason the others have come back to us is because they might not be able to survive alone.

I should feel bad.

I should feel guilty.

But I'm feeling especially petty right now. I want them to regret their actions. They act like they're saints, but they're the ones that up and left Penelope and Creed to die. They didn't try to help Jack as he was mauled. They probably didn't even know Freddy was dragged off.

Sure, we were prepared to run to the waves, but we were still also prepared to help. We tried.

"Whatever. We'll manage just fine." Alicia takes a step back, shifting in the sand to look around. "Maybe you can just stay out of our way until you come to your senses and return to being civilized people and not savages. You'll come to us eventually. You think that you know everything, but you don't. And when you do need help, don't expect any."

Wow. I don't even know how or why we came to this position. I should've expected it. I know how the world works. I just hate that people have died. I hate that we're in this position to begin with.

Evander looks at the rest of their group and lifts his chin. "You guys don't have to hesitate to come to us, but we do expect an apology. We also expect you to understand that some things must be done. We're not going to jeopardize everyone with just the hope of things turning out to be okay."

Adam motions his fingers, wiggling them. "And if any of you guys want to stay now, you're welcome to. It's going to be dark soon. You might not even make it back to your camp by sundown. I bet you didn't even think about that, huh?"

Alicia's stern expression breaks, and she frowns. Adam was right. They were probably so caught up with themselves that they didn't even think about the fact that the sun sets.

"We're going to be fine," Alicia says, holding her hand out to Ian. "We can take care of ourselves. Don't let them get into your head. Come on. Let's go."

Chase glances at me with his peripheral vision, squeezing my fingers. The six of us watch their group turn around and stalk away. I bet the second they get out of our view, they'll make a run for it. I can't blame them, but I can find amusement in their attempt at getting us to return and banish Chase.

We let silence fall between us for a couple of minutes. I wish I knew what everyone was thinking. It would make it easier to come up with something to say. I don't know any of them well enough to know if they're on the same wavelength as me. They were listening too much to their human rationale to even consider that maybe we need to act as vicious and wild as the creatures on this island that hunt us. Because I don't think the wolves here are normal animals. They're something else. I've never seen or heard of anything like it.

Adam groans under his breath, breaking the quiet of the world first. "Goddamn. This is like every book I've ever read about people getting stranded on an island. I always hoped that things wouldn't be like this in these types of situations. No wonder my family was so crazy."

"Hard situations bring out the worst in people," Chase says, staring past me to look at Adam. "My first instinct is not to kill someone to protect myself. I hope you guys know that. I was trying to save us all."

I can't stop my mouth from pouting. "You don't have to explain anything, Chase. They were right. I was the one who brought it up."

"Well, I'm not a fucking saint. I was thinking about it. Jack was gruesome, and if he was about to be whatever the hell Freddy was in the forest...I'm just glad he's dead. Rest in peace." Adam looks at the others, remaining serious.

"Rest in peace," Davian repeats. He turns to me. "Come on, Elle. There's still time to get you some extra fruit. It'll be nice to have in the morning even if you don't want it now."

I take his hand and look at the others. "Thank you all for standing beside me. I don't know what I would do if it was just me and those people."

Tristan smiles. "You and Chase are good people. Except for the fact that the fucker got to kiss you."

My face flushes. I was hoping nobody would bring that up.

"So, are you two a thing?" Adam asks, speaking up.

I pull Davian by his hand. "Don't start, you guys. This

isn't island dating or whatever. See you in a bit."

The four of them watch as Davian and I stroll toward the tree line to the path that'll take us to the few fruit trees nearby.

And damn. I love the way they all look at me.

This whole situation might be messed up, but at least they seem to be the good of it.

Hopefully, they don't regret choosing my side or me theirs.

Because if any of us do, it's going to be a long fucking life on this island. Hopefully, we will manage to get away soon. The men with the wolves only mentioned weeks. One down. Hopefully, not many more to go.

"Eliana, my love," a familiar voice whispers, stirring me awake. "Come to me. Pretend you're going to the bathroom. We need to talk."

What the fuck? The voice doesn't hum in my ears. They whirl through my mind. It's Kellan.

I sit upright, stirring awake Evander. I lean down close and whisper, "Go back to sleep. I just have to go to pee."

He nods his head and turns over.

I crawl from between him and Davian, peeking at Chase sleeping with his back to Davian. They got over sleeping so close to each other naked real quick. Actually, all of us have. It gets cold enough that any extra body heat helps combat the discomfort.

Tiptoeing my way out of our shelter, I catch sight of Tristan and Adam sitting beside the fire, staring at the tree line. They murmur quietly to each other, sharpening a seemingly never-ending pile of sticks to use for protection.

I greet them with a smile. "Hey, will you guys listen out for me?"

"I can go with you if you want. A woman pissing doesn't scare me. Nothing about you does, Eliana," Tristan says, smiling at me.

I laugh and shake my head. "Even so, I can't go with somebody listening closely. I need some space."

He shrugs. "The offer stands. Don't ever be embarrassed. There isn't time for that."

"But there is time to get to know you all on that sort of level. Just listen out. I'm going to be fine. I'm a big girl." I grin with my words and traipse away, swinging my hips just because I can. I know they're both watching me. There isn't anything wrong with a little flirting. It helps pass the time. It also settles my nerves over the danger I put myself in. I know I'm being reckless. Stupid, even. Because one of two things will happen. I'm either going to meet with Kellan or I'm going to realize that I have island fever and I'm hallucinating his voice in my head.

And honestly, I don't know which one is better. Kellan

hasn't been around in days. I almost thought he would never come back.

"I've been giving you time to adjust. I never leave you alone, Eliana," Kellan says, his soft voice startling me. "I swore I'd protect you."

I whip my attention to where he stands within the trees. He wears a pair of shorts and nothing else. I kind of wish he were naked only because I am.

He dangles a bag from his fingers. "I brought you some things. For you and your group. I hope you'll accept them as an apology for everything you've been through already."

I stroll toward him, remaining guarded and clenching my fingers into fists. I wish I would've brought one of the spears, but I didn't even think about it.

Kellan unzips the bag and pulls out some sort of fabric. "I hope these necessities will suffice. I'm sure you were uncomfortable with not having everything you're used to from the human world." He says it as if we're no longer there.

I open and close my mouth, a dozen questions swirling through my mind. What does he even mean by that? Fuck. I'm overthinking things. It's impossible we're anywhere else but on some remote island in the middle of...maybe the Pacific Ocean. No one can tell for sure. There are different plants here that shouldn't grow together. Different fish too.

I automatically take the bag from him and clutch it against my chest. A part of me wants to dig through it immediately to see what he brought, but another part of me knows this might be my only chance to interrogate him about everything happening.

I don't get a chance to do either because Kellan drops his shorts and releases a strange growl. Arching his back, he transforms in front of my eyes.

I startle at the sight of the grey wolf. The wolf I thought was Kellan's pet.

I cover my mouth, trying not to scream.

Wiggling to its belly, the wolf whimpers and crawls forward to me. It's the first time that I've seen it submissive and not threatening.

"Kellan..." My voice squeaks. If I talk, I might say something loud enough for the others to hear. This is insane. How will I ever explain it to them?

As quickly as Kellan transforms into a wolf, he turns back into a human man. He remains on his knees, his naked body close to mine. I take a step back. I can't help myself.

"Please don't be afraid of me, Eliana. I would never hurt you. I just thought this was the best way to explain things. Actions are far easier for me than words. You'd never have believed me had I just told you I'm a lykoswulf." Lykoswulf? I repeat the term over and over again, but it only sounds partially familiar. He stretches out his arms, wiggling his fingers while he silently begs me to hold his hand. "I want to explain everything to you. I wish I could've done it sooner, but my pack wasn't ready."

I gape in confusion. I don't know how to react or what to think. He's a wolf. He's a man who shifts into a wolf. My first instinct is to scream my head off and run. But then another part of me—a deep-seated, strangely powerful piece of me wants to close the space to him. To touch him. To see if this is real or not.

"It is real," he says, responding to my thoughts.

"Shit." I shake my head as if the gesture could keep him out. "This is too much. You—you're a wolf. You're with the men who kidnapped me. Are they...?" They have to be. It explains the attacks and the threats about our survival.

"Take a breath. I know it's a lot to think about." Kellan shifts closer on his knees, taking my hands.

I recoil and jerk back, stumbling and falling to the ground. "Don't touch me. I don't know who or what the fuck you are. I don't know what you want with me. I just—I have to go."

Kellan scrambles to his feet and grabs onto me. Spinning me around, he locks me to him, his naked body pressing to mine. He covers my mouth with his hand, stopping me from screaming for help. A low growl rumbles near my ear, the vibration crawling down my throat, striking me in the heart.

Kellan sucks in a breath. "Eliana, please. Don't—"

I swing my hips back, surprising him by bumping my ass against his cock. It gives me the chance to bite his fingers, sinking my teeth into his flesh. He growls again but instinctively yanks his hand away.

I scream, my mind and body battling against each other over what to do. "Let me go!"

"Damn it, Eliana. Give me a chance. Come with me before the others get here." Kellan tries to snatch me again.

I jerk my leg up, kicking his shin. He doesn't falter, unfazed by my efforts.

My breathing quickens in fear. "Stay away! I need to think. I need space. Just go."

"Eliana! Eliana, say something again. We can't see you," Tristan hollers, snapping branches as he heads in my direction.

Kellan charges me, scooping me off my feet. He throws me over his shoulder and runs. I hit his back and thrash, but he doesn't let me go. He carries me away.

CHAPTER 9

LYKOSWULF

I GRIND MY teeth across the soft fabric Kellan stuffed in my mouth. I should be terrified that he kidnapped me, but I'm pissed off. This is too much. He should've left me alone to try to process things. The others should know that we were brought here by wolf men...wolf shifters. For what? I'm about to find out. I'm just nervous about the answers. I don't know Kellan well enough to read him, but I do know he won't tell me everything.

"Here, let me help you put this on. You're probably cold." Kellan pulls a T-shirt out of his backpack and hangs it in front of me. "If you promise not to scream, I'll remove your gag and untie you. I'm sorry I felt like I had to do it. Your shock over my revelation is setting off your fear instincts."

I narrow my eyes at him and mumble, "I'm not scared of you."

His lips curl to the side in a partial smirk. He's amused, obviously able to understand me. Actually, I'm pretty certain he can read my mind.

"I can." He kneels in front of me, slowly pulling the fabric from my mouth.

"Seriously?" This is all so unbelievable. "What about the other assholes? If they could, I'm sure they would've stopped me from jumping from the yacht."

"You're right. They can't. You don't belong to them." Kellan uses a knife to cut the vines he wrapped around my wrists. What the hell does he mean about me not belonging to them? He makes it sound as if I'm his.

I swing my arm out and try to slap him, refusing to be a docile, good little captive. He catches me by my wrist and tilts his head. Locking me in a staring contest, he silently dares me to try again. If I thought he wouldn't restrain me, I would. I'd punch him in the cock too.

"Let me go. Now. I don't like the way you said that as if I might be yours." I heave a couple of deep breaths, waiting for him to release my hand.

His jaw twitches. "You are mine. You might deny it, but you are. That's why I can't leave you. My soul won't allow it. The moment I saw you, my wolf knew who you were intended to be, but I must be careful. I'm not in a position to make such claims. I can't go against my pack either. They are still trying to determine who is worthy and who isn't, but I know you are. We all do, Eliana, my love. My wolf proves it. My alpha will figure it out soon enough."

His love? He's a psycho. "Fuck off, Kellan. You can't just stake a claim on me, whatever that means. I'm not something to be owned. If you even think I'll be with you, you're crazy. I'd pick anyone else over you. You know there are five other guys who want the chance to be with me. And you know what? I plan on giving it to them. There's nothing better to do here." I remain serious with my words. He can't get away with this, and I won't just pretend either. I can't. I've lost the ability to act as if I will obey the second I was taken. This is about surviving, not just trying to live better. I wouldn't even let a client treat me like this.

A deep, guttural growl escapes his throat. "You can do what you want, but it doesn't change anything. Only our goddess decides who is worthy and who isn't. And so far, no one has shown as much. By the time this is over, you might be the only one left."

"What do you mean by that? If you would just give me

some answers, maybe I wouldn't be thinking about the ten different ways I can keep you on your knees so I can run. What are you, exactly? A werewolf? Why am I here? Am I some sort of prey for you to play with? Why was I chosen? Why were the others?" I wish I had a pen and paper to write everything down to make sure he doesn't skip anything. If he's going to keep me here, I might as well try to figure out as much as I can to take back to the others. Because I will go back. He can't just imprison me in this damn cave.

"You're not our prey nor is this a game. Our species goes by many names. Werewolves, shifters, and lycans to those bitten and moon-called. Moonborne, lunarcanis, lykoswulf to those born from the packs." Kellan studies my expression for a reaction.

I try not to give him one.

"You're here because it was your fate and always has been. Shadow Moon runs in your blood." Kellan reaches out and touches my cheek.

I remain utterly still as his warm fingers caress my jaw, working toward my ear. He combs my dark hair from my face, hovering close enough for me to smell the tropical scent of pineapple on his skin blending with the musk of animal and rawness of woods.

It's like my brain shuts down, and my body takes over, triggered by the sudden pleasantness of his fragrance. His touch sends electricity jolting through me. Tingles crawl from my heart and down my stomach. I gasp at the sudden lust blooming between us. His cock hardens, and I shift my eyes to look at it pressing against the soft fabric of his shorts. I don't know how I know, but sudden raw desires come to life with our closeness.

His lips part with his deep breathing, and I stretch my neck, closing the space between us inch by inch. What am I doing? Why do I want to suddenly kiss him? I don't understand, and a part of me doesn't even care.

He doesn't move, drinking me in as I shift my body, squirming under the intensity of his gaze. I lick my lips, silently begging him to make the first move. I don't want to be the one to give in to this intoxicating, feral need.

"You feel it now, don't you?" Kellan murmurs, caressing his thumb back down my jaw.

I swallow and nod my head. "What are you doing to me?"

"That's not me. That is your nature, Eliana. You were always destined to end up on the island. You should've been born here. Your grandmother was the one and only human-born wolf to ever escape." Kellan locks me with his blue eyes, his words stabbing deeply into me.

My grandmother? How can that be? I would know if I was whatever the fuck he claims to be. My parents were human. There isn't a single doubt about it.

"You're lying. I would know if I were like you." It's enough to knock some sense into me, and I smack his hand away and crawl back, hitting my shoulders to the cave wall.

He crawls closer, pressing his palms against the cool stone on each side of my head, caging me in. I should shove him back. I should do anything to put space between us again, but it's as if I'm entranced by his blue gaze.

"You are not like me yet. I said that Shadow Moon ran through your blood. It doesn't have your soul yet. Those bitten by my kind can't create more. Your grandmother started your line with a human. You are human. But you won't be soon enough. My alpha is coming for those chosen. That's why I'm here. I couldn't stand the thought of no one preparing you for what happens next. It is my duty as your mate to ensure you're okay." Kellan leans even closer, brushing his lips to my ear. "You don't understand it yet, but you will in time. You are mine. You just have to accept it."

I press my palm to his chest, getting him to move back. "No, I don't. I don't have to accept any of this. If you say that I'm not whatever the fuck you are, then I'm going to keep it that way. I'm going to get off this island. You can't keep me here."

His eyes flash gold, and a guttural growl escapes his lips and vibrates across me. The sexy noise sends goosebumps over my skin. His primal reaction unexpectedly gets to me in a good way. Who knew I'd like such possessiveness? I've always hated it before. "You're right. I can't keep you here, but the island can. It will. There is no escaping."

Anger rushes through me, and I push him back. He doesn't try to grab me or fight me this time, and I scramble to my feet and get up. Bolting toward the cave entrance, I run in the direction of the forest. I have no idea how to get back to camp, but I will figure it out. Knowing that Kellan never leaves me gives me the nerve to escape him. It gives me the bravado to face whatever threat might be lingering within the forest. I need space from him. I'm afraid if I allow him to keep me any longer, it might weaken my resistance.

"Head north. You'll run into your group." Kellan's words swirl through my mind as he gives me directions to find my way back. I don't know why he does it, but it slows me down, my need to flee lessening. It makes me consider turning around and sticking it out a bit longer. He is the one with answers after all.

I just don't know if I'm ready for them yet.

We need to get off this island. And soon.

I'm afraid if we don't, we never will.

I'm not ready to die here.

If my grandmother left the island, she had a good reason. I will heed to her unintentional warning. Shadow Moon can't have me too.

I jog through the dark forest, seemingly lit by the bright moonlight even though the canopy of trees overhead doesn't allow much light in. It's ethereal and magical, different than the area right around the shelter.

A figure appears within the trees, and I nearly slip on the loose dirt. I can't see who it is, but I know it's a man. My fear instincts say to keep my mouth shut, because what if it's not one of the guys? What if it's one of the monsters?

The figure pauses and raises their spear. "I don't want any trouble, but if you're here to threaten me, I will fight." I recognize the deep, smooth tone of Evander.

I blow out a breath of relief. "I fight back," I say, my nerves settling.

"Shit, Eliana. We were so fucking worried. Are you okay? We heard your screams and then you were gone." Evander strides closer, maneuvering effortlessly through the dark forest, unfazed by the untouched terrain.

My first thought is to lie. It has always been an instinctual and automatic response over the years. I'm supposed to say what they want to hear. Evander will freak out if he knows that Kellan snatched me only to release me. If I didn't want to lose the little ounce of trust we've already built, I'd fall into old habits.

"You're wearing a shirt. A man's shirt. What happened?" Evander touches the sleeve, rubbing it between his fingers. In the dim lighting shining through the branches of the trees, I stare into his dark eyes.

His concern gets to me on a deep level I'm not used to. Like with Chase and Adam, I'm not used to people worrying about me or caring what happens to me. It feels both amazing and terrifying.

Instead of answering right away, I throw my arms around him and hug him until he engulfs me in an incredible embrace. I breathe against his neck, standing on my tiptoes. Neither of us says anything for a minute, and I just listen to his soft breathing and his beating heart. I listen to the world around us and how silent it is as if a veil circles the forest, protecting us.

"I was taken by one of the natives here. Kellan." I realize that I haven't told everyone about the mysterious man who keeps stalking me in the woods. "He's the one who helped me and Adam. He also interrupted me and Chase. You're not going to believe any of this. He took me to a cave and gave me the shirt. He claimed that I belong to him."

Evander stiffens, his muscles rippling with my words. He groans under his breath and pulls back only to give me another once-over. "Did he hurt you?"

I shake my head. "No. I don't think he would. He didn't chase after me after I broke free. He just wanted to talk."

"If the fucker wants to talk, he could talk with all of us. Doesn't he know how terrifying it is to have a stranger kidnap a woman? You don't do that kind of bullshit. Especially not out here." Evander squeezes my fingers. "You said he took you to a cave? Do you think you can show me?"

I shrug my shoulders. "Maybe. It's south of here. He wasn't living there or anything. He was just using it as a hiding place, I guess. He had a bag of some gear and supplies. This might sound crazy, but he said that his pack was planning something."

It's hard for me to wrap my mind around. But strangely enough, I know Evander will believe me. He's seen the weird-ass things going on. He's been through everything with me so far.

"His pack?" he asks, shifting on his feet and looking around.

"Werewolves or...moonborne? Lykoswulf? It was a word I've never heard. I don't think it's human." I replay my conversation with Kellan over and over again, searching for clues or something I might've missed. But nothing changes. All I know is that we were taken from the human world onto this island. We are expected to fight for our lives and to survive turning like them.

Something cracks and leaves crunch to our right. Evander holds his index finger over his mouth and tugs me along, heading in the direction I came from. I race to keep up with his long legs. All I can think about is what Kellan said about the different packs coming for us.

What if they attack before we can make it back to the others? I need them to know everything I do. We need to come up with an escape plan instead of waiting around.

"Is that the cave?" Evander murmurs, keeping his voice low.

I can't be sure, so I shrug my shoulders. "I didn't look

behind me. I just ran."

"Did he have any weapons?" Evander slows down and pulls me into the crook of his arm protectively. We stroll a couple more feet in silence, staring at the flickering light within the cave. I hadn't really thought about it before, but there was light inside. Was it a fire? I can't even remember.

"He had a bag of supplies. The restraints he used were made out of vines. I don't think he needs weapons. He—"

A snarl rips through the air, and a grey wolf barrels from the cave. I shriek in surprise, and Evander scoops me up and pulls me out of the way. But the wolf—no, I mean Kellan—doesn't attempt to attack us. He runs past us and into the trees, hiding from view.

"Go back to your camp, Eliana," Kellan says, his voice whispering through my mind. "Their time will come to find out information. You don't need to be the messenger."

Rage rushes through me and I tug myself away from Evander. I stride away from him and in the direction Kellan ran in his wolf form. "Like hell. Come back here and face us. You can't just kidnap me, force me to watch you transform, and then tell me that this is all part of my fate and not expect me to talk to those chosen to face this bullshit with me."

Evander clears his throat. "Eliana, who are you talking to?"

I ignore him and place my hands on my hips. "Kellan, I mean it. You either come back here and show yourself to Evander or you just leave us alone and stop trying to be the good guy you think you are. I know you think you're helping, but you're not. You're one of them."

Evander slides his fingers through mine, staring at the trees where I look. "Eliana..."

And then I see him. The grey wolf strolls in our direction, his blue eyes shining brightly. My heart skips, just knowing that at any second, this wolf will turn into Kellan. I hate how much my feelings mix when I think about him. I hate him, but I'm attracted to him. I fear him, but I also know that he would protect me. How do I know that? It's just an instinct. And my instincts have never led me wrong.

"It's okay, Evander. The wolf won't hurt us." I ease away, pulling my hand from his.

He tries to grab the back of my shirt, but the wolf growls.

"I won't hurt you," Kellan says, using his telepathy to communicate with me in his wolf form. "I never promised anything about him."

I swivel and hold my palm up to Evander. "Give him space. Let me show you."

I swear this wolf better be Kellan and not just the island messing with my sanity. But I saw him. I know that he changed into this wolf.

Taking a deep breath, I shuffle forward, extending my hand out. Kellan sits back on his haunches, staring at me without growling or lunging. I treat him as I would any animal—with caution and respect—and wait for him to pad closer and sniff my fingers. Once more, he sits back down.

He licks my fingers, releasing a small whimper. If I didn't know he could turn into a man any second, I'd change the tone of my voice and scratch my fingers between his ears. Because now that he's not growling and baring his teeth, he's fucking cute as hell. I want to cuddle him. Feel what it's like to have him sleep next to me and keep me warm.

Kellan jumps forward and knocks me onto my back, pressing his big paws to my chest. Evander yells my name, but neither of us can react before Kellan transforms into a man on top of me.

Our eyes meet, and he graces me with a smile that leaves me breathless. And it's not because one of his palms rests on my chest, feeling the rapping of my heart.

"Oh, fuck. Fuck!" Evander shouts from behind me.

Kellan glares and eases off me. "Shut up, or someone will hear you. This is why I only wanted to show Eliana, but since her stubborn attitude and strong will make her so insistent, I felt I had to show you too. I'll make myself clear, though. I only did it for her. Not for you. I don't know if you're worthy of knowing such things yet."

"Fuck," Evander repeats, placing his hands on the back of his head. He is more shocked now than he was after realizing what the plan had been from the men who dropped us off here.

I close the space to him and rest my hands on his shoulders. "I can't wrap my mind around it either. It's insane. But it's real."

"I don't know what to say." Evander stares up at the trees.

"You don't say anything. You need to go back to your camp now. Take the rest of the night to process. I will try to come by in the morning." Kellan strolls closer and walks past us into the cave. We stare at the entrance until he returns with the backpack of supplies he tried to give me earlier. "Take this. It'll help you until it's time."

Evander automatically takes the backpack. "Time for what exactly?"

"To see if you are as worthy as Eliana. It'll all be clear soon enough. Now I have to go. I've already been here way too long." Kellan stretches his arms over his head and bows forward, transforming into a wolf once more.

He circles around me and licks my hand before charging off into the trees.

I stand next to Evander in silence, staring as if the wolf will turn around and return to us. But he doesn't.

Someone else does.

I release a breath when I realize it's Alicia. Hank strolls behind her, and the two of them stop short a dozen feet away.

They're fully dressed. Clean.

Alicia pulls something from a bag on her side.

Shit. She pulls out a machete and grins.

I wring my hands together. Something in her eyes scares me. "Alicia. Hank? What are you guys doing here?"

Alicia glances over her shoulder. "Surviving this hell hole. Now get on the ground and don't move."

Evander tightens his hand around mine. "Eliana, run." He shoves me toward the trees. "Go!"

CHAPTER 10

Evander

PROTECTIVE

ALWAYS PROTECT HER first. My dad's voice swirls through my mind, reminding me of what he taught me long ago before he died. Whether it's my mom, my sister, my aunt, whoever. Dad said that it's my duty to ensure a woman's safety despite the threat upon my life. If only his advice had prevented the car accident that took my family.

Control what you can, son. Accept the things you can't. Remember, it's a man's job to take care of those who need it.

It is a man's job to teach her how to take care of herself if something ever happens. I'll never forget that advice for as long as I live. And I'll try my best. I will not let another person in my life down. Especially not Eliana. Because I can control the situation. I can face the threat head-on.

"Go!" I repeat, turning my back on Eliana to face Alicia and Hank.

Something has gotten into them, and I'm pretty sure it's this island. It could very well be Kellan, the fucking wolf man, who is trying to steal Eliana from us. I don't know what his plan is, but he has to have something to do with them. They're wearing clothes. They look prepared to murder us. It's as if they've been brainwashed. Because murder was the last thing on their minds before. But now they see what we see. Except now they're coming after us.

Eliana listens to me and runs toward the trees. I pray that the others aren't surrounding us, ready to hurt her when I face these two fuckers. The psychopaths.

I tighten my fingers around the strap of the backpack Kellan gave us. A thought dawns on me. The last one had a knife in it. This one better have one too. I'm screwed without it. I can throw a punch, but it's a little bit harder when my opponent is armed, and I'm outnumbered.

I hold my hand up toward Alicia and Hank. "Stay the hell back. I don't want to hurt you."

Neither of them listens to me. I don't know what the fuck

is wrong with them, but they move in sync and almost robotically. Alicia swipes her machete in front of her, clearly not knowing how to use it, just hoping that she manages to cut me. Hank breaks away from her and starts to circle as if he's going to try to attack me from behind.

"We're so sorry. You were right. We must do what it takes to survive, even if it means doing something unthinkable." Alicia charges me with a holler, and all I can think about is how this is it. It's a kill or be killed situation, and I don't plan to die.

I pull a small blade from the backpack and throw it at Alicia, sinking it into her shoulder. She screams in surprise, obviously not expecting the fact that throwing knives was a hobby of mine along with axes. I haven't said much about it to anyone because it's not like we had those types of weapons. It's always been for fun. But in this moment? It might save my life. Except now I don't have a fucking weapon. I'm an idiot.

Alicia grabs the hilt of the blade and yanks it out. Big mistake for her. I think I hit an artery, because blood gushes and stains her white T-shirt. She drops to her knees, clutching her skin. If I didn't hear Hank behind me, I might've rushed to try to help her. I know I shouldn't, but my dad's advice flows through my mind again. It doesn't matter who it is. She was obviously put in a bad situation. Now it's the death of her. Death by my hands. I almost don't believe it. I never knew I was capable of it. But I guess there's a first time for everything.

"No! You fucker!" Hank charges me, and I brace for a wrestling match.

He doesn't make it within my reach. Eliana crashes into him, knocking him off his feet. The two of them roll across the ground together, and she manages to climb on top of him. Fisting her hand, she swings and sucker punches him in the throat. She jabs his nose next and scrambles up, only to kick him between the legs. Her fighting surprises me, and I watch the fierce woman turn feral with her need to protect us. I didn't know that I had killer instincts, but Eliana? Damn. I wasn't expecting her to be able to fight like this. She's been holding out on us. And it makes me even more attracted to her.

It kind of hurts my ego just a bit too. It should be me punching Hank and not her.

"Stay down. If you try to get up, we will kill you," Eliana says, her voice deepening with her anger. "I don't know what the hell has gotten into you, but whatever it is needs to stop."

Hank coughs and spits blood, but he obeys her and remains on the ground. "The only way this will ever stop is when we die. This is it. There are things about this island that none of us understand. We were visited by some of the natives. They came with a warning and an opportunity. We have to take it. We can see if you two can join in. They need a female." Darting his gaze to Eliana, he acknowledges her. "They won't be happy that Alicia is dead."

Eliana wrings her hands together and glances from me to

Hank. "We need to tie him up. He can give us more answers."

"Tie me up? Come on. This is your chance. You could join us. We could go after the others to do the trade." Hank sits up, gathering dirt in his hands. The fucker looks ready to throw it in Eliana's face.

I snatch her hand and yank her toward me. Hank does what I expect him to and tosses the dirt, but it only rains through the air, missing Eliana. I tackle him, sending him back to the ground. He tries to grab my balls, but I lock my hand around his wrist and twist it hard enough to break. He screams, his voice piercing the air. This fucker has a lot of nerve and bravado.

Eliana rushes toward Alicia, the woman's body now face first in the dirt. She picks up the machete and the small knife and returns to my side.

"Hold him still. I want to be as humane as possible. He's a dead man already. Look." Eliana grabs Hank's arm and drags up his sleeve, revealing a bite mark. "He's been bitten. That's why he is so aggressive. Maybe whoever put them up to this offered him a cure or something."

I hesitate with her words. What if whatever happened to Hank doesn't lead to that strange monstrous form? Should we really kill him?

The fucker snaps his teeth at me, trying to bite me. My unsettling thought might be coincidental, but it seems as if it triggers Hank. Unease stirs through me. Eliana is right. Hank is a dead man trying to negotiate. His skin ripples and he arches his back, breaking away. Swinging his arm, he knocks me off him.

Eliana jumps onto his back and uses her bodyweight to throw him off balance. They fall to the ground again. She doesn't hesitate, jabbing the machete into the back of Hank's neck, killing him. His writhing body face-plants, twitching for a second.

My chest clenches as she scrambles to her feet and covers her eyes. I think this might've been the first time she's killed someone too. Her body trembles with her heavy gasps. The color drains from her complexion like she might be sick. I rush to her and pull her into my arms, not afraid of her body's reaction. I just want to hold her and help her suppress the shudders. I want her to know that what she did was a necessity. Hank was infected. He was rapidly changing. If she hadn't done what she did, he could've gotten either of us.

I rub my hand along her back, holding her close. Her warm breath tickles against my chest. Remaining steady, I wait until she slows her breathing to guide her chin up, so she looks at me. I want her to feel my words in her very being. She needs to know she did the right thing. "You did good, Eliana. He was changing. You protected us."

She sniffles but doesn't cry. Blinking her eyes, she clears her vision. A dozen thoughts cross her expression, her frown morphing into anger and then relaxing until I can't read her cues.

"You're my hero, you know." I offer her a smile, trying to think of something comforting. "Chase better watch out. Adam's going to ask you to carry his pansy-ass instead."

She laughs in exasperation, her voice hoarse and cracking. "You're ridiculous. I'm not a hero."

I ease away from her and clutch her face, staring deep into her beautiful golden eyes. "Like hell you're not. You came back and tackled a man to protect me. You should have run and hidden, but you didn't. You came back to fight by my side."

She licks her lips, and I can't stop staring at her pouty mouth. "I wasn't going to leave you. We're in this together, remember?"

Something raw comes over me, and I lean forward and press my lips to hers as if my body takes control without my permission. I know better than to surprise kiss her. I fully expect her to knee me in the balls for it, because I'd deserve it, not knowing exactly where she and Chase stand. The adrenaline coursing through me turns me stupid with desire, and I want to test her. Distract her. Thank her for staying.

I try to pull away to apologize, but Eliana responds with passion, kissing me back instead of pushing me away. She slides her hands up my sides and to my shoulders, hooking them around my neck.

I rove my hand lower down her back and pull her closer until she can feel how hard she makes me. She gasps and slides her tongue into my mouth, brushing it over mine, the sweetness of her lips surprising yet intoxicating. I want her so badly that it's all I can think about. My body aches in need.

As if she knows what's on my mind, she breaks away from me and looks into my eyes. "Let's get out of here. Go somewhere safe."

I scoop her up, carrying her in my arms as I leave the bodies behind. She latches onto the bag of supplies, treating it as if it's the most valuable thing in the world, which it might be. I peer around the forest, my good senses trying to persuade me out of following her lead. I should take her back to camp, but then I think about the other guys. I want more alone time with Eliana. I can create something more private.

Screw it. I'm all in. If this is what she wants...goddamn. It's what I desperately fucking want too. I stride with her to the beach, savoring the sensation of her lips on my throat. It's better to be on the sand than in the woods. Eliana works her way back up my jaw and kisses me under the moonlight. I blindly carry her to where a cluster of boulders forms a small cove away from the water. This would be an incredible shelter if it was just a bit larger, but for this? It's perfect.

She laughs as I set her on her feet and hold up my finger, telling her to wait here. I rush toward the trees and snag a couple fallen palm fronds from the ground. I will do whatever I can to shelter us, especially because I don't know where her stalker is. She deserves—we deserve privacy. If only I could give her so much more.

I turn around and look at her. My body flexes at the sight of her. She stands as naked as I am, biting her lip, so incredibly sexy. The big shirt she wore now lies across the sand at her feet, and she curls and uncurls her fingers, getting me to hurry back to her.

I don't even get within a foot of her after shielding the opening with the palm leaves before she laces her cool hand around my cock and strokes me. Crashing her mouth to mine, she kisses me again, familiarizing herself with my body. Damn. I want more of her. I want to do the same to her.

Grazing my hand along her stomach, I trail my way down to the apex of her legs. I groan under my breath, feeling her slick wetness for me. She's so hot and beautiful. So fierce and protective. I plan to kneel at her feet and make her scream my name. I want to bury my face between her legs and taste her. I want—

Eliana drops to her knees and grabs me by the hips, guiding my cock into her mouth. I comb my fingers through her hair, wishing I had the chance to get her off first. The second her tongue glides across the bottom of my shaft, I lose my brain power and ability to do anything except moan her name. All I can think about is how incredible her mouth feels as she sucks and licks me in a way that strikes me right in the nuts. Her tongue caresses across the bottom of my shaft to my balls, and she sucks them, teasing me even more. It's been too long. It takes everything in me not to come in her mouth after only a minute.

I brush my fingers through her hair, and she looks up at me, her heavy-lidded eyes sparkling in the silver moonlight coming from overhead.

"Don't make me come. I want to take care of you first." I slide my tongue over my lips at the thought.

She hums in disagreement, bobbing her head faster and purposely denying me the chance. I clutch onto the side of the rock, my heart pounding as pleasure courses over me.

"Eliana," I murmur, my breathing quickening as I'm near my peak.

My balls tighten, and I try pulling away, but she locks me in place, digging her fingernails into my ass cheeks in a way that makes me explode. I moan as I come in her mouth, my orgasm so intense that my knees weaken.

She licks her lips and swallows, getting me good. God-damn. How is it possible that my dream woman is with me on this island? How did I manage to have the best and worst luck?

I don't want to think about it. All I want to do is guide Eliana to the sand to have my way with her. I join her and kiss her again, not caring that she just swallowed. Nothing about her will turn me off. It's as if her presence alone is enough to entrance me. Like I said, I'm all in.

I break from her lips and lick my way down her throat, nudging her to lay back on her shirt while I suck one of her tight nipples into my mouth and roll my tongue over it. She gasps and arches her back, wiggling beneath me. With my other hand, I make my way between her legs once more, sliding my finger between her pussy lips until I can rub her clit.

Her breathless reaction turns me on and makes me hard again. I just want to hear her moan more. I want to hear her plead my name. I need her to forget about the other guys completely. I can't help craving to have her to myself. It's all I want.

"I'm going to make you come with my finger first and then my tongue," I mumble, kissing her other tit and sucking her nipple. I add pressure to her body with my finger, listening to her reaction to guide me into doing what she likes.

"Evander, it's taking everything in me to be quiet." She shifts, rotating her hips back and forth like she can't stay still.

I arch away and meet her gaze, her eyelashes casting shadows on her cheeks. "I'll help you." Bowing down, I kiss her again, silencing her moans with my mouth as I work my finger over her until her body tenses beneath mine. She moans against my mouth and nips my bottom lip, sucking it between her teeth. I ache in the best way. I imagine my mouth will be bruised from her, the reminder of our moment lingering with me for days. Maybe forever.

I want so badly to continue. I want to align our bodies and sink inside her, feeling her heat and wetness. But I know I should stop. I don't want to risk her regretting this despite how we feel in this moment. We should try to find the others. I'm sure they are freaked the fuck out and will be pissed when they realize I didn't take Eliana immediately back to them.

"What? Is everything okay?" Eliana touches my cheek, stealing my attention away from my thoughts. Concern laces her words, and I force myself to smile and kiss her again.

"It's better than okay. I was just thinking...I might regret this, but I'm starting to worry about the others. What if the rest of those assholes come looking?" I lean my elbow in the sand, staring into her eyes. "You have no idea how hard it is for me to stop right now. I want you so fucking bad, but..."

"You're right. I don't know what got into me." She presses her lips together with her words.

I regret my comment immediately. I don't want her to feel bad. Because really, I don't. The others can take care of themselves. And I just want to take care of Eliana.

"No, don't sound like that. This was incredible, and I want more of you. Whatever I have to do to ensure it. Nothing got into either of us apart from the island. It's as if it wants us to be together." It's hard to explain but it's true. Every event that led up to this moment happened so it could bring us together.

"Evander...we can't be together like that. This was fun, but..." Eliana swallows and shifts beneath me until I slide off her. "I'm just...I don't want to get attached."

Damn. It might be too late for me.

I push the thought away and out of my head. "I get it. You're right. No attachments. But we can have fun, can't we?"

She smiles and rubs her fingers along my jaw. "As long as you know. I just…this whole situation is crazy." She kneels and gets to her feet, offering me her hand.

I grab the shirt with me and help her put it back on. There's something about this moment that makes me want to shield her from the rest of the world. A part of me wants to deny everyone else the chance to see her sexy body in the way I have. But she just made it clear that I don't have that right nor does she want it.

I try not to let the disappointment get to me.

She slides her fingers through mine. "Maybe if we get off this island alive." Shrugging her shoulders, she offers me a smirk.

I bob my head and kick the palm fronds out of the way, guiding her from the small cove between the rocks. "I'd like that. Take you out on a real date."

Her smirk turns into a full-on grin. "I'd love that. I look forward to it."

A howl hums through the air, drawing our attention toward the forest.

I spot a grey wolf in the trees, but it backs away and hides in the shadows. Yeah, fucker. I knew it. He was probably watching us the whole time. It makes me wonder if there are others watching too.

Eliana stops and takes a short breath. "Tristan?" she asks, and I realize she's not staring at the forest any longer. I spot a figure on the beach.

"Tristan!" Eliana yells. She dashes away from me, running toward the others as they come out of the trees. "Chase!"

Fuck me. I shouldn't be so jealous.

I shouldn't be a lot of things.

But all I can think about in this moment is how I want to make Eliana mine. I need her to be mine. I don't think I'll survive any of this otherwise.

CHAPTER 11

Eliana

FIGHT TOGETHER

"THE BODIES ARE gone. Are you sure this was where it happened?" Tristan shuffles outside of the cave, searching over the terrain for signs of disruption to the dirt.

"Yes, we're fucking sure. It happened here. I killed Alicia in this exact spot. She was coming at me, and I threw a knife at her." Swiveling on the balls of his feet, Evander motions toward another spot. "That's where Eliana took Hank. He was turning into one of those things...what did you call them?" His eyes meet mine.

"I don't think Hank was turning into a lykoswulf. He wasn't anything like Kellan." And it's true. Kellan transforms into a beautiful grey wolf. Whatever the fuck was happening to Hank? Not even close. It was more like Jack and Freddy.

"Well, either somebody took the bodies, they weren't actually dead, or this is the wrong spot. There isn't any sign of foul play that I can see." Chase messes with the waistband of his shorts.

There were enough pairs for all of us. Though mine are too big and definitely intended for a guy. Evander's fit a bit snuggly, showing off the outline of his dick. Chase's reveal just as much. But at least I'm not as distracted anymore. I can finally find some normalcy with them being partially dressed. There weren't any other shirts except for the one I'm wearing, which they were fine with. Apart from the clothing, Kellan gave us a bar of soap that we managed to cut pieces off to wash with. I never thought something like that would be such a luxury. What I wouldn't give for a hot shower.

"Who knows with this island. Maybe it just devoured them. As long as they're not coming after us again as zombies or something, I think we need to explore more. We should head toward the other camp and see if anyone is still alive." Davian crosses his arms over his chest.

"I don't know, man. You didn't see them. They were savages. I don't know what the hell happened to them but they're not the same people who were shouting that we were monsters." Evander closes the space to me and brushes his fingers to mine, seeing if I will take his hand.

I don't know if I should or not. Everybody watches the gesture in anticipation.

So, I do the only thing I can think of.

I grab both his hand and Tristan's, pulling them to me. I'm sure Evander thinks what the fuck, but I was honest with him. I don't know what is wrong with me. I just can't think about someone getting hurt because of me. Everything is too serious. I don't want anything else to be. "It's probably a good idea."

Davian twists his lips to the side. "We don't all have to go. If you're concerned, you can start gathering supplies."

Chase drapes his arm over Davian's shoulder. "We need to stick together. It's far too dangerous to separate."

"Don't be scared, doc. I'll protect you. Though, we still need to make arrangements for you to protect me like you do Eliana. I'm fucking tired of being on guard all the time. I just need a strong man watching my back." Adam chuckles with his words.

"I think I'd prefer this badass protecting me. You should've seen her go. She's holding out on us. She can throw a punch." Evander gives my hand a little shake. "If I didn't know any better, I'd think you were a fighter before this."

I lift and drop my shoulders. "I've gotten into a few fights.

Mostly self-defense."

"What did you used to do that required you to use self-defense, little badass?" Adam steps closer to me, holding his hand out.

I don't have enough hands to give in to everyone's desire to stay close to my side, so I release Evander and Tristan but only give Adam a playful high-five. If this attention and affection keeps up, we're all going to have to have a talk. They don't say it, but I can tell they're all competing with each other.

Maybe I need to chill out.

It's so hard. They're all gorgeous, sweet, and way more caring than any man I've ever met. I don't even really know what to do with them at this point. I've never been treated this nicely. They don't even expect anything from me.

"I mean, before you lost your job." Adam nudges me with his knuckles, pulling me from my thoughts. "Since that seems to be the thing that we all have in common. No ties."

I realize they're all listening intensely while I'm sitting here fantasizing about them lusting after me. I'm fucking crazy. What is wrong with me?

"So fucked up, right? They had to be watching us." I try to change the subject without being too obvious. I feel self-conscious about where I was before the bastards kidnapped me. "I was walking...home when they attacked." If you could call the vacant house I'd been squatting in my home. Without a job, I couldn't afford anything. I managed to keep my gym membership for showers because the owner liked me. A favor for a favor was our agreement.

"You're avoiding the question, Eliana. You don't have to be shy. We're not going to judge you." Adam tilts his head close to mine. "Promise."

Evander punches Adam in the arm. "Leave her alone, asshole. If she doesn't want to tell us—"

I hold my hand up, stopping the two of them from arguing over this. "I was...unstable. Most jobs I took were under the table. I was a nanny for a bit. Worked in retail. A personal shopper for..." I let my voice trail off. "I was a lot of things. But stable? No. I've been on my own since I was a teen. Life sucked and then this shit happened."

"That doesn't explain how you're such a badass," Tristan teases, offering me a smile.

"I wasn't always. A job I took last summer...persuaded me to better my skills." I suck my bottom lip between my teeth. "You know how it goes."

They greet me with absolute silence. I don't know what they fill the blanks in with but it's probably close enough. I don't even like thinking about it. The world has been brutal to me since my parents died.

They look at me with various expressions ranging from pity to anger. This is why I didn't want to say anything. That's why I still don't. Obviously, whatever happens now has changed everything. I won't go back to the real world to be the same person that I left behind. Not with the knowledge I have. I will seek answers. I need to know more about my parents, but I don't want to find out anything from the fuckers here.

I laughed nervously. "Please, guys. Stop. I'm okay...well, sort of. All things considered."

"I want to make a pact here and now. Between us. Whatever happens, we're in this together. We need to protect each other and fight for each other. We need to work together to get the fuck off this island." Chase speaks for what feels like the first time in a while. I wonder what goes through his mind, especially because he probably senses something happened between me and Evander.

"I'm in. I don't want to be whatever the fuck they planned for us to be." Davian holds out his fist, waiting for Chase to bump it.

"Damn straight. We live and fight together. We protect each other. All of us come first." Tristan does the same as Davian and bumps his fist.

Adam claps his hands together, rubbing his palms. "Hell yeah. We're going to make them regret this shit."

Squeezing my arm, Evander meets my gaze. "Are you in? I'm in."

I nod my head. "I'll do whatever it takes. I'm in." For the first time in what feels like forever, I feel powerful. I feel as if I am taking back control of my life.

Fighting to live or die trying—there is no other option.

Tristan drapes his arm over my shoulders, strolling next to me as we walk along the shoreline. We might be exposed out here, but it lessens the chance of something or someone sneaking up on us. Right now, we need to find the rest of the group we left behind. If they had a run-in with the monsters that control this island, they might have answers that we can use to our benefit.

"Our old camp should be up ahead. If they're not there, they still won't be far. We can head to the creek if we have to. We might also have the advantage. Only Tiffany, Ian, and Reggie might be alive. That's six against three." Chase clutches the machete, peering at us from over his shoulder.

"I doubt they're where we left them. They had to have gone somewhere they thought was safer. Maybe there's some more caves or trees separate from the forest that they could have built a shelter from." Evander scratches his fingers across his head. "It's what I would do. Better to take higher ground or to the trees. It would be easier with so few of them."

"Damn, why don't you make us a fucking treehouse or something?" Davian scoops up a smooth rock and tosses it into the waves.

"Figure out how to plant us a garden or some shit then, farm boy." Adam grins with his words. "I need you all to fucking Gilligan's Island this shit."

"Nah, man. We're like Lost." Tristan tugs me with him until he surprises Chase and hooks him in a headlock. "We even have a doc."

The others laugh, the sound of their playfulness helping to ease my nerves. It's easier not to think about all the possible outcomes with them teasing and playing around with each other, acting as if they've been friends forever.

"What do you think, Eliana?" Adam asks.

I look at the five of them, stopping on Davian. "We have a ginger," I tease. "Just as hot, too."

Davian chuckles and rushes me, lifting me off my feet. "That's what I'm talking about. You hear her, assholes? I'm the hot one."

I laugh as Davian spins me around, his eyes sparkling in the sunlight. We have at least an hour or two until sundown and plan to relocate our camp from where we previously were. It's safer to keep moving. That was the first thing we agreed on. If we can't find the others, there is no way we want them to find us and catch us off guard.

"Shit. There it is." Chase's voice lowers. "Is that a body?"

"Two. There's one over there." Tristan points toward the crashing waves. Whoever it is looks as if they were trying to run toward the water.

Davian swears under his breath and sets me on my feet. "Get your weapons ready. Stay close."

"Eliana, get in the middle." Evander holds his hand out to

me.

I honestly don't have a problem with that. It might be wrong of me, but if they want to protect me between them, I'm here for it. I don't need to test my ability or prove my strength. I just want to survive.

We shuffle through the sand as a group, keeping our eyes trained on our surroundings. I can't take mine off the first body though. It looks normal. It's not one of those things—the half transformed. It's definitely human. Male.

Chase strides ahead and uses his spear to push the body over. Leaning over, he checks for a pulse even though there is no way someone could survive with...ugh. I think part of his insides hangs out.

Swinging his attention to us, Chase furrows his brows. "It's a stranger. I think human. He's naked like we were." Chase bends down and lifts up the man's hand. "Looks like he was restrained as well. There's bruising on his wrists from trying to break free of something. Looks fresher than ours. They must've come to the island after us."

Adam tenses next to me. "So, there are more people on this island. What the actual fuck is going on? They're kidnapping humans and trying to turn us like them. Why?"

"Maybe for population growth? To hunt? It could be for a lot of reasons. Eliana's stalker wouldn't say anything, but I know he knows." Evander looks at me. "I bet you could get the answers out of him. We keep intercepting his attempt at alone time with her, but maybe if we just watch and wait, he'll let his guard down and you can find out more for us."

I dart my gaze toward the water, where a body lies in the sand as a wave crashes over it. I know that we need the answers, but the thought of finding Kellan instead of just getting off this island freaks me out a bit. Especially knowing that my grandmother was the only one to have ever escaped.

"No way. I don't want to put her in that position," Tristan says. He grazes his fingers over my arm. "He already thinks she belongs to him or some bullshit."

Evander frowns. "But—"

Something rustles from the trees and a net falls over Chase and the body he inspects. No one has a chance to react as a man jumps from the trees and tackles him. He hollers and tries to shove them off. A blade sparkles in the sunshine a second before the man stabs it into Chase.

I scream and run forward, my fear getting the best of me and stealing away my good senses. I beat the others to the man and swing my makeshift spear at him hard enough to get him off Chase.

I jab it into his leg, piercing his skin. The man screams, his voice higher than I think even mine can go. He locks his fingers around the spear and snatches it away from me.

Chase manages to get his knife through the netting and cuts it open to free himself. "Eliana, behind you!"

I spin around in time to see another man charging me.

Tristan tackles him, and I realize there are three other guys. Davian struggles underneath another net, thrashing around. Adam faces another man, trying to get close enough to stab him.

My mind races. Why are they attacking us? Who are they? Did they kill Tiffany and her group?

I spin on my feet, looking for the next threat. Hopping over a body, I go after the guy fighting Adam. A net falls over me, tangling around my limbs. The weights hit the ground beside me, stopping me from throwing it off. Another man jumps down from the tree in front of me. I don't get a chance to even try to escape before he grabs the bottom of the net and scoops it up, snatching me off my feet. My body curls in on itself, and I scream and thrash, trying everything I can to get him to drop me to the sand.

"Don't fight. I don't want to hurt you, but you have to come with us. We need a woman." His gruff voice strikes fear into me. Why do they need a woman? Hank said the same thing after Evander killed Alicia. Why does it have to be my luck that others want me like this?

"Let me go! I'll fucking kill you!" I thrash harder, clawing at the man through the net. My nails bite into his skin as I scratch him, drawing blood.

He flips me over and slams me into the ground. The air escapes my lungs and I can't even scream. I can't breathe. The edges of my vision shadow.

"Keep it up, little girl. I hear they like them feisty." The man grabs the net again and hoists me up. "Now, why don't you take a nap?"

He swings me toward the ground again, hitting me hard enough to make my head spin.

I blink through the stars peppering my vision, but I don't pass out. I can't fight though. The man swings me back over his shoulder and carries me away.

I hold onto my consciousness the best I can. The world jostles around me and a massive headache pounds against my skull. I try my best to memorize the way the trees look as he trudges through the thick vegetation. The sounds of fighting continue behind us, but they grow quieter and quieter the deeper he carries me into the forest.

How am I going to survive this? Do I want to?

Fuck yeah, I do. I'm not only going to survive this, but I'm going to murder this guy the moment I get the chance. I'm not dying here. I'm not going to let my grandmother's escape go to waste. These monsters don't control me. I'm starting to realize that now. They can try all they want, but in the end, it's up to me.

"Where did you find her, Chad? That's not the one we've been watching." Another voice cuts the air, and I try to stretch my neck to look around.

"It was luck. Fate. Another group found the abandoned shelters." The man holding me, Chad, swings me in front of him and drops me on the ground again, hitting my back on tangled tree roots.

I can't control my gasp of pain. I squeeze my eyes shut, thinking about how I'm going to take on two men. I'm not strong enough if they work together.

"Damn, she's a looker. I hope that the Windshore pack was right. I'd like her to be our little bitch." The other man stands over me, tilting his head and leering, lust and something dark in his eyes. "What do you think, honey? Do you want some big strong man to take care of you?"

I manage to free my leg from the net. Jerking up my foot, I kick him hard between the legs and feel his balls squish with the force.

He hollers and clutches his junk, wheezing with his anger.

I don't get a chance to protect myself as Chad lifts a rock and bashes it into my head.

I fall limp, agony swelling through me.

These men are now out for my blood and body. I prepare for the worst.

CHAPTER 12

Eliana

KIDNAPPED

"TAKE OFF THE net and hold her still, Mark." Chad glowers at me as he crosses his arms. "She needs to be taught her place."

My breathing quickens with my fear. A dozen thoughts paralyze me long enough for Mark to untangle the net. He manages to grab my hair before I can react. I buck my body, refusing to make it easy on them.

Screaming, I project my voice as loud as possible. We can't be far from where they took me away from the others. And then I remember Kellan's words. He's always nearby.

I open my mouth to call for him, but Chad slaps his hand across my face, covering my lips with his dirty fingers. I gag, his disgusting body odor assaulting my nose.

My stomach twists, and I bite him as hard as I can, refusing to let go even though he slaps me again. Adrenaline numbs my pain, and a feral part of me awakens. The part of me that will do anything to survive. The part of me that excuses murder as long as it's me or them. And right now? I pick me.

"You bitch!" he shouts, trying to tug his hand away. "Mark, get her now, you asshole!"

I continue to bite harder and harder, knowing that if I keep at it, I can bite the fucker's finger off. The thought grosses me out, but it also satisfies me. I want nothing more than for him to feel the fear he instills in me. He deserves to feel the pain he's already put me through tenfold.

I grind my teeth into Chad's flesh, turning my gaze to Mark. He doesn't see the figure stalking up behind him. A machete chops into the side of his neck, and Mark's eyes widen. He opens his mouth in a silent scream, but he can't get his voice to work. The machete slams into his neck again, and then again, and I bite Chad so hard at the same time I watch Mark's body fall that his finger tears away in my mouth. Blood drips across my tongue, and I spit and gag, finally releasing Chad's hand. He trips over one of the roots of a tree and lands hard on his back.

I don't let him get up. I scramble and get on top of him, jabbing my fingers into his eyeballs, feeling the heat crawl up my hands as blood gushes from his sockets.

"You monster!" I yell, ripping my hands away. I swing my fists at his face over and over. A part of me breaks, stealing away my human rationale, leaving me broken and wild. Bloodthirsty and in need of revenge and justice. They might not have done the worst they could've to me, but they would have if they hadn't been interrupted.

A deep growl reverberates down my spine, but I still don't stop. I'm going to kill the son of a bitch with my bare hands if I have to.

Chad screeches, his voice turning high-pitched to where I'm sure ocean animals can hear him. Something locks to the back of my shirt, the strength managing to drag me away from Chad. I kick and fight, training my gaze on Chad as he clutches his bloody crotch. The shock of seeing his pants down and his cock a bloody wound freezes me and knocks sense back into me. And fear.

Teeth graze my fingers before a cold nose nuzzles the palm of my hand. I gasp and jerk away, meeting the bloody snout of Kellan's grey wolf. It's still hard to acknowledge that it's not his wolf. It's him.

Hands slide under my arms, and a muscular body engulfs me in a hug, lifting me off my feet from behind. "Chase, quick!" Davian yells, his voice booming in my ears.

"Someone end him. His screams are going to draw attention. Put him out of his suffering," Chase commands, coming into my view.

Silence falls after his words. Chad no longer screams in pain. I don't even have to look at him to know that someone obeyed Chase and killed the man.

A part of me—admittedly a monstrous part of me I didn't even realize I had—wishes that it could've been me.

"You have enough blood on your hands, Eliana. Allow someone else to handle the mess." Kellan's voice trickles through my mind.

I don't get to look for him because Chase fills my vision, clutching my cheeks between his hands to search my eyes. Blood stains his face, and a bruise purples his cheek already. Davian doesn't fare any better. Blood trickles from a cut on his lip, and bruises in the shapes of fingers darken around his neck as if someone tried to choke him to death.

"Where are you hurt?" Chase steps back with his question, running his fingers over my arms, trying to inspect me the best he can. "Turn her just a bit. There's blood in her hair. I need to see if it belongs to her."

Chase touches a spot on the back of my head, and I wince in pain. It's where Chad threw me on the ground. Combing his fingers carefully through my dark tresses, he finds the cut from the rock used in an attempt to knock me out.

"She's scraped up pretty bad on her legs," Davian

murmurs, keeping his voice soft as if he says the words out loud that he might explode. Anger laces his voice, but it's not directed at any of us.

"Those will be okay. I'll clean them. I'm more concerned that she might have a concussion or might need stitches. We aren't equipped for the latter. I'll know for sure when we get her cleaned off. I need water." Chase guides my head back a bit until sun shines in my eyes. "How much pain are you in?"

I blink a few times, my mind and body finally aligning. I ignore his question and ask, "What about you? You were stabbed. I was so scared."

Chase doesn't have a chance to brace himself before I fling my arms around him and hug him, forcing Davian to let me go.

Chase chuckles and groans, but he doesn't put me down. I find my mouth against his, and we kiss each other in a rush of emotions. Relief and lust, excitement and a bit of fear—so many things crash through me that I can't help myself.

"Damn, I was stabbed too, Eliana," Adam teases, ruffling his hand through Chase's messy hair. "I mean, look at this."

I jerk my attention from Chase, my mind catching up to me. Chase sets me on my feet, but my legs wobble, and I stumble. A furry body darts in front of me, and I land on top of Kellan in his wolf form. He transforms beneath me, turning into a man as we hit the ground. Our eyes meet, and he grazes his fingers across my cheek, sending tingles of pain and something else, something more intense, across my skin.

"Eliana…" His voice trails off.

I flare my nostrils and shove my hand to his chest, pushing myself up. The edges of my vision blur, and I sink back down. My head throbs along with the rest of me.

Chase kneels beside me. "Easy now. He helped us and led us here."

I rest my head on Kellan's shoulder, begging the world to slow down. "He h-helped? Why?" I stutter with my words.

"Because you need each other. You need the protection and they need a female to show their capability. Something shifts among the pack alphas, but mine isn't telling us anything. I happened to overhear some things. I know I shouldn't get involved, but my very soul demands it." Kellan tests me by resting his hand on my lower back.

"Is that an island thing? Because I feel that shit too." Tristan tightens his jaw, staring at me as I lie limply on Kellan.

"Could be survival instincts…or maybe because Eliana is a sexy little badass. Just look at her. I don't even care that she's on top of that asshole. I still want her." Adam squats beside me, shading me from the sunlight breaking through the trees. "What do you say? Let me carry you to where we're going to build tonight's shelter?"

All I can do is nod. I want nothing more than for someone to hold me. Feeling the weight of their arms around me will help keep me together when a part of me—the weak, scared little girl—begs to fall apart.

"Then I will clean you up and see what I can do about your injuries," Chase adds, flicking his gaze to Kellan. "Is there any way you can get me any first aid supplies?"

"For Eliana, I'll do anything." Kellan hands me to Adam, and he strokes his fingers over my cheek. I automatically cup his hand, pressing his skin into mine. I don't know why I do it or why I feel like I need to, but it's as if his strength can somehow seep into me through touch alone.

I clear my throat. "Thank you. I know you didn't have to."

Kellan offers me a soft smile. "But I did. I'll do anything for you." Leaning in, he presses a kiss to my forehead, sending tingles blossoming over my body.

No one says anything as he transforms into his wolf form and darts away. Slowing when he gets a dozen feet from us, he turns his head and looks at me, releasing a low howl. I wave at him, wiggling my fingers. The others stand around me silently, watching and waiting. This feels so surreal.

"Kellan said to head south toward shore. There's a cave hidden where we can build our shelter. It's near water and some fruit trees yet still beach accessible. We'll be able to have a look-out in the trees. No one will be able to sneak up on us as long as one of us is always on guard." Evander crosses his arms, broadening his body as if he can't help himself from wanting to stand tall.

"Are you sure we should trust the guy? Convenient that he showed up and all of a sudden decided to help. What if it's a trap?" Davian rocks on his heels. "What does he get out of it?"

Tristan scratches his fingers through his hair, mussing the strands. "We all know he wants Eliana. Maybe he sees how close we're getting to her."

Evander tightens his jaw and looks at me. "Don't feel obligated to do anything with him. He deserves nothing."

"I don't," I murmur, training my eyes on my hands. "I honestly don't even know how to think or feel. This is all so confusing and complicated. I just want to figure out how to get out of this place."

"And we'll make it happen. There's no fucking way I'm staying here. Starting tomorrow, we're going to set a plan into action." Chase touches my hand, getting me to look at him.

"Hell yeah, we are. They can't keep us here forever." Adam adjusts me in his arms.

I don't respond. I can't.

If only I believed that to be true.

Strange neon colors paint the cave walls, illuminating the world around us. It's unbelievable and magical. I've never seen anything like it. There's no black light to set things a glow, yet it still does. I knew something was different about this island, but now it's almost like another world.

"Do you think we're still on Earth?" I can't stop my voice from sounding out my thoughts. If I continue to think about it without answers, I might go crazy. "This island doesn't make sense."

"Who knows. I've given up trying to make sense of anything." Evander strolls beside Adam, clutching a knife in one hand and his makeshift spear in the other.

Chase leads the way, slowly but confidently, as if he's ready for any and all threats. "I can't. I know there has to be a scientific explanation."

"This island is like a gateway. It's in between worlds, but not as if it's another planet. You will find out eventually, but you can't see it until you've been chosen." Kellan's voice sounds from behind us.

Tristan aims his spear. "Don't sneak up on us, asshole."

"Davian allowed me in." Kellan dangles a bag from his fingertips. "But perhaps you should still pay attention to your surroundings."

I hold my hands up, stopping the two of them from arguing. I can tell that Tristan already goes on the defense with Kellan around. He has no reason to trust him. I don't either...except that I can't help it. I don't know why. He has been around and has done a few things for us, but he still is with the packs who have kidnapped and abandoned us here. He is a lykoswulf.

"Kellan, give us a break. We don't have your super-hearing and whatever other abilities you have. You probably can turn on some sort of stealth mode." I tip my head with my words, giving him a long look.

He flexes under my attention, unfazed by the fact that he strolls in naked. Now that the rest of us have clothing, it's a bit odd. He's so comfortable in all his delicious, muscular hotness.

"Of course, he has super-hearing," Adam mutters under his breath.

Kellan smirks but he doesn't respond. "I suppose you're right, my love."

I try not to react to his term of endearment. It's not the first time he's said it, but it doesn't get any more familiar. I don't know how I feel about it. Why is he calling me that? I know he thinks I'm his mate and he believes we belong together, but I don't believe in that bullshit.

"Let's not worry about that. You're safe here, and I brought what I need to take care of you." Kellan tilts his head, training his eyes on me.

Chase holds his hand out. "I can take it from here."

Kellan doesn't give him the bag and instead closes the space to me and smiles. "I brought some things that have been passed down through my pack. It's not human medicine, but it will help you. You don't need stitches or anything of that sort."

"I think you should let the doc determine that." Adam

slides his fingers through mine, trying to tug me out of Kellan's reach, but I don't allow him.

It's like my feet are glued to the ground. I'm caught in a magnetic pull, and I want to know more. It's my curiosity that leaves me open and vulnerable to Kellan. Hopefully, it won't be my undoing in the end.

"What about them?" I ask, reaching for the bag next.

Kellan allows me to take it without protest. "It will help them too. But you first. I can't stand seeing you injured like this for another moment. It's testing my willpower not to disobey the command of my alpha."

Tristan scowls. "And what command is that? You're already here, so be straight with us. What the fuck is going on and why are others trying to kill us and kidnap Eliana?"

"I'll give you as many answers as I can, but first...our girl. She needs my attention and care. Then you, Chase, will go next. I don't want your stab wound to become infected." Kellan holds his hand out, and I automatically take it. His comment stirs something inside me. *Our* girl. I'm not sure how I feel about it.

"I thought you'd prefer that over being called mine." Kellan's voice swirls through my mind as he extends his hand to Chase next. Chase raises an eyebrow and doesn't take his hand. I offer mine to him instead, and I let the two of them walk me deeper into the cave. Tristan, Adam, and Evander follow behind us. I whisper a silent prayer that Davian is okay outside alone. I don't know if he's injured like the others, but I'll make sure that Kellan checks him out as well.

Kellan picks up his pace, and I let him tug me along because my feet won't keep up. It takes a moment for my eyes to adjust to the constant change in light. I find myself standing in a beam of sunshine coming in from above.

And then I see it. A small pool bubbles within this cave. The water flows but not fast enough to sweep any of us away. It must be connected to the creek or something. I can't really tell where it comes in from, but I realize it's not freshwater. The scent of salt permeates the air, and I stare at the crystal-clear seawater.

I knew this cave was near the shore, but I hadn't realized that it must exit into the ocean.

"You don't have to worry about getting swept away. The seawater fills the pool with the high tide. There is an opening in the cliff. The drop is too far, so don't try to leave that way. No one can get in through there either." Kellan motions toward the other side of the pool. "I can show you after I take care of your injuries if you'd like."

"I'd like that," Chase says, speaking for me. I know he purposely does it because Kellan acts as if none of the others are here. His attention remains completely focused on me like I'm the only one he cares about. And that might be the case. I don't know what to think about it. I know that he is being cordial on my behalf, but I want to be able to trust that if I'm not here he would still help these guys. We're all in the same situation, and just because I'm a woman, doesn't mean that I'm the only one deserving of care.

"That's fair enough, my love. My apologies if it seems that way, but I can't get attached to those who have not been chosen yet. It makes things easier. You shouldn't either. Not until the moon calls." Kellan's voice whirls into my mind as he talks to me telepathically once more. I'll never get used to it. Now that I know he can listen in on my thoughts, I can't help but wonder what else he's heard from my mind. It annoys me to an extent. It's as if I no longer have privacy.

"You don't have to worry about that, Eliana," he adds, continuing to listen in on my mind. "I'll never judge you, and I only hear things when you think of me. Your thoughts are your thoughts unless your soul calls."

It takes everything in me not to speak out loud. I choose to ignore him completely and step toward the pool. He and Chase both stay by my side and clutch onto me as I dip my toe in. It feels amazing with the perfect temperature. It's not too cold like the creek water but it's not hot either.

"Damn, must feel good. Here, Eliana. I'll get in first and help you. Your knee is all fucked up." Adam strides around us and jumps into the water without hesitation. Tristan joins him next, and the two of them each hold out a hand for me to take. I have to tug myself from Kellan to get him to let me go. He acts a bit protective. Maybe even possessive. All I know is that

I'm not going to stand for it.

I side-glance him. "Do you understand? I don't belong to you." I think the words, wondering if he can hear them.

His jaw twitches but he doesn't respond. The bastard. His face is enough for me to know his answer. He doesn't like it, but he will give in to my demands.

"For now," he murmurs under his breath, probably thinking that I wouldn't be able to hear him, but it's like I'm ultra-aware of his presence. Even when I take Tristan and Adam's hands, letting them help me into the water.

"Looks like there's a rock shelf. Come here. You can sit on my lap since it's a bit deep and rough." Tristan pulls me with him.

I tip my head back and laugh. "Just the way I like it." Heat flushes my face at my comment, and I realize just how comfortable I am with everyone. I can't believe I just said that out loud.

They obviously can't believe it either, because the expressions they give me...damn.

"Shit. Move over. She's going to sit on my lap. I'm the doctor." Chase splashes into the water, sending a wave at my stomach, soaking my white shirt.

I tilt my chin down and look at the sheer fabric and how my boobs press against it. This might have been a terrible idea. But also a fun one. I could use some entertainment and light-hearted teasing. Flirting. I hadn't realized how much I truly enjoy all the attention. It's different than back home. I want it, not like with other men or clients. Before, I just accepted it and fake-smiled my way through it. Now? My cheeks hurt from the genuine smile crossing my face.

I swing my hand through the water and splash Chase in the chest. He scrubs his palms over his scruffy face, grinning the whole time. I let Tristan pull me onto him, and I feel the hardness of his body awaken beneath me. Obviously my comment got to him. It got to me too. Now that I can feel his cock pressing against my ass, I can't help remembering what he looks like naked. How hot he is.

"Keep squirming, and we're both going to get in trouble," Tristan whispers in my ear. "I know all these guys have a thing for you, but so do I. I'm willing to do whatever for my chance with you. I don't even care if I sound desperate."

Should I feel like a whore? Many people would think as much. Maybe even the guys. But I don't think they do. They don't seem like the double-standard type despite them being chivalrous and macho. It makes we wonder what they were like before all of this. Would they have given me the time of day then? Or is it because I'm the only female here? I know I'm not ugly but is it possible that I'm all their types? I know they're all different, but I find them attractive in their own way. Smart and funny too. Talented and sexy. Maybe it is this island.

"No, Eliana. It's all you." Kellan's voice tugs at my attention, trying to drag it away from Tristan.

"You don't sound desperate," I murmur, answering Tristan, shifting to look into his eyes. "And as for giving you a chance...that's what makes this so complicated. I like you all, except it makes me feel...easy. I don't know. You know how it is for women. You guys get to be fuck boys while I'd be shamed."

"Never with me. Fuck that. We're on a damn island. The rules have changed." Tristan darts his gaze to my mouth. "I'll prove it."

I know what he's thinking before he even closes the space to my mouth. Everything happens so fast that I don't have a chance to react as something locks to the back of my shirt. I scream out as I sink underwater, and I nearly inhale a breath. Just as fast as I go under, I pop to the surface.

Warm arms wrap around me protectively, and my body buzzes.

"They're not ready, my love. You can't test them just yet. They all have different boundaries." Kellan's voice hums in my ear. "Human men tend to be greedy. They want it all and for you to only have them."

I swipe the water from my face, ignoring his comment. Yells echo through the cave. Evander shoves Tristan underwater, calling him out for trying to kiss me. Splashing, Tristan swings his arm, missing Evander by a few inches.

"You know I like her, man," Evander says, his voice deep with his annoyance. He punches back, getting Tristan in the shoulder.

"You don't fucking own her. She made it clear already. If she wants me, you need to deal." Tristan whips his head, sending water cascading from his hair.

Charging Tristan, Evander locks him in a chokehold and drags him under again. No one does anything, and Tristan thrashes, unable to break the surface. Evander doesn't let him up, either.

"Stop!" I shout, thrashing to break from Kellan's hold but he doesn't let me go.

Evander doesn't stop.

If I don't do something, they're going to kill each other.

Fuck. I can't let that happen.

Not over me.

CHAPTER 13

Eliana

ISLAND FEVER

"KELLAN, PLEASE. DO something." My voice cracks with my words. "Please."

Sighing, Kellan helps Chase drag Evander off Tristan. Adam blocks Tristan from trying to retaliate.

"Evander, go find Davian and join him on watch. You need to cool off." Chase shoves Evander toward the side of the pool. "I don't know what the hell has gotten into you, but it needs to stop. Eliana made it clear. She wants things to stay casual. You can't start picking fights now, especially because you weren't even with her first. You don't see me beating your ass for it, now do you?"

Evander flares his nostrils in silence, flicking his gaze from Chase to Tristan and finally to me. We stare at each other, and I try not to give anything away. Annoyance and sadness weigh heavily on my chest. I didn't intend for things to be this way.

"I'm sorry, Eliana. I don't know what came over me." Evander plants his hands to the ledge of the pool and hops up, still facing me. He clenches his jaw and turns to Tristan. "Sorry to you too, man. Fuck, this place is making me lose it."

He gets to his feet, not waiting for any of us to respond. Silence blankets the air, and I lean my back against the rock wall, trying to settle my racing heart.

"I think it's best if everyone starts setting up camp. I'll take care of Eliana and call the rest of you when it's your turn." Kellan grabs the bag he brought from the side of the pool and motions for me to cross to the other end, where the cave continues.

"Are you sure you don't need me?" Chase asks, his muscles flexing as if he's ready to argue.

"It's best if I take this moment to care for Eliana alone." Kellan climbs out of the pool and reaches down to lift me up. I don't complain or try to argue.

I don't know if it was the fight or what, but suddenly, I feel defeated. Tired and exhausted. So much so that I don't realize Kellan sprawls out a blanket and helps me sit on it. It takes him kneeling beside me and touching my scalp to get me to react.

"Shit. Be careful. That hurts." I try to swat his hand away, but he catches my fingers and closes his hand around them.

"I wish those men weren't dead so I could make them suffer for doing this to you. The Windshore pack won't get away with this. I'll ensure it, even if I have to take care of things myself." Kellan sounds like he's talking more to himself than me.

This isn't the first time I've heard about the Windshore pack. The men in the forest mentioned them. It brings up so many unanswered questions I have.

I inhale a soft breath and meet Kellan's gaze. "You have to stop doing this. Every time you mention something, it only makes me angrier for the lack of answers. You keep saying that you can't tell me, but I think it's because you don't want to. I need to know more. Give me a reason to trust you."

"There's no reason to trust me. That's why I'm here and why I stay nearby. Trust is built on actions and not words, my love." Kellan pulls out a bottle from his bag and shakes it, turning the blue liquid inside purple.

He has a point, but I still don't like it. "Trust is also built with communication," I say. I cross my arms over my chest, not allowing him to take my hand.

He groans under his breath and pours some of the liquid

into the palm of his hand. "We'll get to that. It will take time because some things are better left unsaid and shown instead. We have rules and laws to follow as well, and some things aren't my place."

"Where is your place exactly?" I ask, trying to pry without getting angry. I need to ask the right questions to get him to open up to me.

He shrugs his shoulders. "Hold still," he says, not responding to my question. "I'm going to lather this in your hair. It's an old recipe that will heal your wounds. It'll tingle."

Without waiting for me to respond, he smooths the liquid over my head, kneading his fingers into my scalp as if he's washing my hair. And holy fuck does it feel amazing. A moan escapes my mouth, and my body relaxes as the pain dissipates.

It feels like magic. It is magic.

"No one has ever cared for you like this before, have they?" Kellan shifts and guides me to rest against him.

The closeness of his body leaves me fighting against my rationale, screaming not to get comfortable with him. "Does it matter? I've had a difficult life. But you know that, don't you?" I tip my head to look at him.

His piercing blue eyes search over my face, and a flicker of sadness sheens over his gaze. He blinks it away and shakes his head. "I didn't. Only the pack alphas pick the chosen. I didn't know about you until you arrived."

"But how did they find me? I haven't exactly been on the

grid. I have no social media. I had no permanent address. All of the work I've done has been off the record. After my parents died, I kind of just disappeared." I never really thought about it much until now. It wasn't by choice. I couldn't hold a job that offered a living wage. It was like I had been cursed with bad luck. It was one thing after another until I just existed. There was no meaning to my life. It feels like this is the most purpose I've had in a long time, and it sucks that it's just about surviving.

Kellan grimaces, and I realize he's listening to my thoughts. I try not to react. I don't think I'll ever get used to him having the ability.

"Your purpose isn't about surviving, my love. It's so much more. I want to tell you everything, but you have to discover some things for yourself. And as for locating you...we can track your blood line. It's a gift. Every alpha who creates new pack-mates is gifted with a sense. You were found by an ally. You can't join their pack as a mate, which is why you were given to us." Kellan pours more liquid into his palms and begins massaging it into my shoulders next.

"And who are you exactly? Which pack are you from?" I shift until I sit sideways. Draping my legs over his, I practically crawl onto his lap. I don't know what it is about this moment, but he's distracted me enough to forget he's naked until now.

Fuck. Me.

I beg my eyes not to look away from his, but I fail

miserably. Kellan tenses under my attention, his body awakening with desire. Something snaps inside me, cracking me open, and I explode with unexpected lust.

Kellan clears his throat. "I'm part of the Twilight Cove pack. Your grandmother was brought into Crystalrock."

His words should distract me enough, but I can't shake the longing feral need humming through me. And then I kiss him. It's as if my body takes control and my mind decides to say fuck it and follow along. It helps that I'm no longer in pain, and Kellan feels so open in this moment. Honest. It's hard to explain, but I want to prod deeper into his mind. I can do so by getting close to his body and using that to my advantage. Part of me knows it's wrong, but another part of me has lost control. I can't think rationally with the heat of his body close to mine and how his scent, like salt and woods and warm musk permeates the air, being the only thing I can breathe.

"You could never take advantage of me, Eliana," he murmurs, guiding his fingers lower down my arms until he reaches my legs and massages my thighs. "I do fear that you might feel as if I do that to you. These emotions...they're not all yours."

My body trembles in anticipation, and I squirm, wishing he'd continue to explore my body in all the right places. I crave it. I feel as if I'll explode if he doesn't.

"I don't care. This is the first time I feel as if I have control." I lean closer, leaving only an inch of space between our mouths.

"It's not in my nature to give you so much. If it will help you see things more clearly, do what you feel like. But fair warning. This will change everything. My soul claims you, but I can't. It goes against the arrangement." Kellan grazes his lips to mine, sending sparks across my body and zinging right between my legs.

"You think I care about some arrangement? It makes me want to do this more." I kiss him harder, shifting to straddle his lap. "I want you. I want to show the alphas they can't control me. You're going to help me."

"Goddess, guide me. I can't resist." His words trickle through my mind, and I'm nearly certain they were never intended for me to hear.

Is it wrong of me to push him? Maybe. But it's wrong that he has gone along with kidnapping humans and bringing them here. It's wrong that he keeps answers from me. There is nothing right about the situation except for how I feel in this moment.

"She's mine." The thought strikes through me, shoving away my thoughts about the island and the packs and whatever they intend to do with us. All I can think about are the words that Kellan projects into my very being.

It's as if he fills me up with something unexplainable, and I feel an imaginary rope tangle around the two of us, bringing us together. A wave of emotions crashes over me, and I moan. Kellan's hand travels from my thigh and slips between my legs.

I push him back, not letting him take control.

Grabbing my knees, he slides me up his body until I sit on his chest. I arch my hips and let him tug off the shorts. He abandons them beside us, and I strip out of my shirt and toss it into the pile. Dragging me closer, Kellan growls as he licks between my legs, drawing his tongue over my clit, making me arch in pleasure.

I squirm and moan, rocking my body as he digs his fingers into my ass cheeks. Ecstasy steals my breath. I lose myself to every sensation he creates with his mouth. I play with his hair, trying to stay still. He keeps me in place, making me sit with my weight on him. Our eyes meet and gold flashes in his gaze. He enjoys this as much as I do, his need to get me off, sending me over the edge until I orgasm. I smother him with my body, rocking and tugging his hair as I ride through the bliss he elicits in me.

My chest heaves, and I shimmy back, fighting against his strength to keep me on his face to make me come again. But I want more. A soft growl hums from his pouty lips, and I press my index finger to his mouth, stopping him from trying to have his way.

I scratch my nails lightly down his taut chest, memorizing every muscle and groove of his body until I feel the hardness of his cock tap my back. Stretching up, I align my body with his, not even taking a moment to think things through. I'm tired of thinking. I'm tired of constantly having to strategize and plan. I just want to feel good. I want to make this man weak in his knees.

Bowing forward, I brush my lips to his ear and suck his lobe into my mouth. "I want you to know that I don't belong to you or anyone else. This is purely for me."

Kellan narrows his eyes. "For now, Eliana."

I shake my head, glaring at him. But it doesn't stop me. I align my body completely and sink on to him. Kellan grabs my hips with a groan, his eyelids heavy with pleasure and lust.

There might've been a time in my life where I thought I was crazy for fucking a man like Kellan and not even because he transforms into a wolf. But the reserved, lovesick girl I used to be died a long time ago. I've had one-night stands and have done things with strangers to survive. Something about this is different. Kellan is—

Flaring his nostrils, Kellan growls lowly at the same time he hooks his arms around me and rolls, forcing me onto my back. He crashes his lips to mine with a deep thrust, nipping me while stretching my leg over my head in a position that makes my body ache in a good way.

"Those memories will be fleeting and unimportant. That life will have felt like a dream. I will ensure that you only think of me when we're together. I promise you that." Kellan's words rush through my mind as he silences my unbidden memories.

I gasp in pleasure, his body sinking into mine over and over, fast and hard, feral and completely wild. I scratch him with my nails and break from his kiss to graze my teeth along his shoulder. My moans echo through the cave alongside Kellan's grunts and growls. He sounds monstrous in a sexy way, each guttural moan of my name sending my heart racing. Grabbing my other leg, he curls my body, guiding my feet to touch the cool rock floor above my head. He tightens his jaw and looks between us, watching himself as he enters me. He strokes my exposed clit with his thumb, increasing my pleasure. I've never been with a man back home whose mission felt like my pleasure was his sole purpose. It sends a rush of energy through me as my body spasms and I come. I scream out and scratch Kellan harder, only to have him snatch my wrists to pin them over my head. I feel so vulnerable yet safe and sexy beneath him. I don't even care if he stole control from me.

All I care about is how he makes me feel in this moment. How I can forget that a treacherous world exists outside this cave. Here, I'm safe. I'm protected.

"Because you're important to me," he murmurs, slowing down with a soft moan. "You're my soulmate. You'll see."

I close my eyes, wishing he'd have kept that to himself. It's like with the others. I don't want those types of strings or attachments. Not here. Not on this island. I especially don't want Kellan to start treating me like his beloved.

"There are many things I've been forced to keep from you, but that truth I cannot, Eliana. My heart won't allow it." Kellan strokes his fingers over my jaw. "You can try to reject our innate bond all you want, but only your soul can do that. Not words. Not your hesitation. Especially not your human rationale."

His blue eyes capture mine, and he silently dares me to argue. Except I don't have the will to do so. He sounds so certain that it feels pointless even to try. If he wants to set himself up like this, there isn't much I can do apart from keeping my guard in place and making myself clear.

"I'm not rejecting you, but I'm not accepting whatever bond you think we share. I'm not just going to start ignoring the guys either. I like them."

Kellan surprises me with a smirk. "What if they don't accept your free spirit, my love? I know desire and companionship know no bounds but look at the jealousy already arising. And when they find out about—"

I press my hand over his mouth, shutting him up. "For one, I think the whole island heard us. And two, I already told them I wasn't interested in anything besides some fun."

"You don't think that will change?" Kellan holds his weight above me and only moves off when I push my palm against his chest.

"Maybe when I get off this damn island." I sit up and grab my clothes, hurrying to put them on. "But first, you promised to heal the others after me."

Kellan's inquisition prods at my being. I don't even want to think about this shit. Not now.

"Are you sure you want to find them so soon?" He sits up, following me to my feet, not allowing a foot of space between us. "They'll be okay a while longer. You, on the other hand...your mind is racing. Please, I didn't mean to set you off. I can sense your desire to flee. Let me help."

I shake my head, stumbling away, trying to get enough distance between us to make a run for it. I don't know what's up with me. I was fine only moments ago, but now I can't seem to get away fast enough.

Kellan jerks his attention from me and toward the ceiling of the cavernous cave.

Then I hear it.

Howls.

A man hollers.

Spinning on my feet, I bolt away from Kellan. I pray that the scream wasn't from the others. My heart races, and I jump into the pool, splashing my way across.

"Eliana, slow down," Kellan calls. "Please."

I ignore him, rushing toward the opening of the cave. I don't see the figure emerging from the shadow until it's too late.

The world spins, and my back hits the wall of the cave. A warm hand covers my mouth, and it takes a moment for my mind to catch up and realize Tristan's not a threat.

"Shh. They're close by," he whispers, his breath tickling my ear.

"The wolves?" I can't stop the question from sounding through the air.

He shakes his head. "More humans. We think they're getting dropped off like us. Chase went to look."

My heart flutters at the thought. "Alone?"

"No, with Evander. You were...a bit noisy. They left when Davian caught sight of the boat entering the waves. If the fuckers leave it like they had with us—"

My eyes widen. "We could steal it and get the fuck out of here." Hope rises inside me, and that's all I can think about now. If we had a boat, things would be so much easier. I wonder if that's how my grandma had managed to escape. "Tristan, we have to go to them. If it's unattended, we need to take it. Now. Together."

Footsteps slap against the rocks, and I jerk my attention to Kellan as he rushes toward us. I can still feel his raging emotions, and fear explodes from him. He's not afraid of anything outside of us. He's afraid of what I'm thinking. Of what I want to do. Because he doesn't want me to leave the island.

No, not the island. He doesn't want me to leave him.

But I can't stay. I can't just accept this is my life now. I'm not a lykoswulf. I'm human. I was born in the human world, and I plan to live the rest of my life there. It's the only thing I can imagine. Even after all of this, I still want to go to the place I'm familiar with. The place that used to have people that cared for me before my parents died. There is a reason I ended up there and that my grandmother left this place. I must follow her lead.

"Eliana, please. Don't go yet." Kellan picks up his pace and comes in to view, emerging from the shadows of the back of the cave. "What you're planning won't work."

I glare at him. "You don't know that."

He raises his hands up in surrender, slowing down. "But I do. Please, just listen to me. If you go—"

I point my finger at him. "You can't keep us here. We don't belong." Tightening my fingers around Tristan's, I pull him closer, getting him to silently follow my lead.

Kellan growls and shifts into a wolf before our eyes. He stalks forward, his body rippling with his movements and his thick grey coat stands on end. He's not going to let us leave. Well, he's going to try.

I shift my eyes to Tristan. Leaning close, I whisper, "We have to try. We can't let him stop us."

Tristan bobs his head. "You know I'm with you. We're going to get the fuck off this island. I won't let anyone stop us." Slowly reaching behind him, Tristan pulls something from the bag on his shoulder. It was one that Kellan gave us, but what he pulls out of it...shit. I had no idea anyone grabbed the net.

"Eliana, be smart about this. You don't want them to come after you. It's not my pack, and I can't fight them off on your behalf." Kellan's voice projects through my mind, and he inches closer in his wolf form, looking ready to launch in our direction to pounce on me.

I wag my finger at him. "Stay back. You're not in charge of us. You're either beside me or in my way." It pains me to say the words, but the truth to them sinks deeply inside me. I don't need someone to tell me what's best. I need someone who can tell me that I can achieve anything I want.

Kellan releases a growl, the threatening noise igniting my human fear instincts.

Tristan expands the net and chucks it at Kellan, managing to blanket it over him. Neither of us waits to see if it traps him. Tightening his fingers around mine, Tristan pulls me in the direction of the mouth of the cave.

I run hard on my bare feet.

Sunshine blinds me as we exit. Ignoring the cacophonous noise of the wolves in the forest, we run together toward the beach.

We break from the tree line and rush into the sand, kicking it up around us. And then I see them. Three men lead a couple of humans from a motorized raft.

Arms lock around me from behind. Tristan covers my mouth, stopping me from screaming out.

We duck into the thick vegetation.

"Look, there they are." Tristan motions a bit down the beach to where we spot Evander, Chase, Davian, and Adam all lurking behind a couple of trees.

They don't see the wolf sneaking up on them.

Fuck.

The black wolf launches into the air, pouncing on Davian's back.

I cover my mouth to stifle my scream.

The wolf sinks his fangs into his arm. It drags Davian away from the others.

Three more wolves attack.

"Eliana, we—" Tristan snaps his mouth shut.

A figure appears behind him, and I gasp at the sight of Tiffany standing a foot away with a bloody knife. Tears stream down her eyes, and she shakes her head.

"I'm sorry. I had to do that. I didn't have a choice." Dropping the knife, Tiffany takes a step back.

Tristan drops to his knees.

CHAPTER 14

Davian

DO WHAT IT TAKES

PAIN EXPLODES THROUGH me, and I can't stop the yell from sounding through the air. The black wolf snaps his jowls on my arm, refusing to let me go. The massive beast shakes its head like it wants my arm, and I try to swing my fist to punch it away. But it's no use. It's stronger than me.

I thrash, trying to find my footing, but it drags me away from the beach and deeper into the forest. I use my free hand and reach out, grabbing at anything and everything to find something I can use as a weapon. This fucker will kill me otherwise. It'll do exactly what it did to the others, and I refuse to die at the teeth of this man beast.

I lock my fingers around a tree root, using my strength to slow the wolf down. Its teeth grind across my forearm, shooting agony across my body. The edges of my vision darken, and I shout again as fiery pain licks my skin.

The wolf releases me, but it doesn't run away. It snarls and snaps its teeth, lunging and retreating as it tries to intimidate me.

Glowering at the wolf, keeping my eyes on it, I use my good hand to blindly feel around the dirt until I find a sturdy branch, fallen from the trees. I whip it as hard as I can, smacking the wolf across the snout. It whimpers and backs up, barking once at me.

It bolts away, disappearing into the trees. I suck in a few deep breaths and pull my arm close to my chest, trying my best not to look at my mauled skin. I'm going to pass out. I've never seen something so disgusting and felt something so painful in my life.

Heat burns from the wound, warming the rest of my body, and sweat prickles across my skin. I swallow. My tongue hangs heavy and swollen in my mouth. I struggle to breathe. To call for help. I can barely even think. My chest tightens and my head pounds. Am I going to turn into one of those things? Is my body going to start morphing into something I won't be able to survive?

Fuck. I don't want to die. Not here. Not like this.

It's the only thing that keeps me conscious. I know if I pass out, I'll never wake up. That this will be the end.

"Get up," I mutter to myself, using my good hand to press against the forest floor to get to my feet.

My body trembles with the movement, but I manage to push myself to my knees. Blood drips down my arm and splashes the ground, absorbing into the dirt. I need something to stop the bleeding. I look around and realize that the only thing I have are the shorts I'm wearing. A huge fucking part of me doesn't want to take them off and leave myself exposed. But the part of me that wants to survive says to suck it the fuck up buttercup, because it's either show off my damn cock or bleed out. Risk infection. Die.

Another howl booms through the forest, striking me right in the gut. It kicks me into action, and I stumble to my feet and drag my shorts down to take them off. I wind them around my arm, putting pressure on my wound even though the pain intensifies, and I nearly fall to the ground.

"Tristan! Tristan, stay with me!" Eliana's voice rings in my ears, and I steady myself on the tree trunk, looking around, trying to blink the haze from my vision.

I spot Eliana standing a dozen feet away, obscured by the low hanging branches of the tree. A body lies in the dirt by her feet, and my muscles tense. But it's not because Tristan sprawls out motionless on the ground. It's because another figure rushes toward Eliana.

I recognize Tiffany, and anger ignites inside me, giving me the strength to get my shit together. I stumble forward, barely staying on my feet, until my adrenaline kicks in and helps ease the pain trying to leave me incapacitated.

Eliana spins, evading Tiffany. Sweeping her leg out, Eliana trips the woman, sending her skidding across the ground. I'm not even within a few feet of them before Eliana jumps onto Tiffany's back and locks her fingers through her hair. Yanking her head back, she jabs her fist into Tiffany's nose, sending blood pouring down the woman's face.

"You're dead. You're fucking dead!" Eliana shouts, punching Tiffany again.

Tiffany gurgles a scream, but she can't seem to fight back against Eliana.

A grey wolf surprises the two of them and jumps onto Eliana, knocking her away from Tiffany. It's not Kellan. I would recognize his wolf form now that I've seen it a couple of times. This wolf doesn't have the same blue eyes, and its chest is lighter, almost white.

Eliana shrieks and locks her fingers to the wolf's fur, managing to keep its teeth inches away from her throat.

Rage consumes me, and I spot a blade sparkling on the ground near Tristan. I try not to look at him, afraid that I'll notice he's not breathing. Right now, I can pretend he's okay.

I need to believe that we're all going to be fine. I'll protect us, even if it's the last thing I do.

Eliana cries out, struggling to keep the wolf away from her. I charge toward it and jerk my hand, slicing the blade across its side. The wolf screeches and catapults away from her. I don't even get a chance to do anything as it kicks its back legs into the ground and flies at me, knocking me so hard that I fall back and smash against the tree. Snarling, the wolf sinks its teeth into my mauled arm again, the agony forcing me to release the blade. Eliana screams again, but I can't see anything but her blurry figure moving behind the wolf.

I expect the beast to go for my throat next. I brace myself for an agonizing death. But the wolf stops short. Howls echo around me, and it cocks its head, twitching its ears. Snarling once more, the wolf shoves its paws against me only to retreat. I watch in shock as it goes after Tiffany, locking its jaw to her arm and sinking its teeth into her skin. She screams and falls, and the wolf drags her several feet.

A huge branch swings through the air, smacking the wolf in the face. I blink my eyes, trying to keep conscious. Adam shouts and swings a branch again, knocking the wolf away from Tiffany. The wolf doesn't try to attack. All it does is dart between two trees and disappears into the forest. I inhale deep breaths, trying to suppress the pain, but it's too much. I don't think I'm going to last much longer.

"Doc! Doc, over here. We have three down." Adam kneels

beside Tristan. "Stay with me, man."

I open and close my mouth, but my voice doesn't come. Eliana closes the space to me, and I meet her beautiful golden eyes. They look brighter than usual as if the sun shines in them even though she stands in the shade.

"Davian, it's going to be okay. I know it hurts, but you're tough. Take slow breaths. Chase is coming." Eliana kneels beside me, running her fingers through my hair. "We're going to get you fixed up. It's just a flesh wound."

I can't stop my exasperated laughter. It's all I can manage.

She continues to play with my hair, the sensation helping to distract me from the fire licking down my arm. "And once you're taken care of, I'll be your nurse. I'll get you back into good shape, okay? If you need me to kiss you to make you feel better, I'll do it. I heard that's what kisses are good for."

I open and close my eyes, feeling my mouth stretch at the thought. Thinking about her lips on mine helps ease the pain.

"Fuck, he's been bitten." Evander's voice cuts through me like a knife. "Maybe we should en—"

"Don't you fucking say it. He's still a man." Eliana raises her hand to Evander.

"But for how long?" Evander heeds Eliana's warning to stay back, and he stands upright and crosses his arms over his chest. "If I were him, I wouldn't want to even experience this kind of torture for a second."

"I'll remember that." Eliana glares and turns her attention

back to me. "Don't listen to him. It's going to be fine. You're not going to turn into one of those things."

Except we all know I might. It's hard to even process. If that happens...Evander is right. Maybe I shouldn't wait. The pain coursing through me now is already unbearable.

"Davian, please. Please, keep your eyes open. Chase is going to fix you up next." Eliana cups my cheeks in her hands.

I hadn't realized I closed my eyes. I blink a few times, the weight of my body making it hard to stay awake. I just want to go to sleep. The burden of the pain and the terror gets to me, making me feel weak when I know I'm stronger than this. I don't think I've ever been so close to death before.

Eliana pulls me closer, cradling my head on her lap. She combs her fingers through my hair, trying to distract me the best she can. Tears swell in her eyes, and a few slip free and splash on my forehead. I can't get my arms to move anymore to wipe them away. She shakes, unable to keep herself together.

I don't think anyone has ever cried over me like this. My heart aches for her. Because I know that once this is over for me, that's it. But for Eliana? She'll keep going. She'll have to live with this even if it was out of her control.

It makes me want to fight harder just so she doesn't have to. There is something about this incredible, compassionate yet fierce woman that draws me to her. I know that there is still a lot to learn about each other, but the situation has brought all of us close together. And I can't help the feelings rising inside me for her. All I can think about is how shitty it would be if my life ended here and I never got the chance to see where things could possibly go with her. I know she wants to keep things casual and not start anything romantic with any of us, but that's just now. That doesn't mean the future. It's a hope of such a future that helps me focus on her and stay awake. It prevents me from succumbing to the pain and anguish rolling through me trying to steal my life away.

"Please, Davian. We can't do this without you. Who will be my farm boy? I never even got the chance to see what it's like to kiss my Ginger of Gilligan's Island." Eliana laughs through her tears, the sound melodious yet heartbreaking.

Another shadow falls over me, and an arm drapes over her shoulders. "If that doesn't keep you the fuck with us, I don't know what will. Come on, Davey boy. Stay awake. Don't fucking die before our bromance even takes off." Adam keeps his voice low, and I want to punch him for talking to me as if he must whisper the words like at a damn hospital when someone is sick. That always bugged me. The quiet that lingers around the ill and dying. It should be noisy as fuck. It should be full of life and not acceptance of death. When I go out, I want it to be a fucking madhouse party. I don't want it to be people crying over me like this. Fuck that.

"Adam, scoot over. I need some room. Why don't you go sit with Tristan? I want you to keep pressure on his bandages. We're going to need to figure out how the fuck to seal his wounds unless Kellan shows himself. Evander went to look for him. Tiffany is doing it now, but I don't trust her not to try to murder him the second our backs are turned. She's been bitten too."

Fuck. Tiffany? I thought she might've been taken. Call me fucked up in the head, but I kind of hoped for it. That bitch is not one of us. She chose the others, and she is responsible for half of this mess. I didn't like her since the moment she opened her mouth. She just seemed like the type to act better than everyone else. It's why I chose to go with Eliana in search of water that first day rather than help with the food, even though I have experience in farming.

I never said I was a good guy. It's probably why my parents kicked me out when I was sixteen, and I recently got out of jail for setting a neighboring farm's barn on fire because the assholes tried to dam up the river that brought water into my boss's farmland.

I can't help it if I hate selfish, entitled people. Even if I might be one myself.

"Hey, Davian. Focus on the beautiful woman holding you. Okay, man? This is probably going to hurt like hell. I need to inspect your wound and clean it." Chase taps me in the middle of my forehead.

I react, my body jumping at the gesture.

Chase glances to Eliana. "It's good that he's responsive. I want you to hold him still and distract him the best you can. I think if we see signs of infection, we should try to remove it."

I dart my eyes to his, opening and closing my mouth. Remove what? The skin? My arm? What the actual fuck? I groan and try to move. That sounds far worse than death. This asshole doesn't have anything for pain. I've seen it done on damn TV shows, and I don't think our machete is sharp enough, nor is he strong enough to sever my limb in one go.

"Shit. Don't we have to move fast? I honestly don't know how it works." Eliana pinches my chin. She leans into me, filling my vision with her gorgeous face. "Davian, we won't do anything without your permission, but if your arm has to go, I'm going to beg you to let us do it. We have to try. I don't want to lose you to whatever the fuck happened to the others. I don't want to have to kill you either."

Do I even want to survive that kind of bullshit? Fuck me. Why is it my luck that I'm the one who has to deal with this shit? I'm kind of attached to my arm. I need two fucking hands to do my job back at home.

"Better being without one arm than being dead, Davian. There's amazing technology these days. And the pain won't last forever." Chase presses his hand into my shoulder, pinning my arm down. He ties a vine around it like a tourniquet. It sends my stomach twisting. Is he fucking prepping me for this? I thought I got to choose.

I open and close my mouth, trying to force the words out. But Chase does something to my arm, sending shooting pain through me. I pass out from the agony, and darkness engulfs me. I don't know how long I remain knocked out for, but when I come to, the pain continues. I'm afraid to open my eyes. I'm afraid to see a missing limb. It makes me attempt to move my fingers.

I regret it immediately, because pain shoots through me with the motion.

"Do you see these? They don't look the same as they had on the others, but I don't like the way it looks. Where the fuck are the others? Where is Kellan? I might have to be the one to pin him down." Chase keeps his voice slow, but I still hear his words.

"You're fucking joking. If you pin him down, then that means…" Eliana pales, losing color in her face. Her mouth trembles, and she looks at me again and then to Chase. She shakes her head. "Kellan! Kellan, you fucker! I know you can hear me!" Eliana shouts the words, her chest heaving as she thinks about what Chase just mentioned.

"You can do this. I think we're out of time. We can't wait for the others and risk it spreading. I don't know what else to do. If we wait, we can lose him. We need him to survive. Davian is one of us." Chase pinches her chin, looking into her eyes. "Your hands are far steadier than Adam's. Davian trusts you."

He isn't wrong, but I also don't want Eliana to be in this fucking position. It isn't fair. It's my dumb ass who got mauled.

Maybe I deserve to die like this because of my actions.

"You're going to owe me something, Chase. You're the doctor," Eliana mutters under her breath, taking the machete from him. He helps her pour water over it, cleaning it off.

"Whatever you want. I'll do anything for you. If you want to smother me with those thighs, you got it. You want me to hand feed you? I'll do it. I mean it. Whatever." Chase leans in and kisses her. "You got this."

I groan, wishing my damn mouth would stop trembling enough so I can tell him to shut the fuck up already. He's offering to lick her pussy for cutting off my arm. That's some fucked up shit right there, though I might have to offer her the same thing if she's my hero. Goddamn it. This fucking sucks.

Eliana shakes out her arms and looks at me. "I'm sorry, Davian. I'm so, so sorry. I just don't want to lose you."

My need for self-preservation kicks in, and I thrash and buck my body. Chase gets on top of me and holds me down, shoving his hand at the top of my shoulder and the other one at my wrist. I'm going to kill some wolves for this. I'm going to kill everyone who isn't a part of our group.

I will fucking save my arm to shove it up their asses. They will regret ever doing this.

"You need to swing with your entire body. Put all your weight and force into it. I want you to do your best to chop it in one swing. No one wants to deal with a second blow." Chase clears his throat, his voice choking with his instructions. "Make sure you hit here." He draws his finger over my arm just above my elbow.

"Fuck. Fuck! Fuck!" Eliana screams, her voice ringing through the forest.

Chase looks down at me, grabbing my shorts and folding them up. "Bite on this, man. I don't want you breaking your teeth."

I don't have a choice, so I let him shove the gross fabric into my mouth. I honestly don't give a fuck about my teeth right now. I give a fuck about the fact that someone is about to chop my arm off without any anesthesia or pain meds or any bullshit. If I survive this...shit.

I yell like a damn baby, and unbidden tears blur my eyes. I'm terrified. I don't think I've ever been so scared in my life. I'm afraid that I'm about to piss myself. Maybe shit myself. My dignity is about to be obliterated by this entire situation. I just wish I could pass out again. I want somebody to suffocate me, so I don't have to be awake.

"On the count of three, Eliana," Chase says, adding more pressure to my arm.

She gasps and nods her head. "I'm sorry, Davian," she repeats.

"One." Chase's voice deepens. "Two."

Eliana releases a sob and adjusts her arms, holding the machete over me. I squeeze my eyes shut, preparing for agony worse than what I'm already going through. I prepare for the end.

"Three." Chase growls with the word, pinning me down with his entire body.

I holler, my voice muffled with the fabric. My whole body cools while sweat pools on my forehead. The pain doesn't come. Eliana doesn't swing the machete. I risk opening my eyes, seeing Eliana looking in the distance. Chase frowns beside her.

She drops the blade by her side and covers her face with her hands. "He's coming. I just heard him. He told me to stop. If we do this, he'll be rejected."

Chase searches her face. "But the infection—"

"He said to let Davian fight it. He's coming with something to help." Eliana reaches down and rubs her fingers over my forehead, smearing the moisture on my face. "Davian, I'm so sorry. This whole situation is fucked up, but I trust Kellan. It's hard to explain. He's in my head. He's in my soul."

"I don't understand," Chase says, voicing my silent question.

"He claims we are soulmates. He can project his voice telepathically to me. He heard my cry. He's coming." Eliana swipes her palms across her cheeks, smearing blood over her skin. "He said the hunt is about to begin. We'll be tested soon. It's what is taking him so long and why he didn't follow us. His alpha called him back. He had no choice but to go."

Her words strike me to my core. A hunt? Fuck. A test? Has

it even been a couple weeks? I don't even know anymore. Time passes sometimes quickly, sometimes slow. I've lost track of days and nights as I've only slept when I've had the moment to.

"Whatever he's talking about doesn't sound good." Chase leans away and links his hands to the back of his head.

He's right. It sounds worse.

"Maybe we should try to get the boat. We can wait until Kellan gets here and then head out. We won't give him a choice if he is who he thinks he is to Eliana." Adam speaks up for the first time in a while. I can't see him with Tristan though.

"What about me?" Tiffany asks.

Her voice enrages me and gives me the strength to sit up-right and push through my shadowy vision. "You can fuck off. You'll be the one they chase first. I'll guarantee it."

Eliana grumbles next to me. "No, I will. You've betrayed us. You're lucky we didn't let that wolf take you."

"You can't do that. It isn't right." Tiffany abandons her spot on the ground and looks around. "I won't allow it." Opening her mouth, Tiffany screams, calling out to the island that we're over here.

She doesn't see the wolf launch from the trees.

Kellan smashes into her back with a snarl, transforming into a man to restrain her. She screeches, only to have him cover her mouth. "Shut up. You've been chosen by the Wind-shore pack, and you'll face their mercy. Now, speak again and find out what happens. You've betrayed my soulmate."

Tiffany sniffles and submits, crying into the dirt.

Kellan jerks his attention to me. "Now you, Davian. Who bit you? Tell me everything."

My mind draws a blank. I can't remember the attack and only the pain after.

"It was a black wolf, I think," Eliana says, absently combing her fingers through my hair.

Kellan flares his nostrils. "Someone from the eastside of the island. Blackshell or Lagoon Hollow. They shouldn't have been in this territory at all."

"What does that even mean? Does it matter?" Adam asks, flexing his muscles.

Kellan trains his gaze on me. "It'll determine where you end up. I can try to intervene, but I have to bite you. It'll be twice as bad."

Eliana shakes her head. "No. Not again. We're getting out of here, so those packs won't be a problem."

Kellan ignores her and presses his hand to my chest. "The choice is yours and yours alone. You'll be the first one to ever have been granted the option. Don't disregard it out of fear. If you want even a chance to be around Eliana, then take it. It's what I would do."

"Davian, no," Eliana says, trying to draw my attention to her.

It pains me to ignore her, but a deep-seated part of me

believes Kellan. I can't imagine a life on this island otherwise, and right now, I have zero hope of ever leaving.

I stretch my arm up. "Do it. I'm accepting your offer."

Eliana and the others don't have a chance to argue. Kellan explodes into his wolf form, snarling and baring his teeth. Opening his jaws, he bites me hard over my wound, making me scream in agony.

I can't keep conscious any longer. This is it.

I'll either wake up from this nightmare or I'll die.

"Blessed be the lunar goddess. May you be chosen and worthy, brother." Kellan's words whisper through my mind.

All turns silent.

CHAPTER 15

KARMA

"WILL YOU PLEASE stay here, Eliana?" Kellan stands near the entrance of the cave, haloed in moonlight. "Someone needs to watch over Tristan and Davian, and it should be you."

I wasn't planning on going anywhere, but his words strike a nerve. "Why? Don't you think it should be Chase? He's the doctor. I have self-defense training. I can help." I don't mention it, but I'm worried that if I stay and something happens with Davian, I don't think I'll be able to perform a mercy killing. I couldn't cut off his arm to save his life if I had to. I've never felt so sick in my life. It's one thing to do something I have to for someone I don't care about. But being in the position I was? I never want to face that again. Kellan bit him. He's been bitten twice by a lykoswulf, and apparently this is now a test of whether his body can handle the change or not. Humans aren't intended to evolve immediately. Many of the ones abandoned on this island to fend for themselves don't make it. Out of the fifteen people from our original group, Kellan said they only expected a handful to make it. That's all that's left right now. Except for Tiffany and Ian. And she's going to lead Kellan's pack to him. She's going to give up information to kill him in exchange for survival from the alpha. Maybe. I can't honestly believe that a man who knows that many of us are going to die here would ever grant that sort of mercy.

"He won't. She'll be given to the Windshore pack, bitten again like Davian. If she survives, she'll be cast out. They would never blend bloodlines with my pack." Kellan answers my thoughts using his telepathy.

I should feel bad. I really should. But she stabbed Tristan. She came after me. She was responsible for Davian getting mauled. All I feel now is relief that she will face karma.

"Which means you'll be blessed for your compassion. These men need you now. Be here for them. Care for them as they've tried to care for you." Kellan closes the space to me and touches my cheek. "Please. I need to ensure you're safe until I return."

"They need your little badass self, Eliana. I'd want it to be you playing doctor over Chase if I were them." Adam strolls from the back of the cave, clean and dressed in the clothes Kellan brought. He hands me the bag, and I pull out the extra blanket, wrapping it around myself.

I sigh. "Fine. But I expect you back before dawn."

Adam comes up to me next and ruffles his fingers through my hair playfully. "You can blame that asshole if we're not. I think he might overestimate our ability to navigate this hellhole island in the dark."

Turning to Kellan, I say, "I trust you to bring them back safely."

He tightens his jaw and nods once. "You have my word."

Chase and Evander stroll from where the saltwater pool is, and Chase offers me a weary smile. I quickly kiss his cheek and tell him to be careful before turning to Evander.

He keeps space between us and crosses his arms over his chest. His rejection stings, but I can't blame him. We still haven't had the chance to talk about him attacking Tristan. And now? Fuck. I can't think about it.

Kellan shakes his head, staring at Evander but no one comments. I shift on my feet, deciding to let them leave the cave together instead of watching after them.

Kellan murmurs softly, and Tiffany releases a breathy sob. I turn my focus toward where Tristan and Davian sleep on blankets on opposite sides of the cave. Vines tangle around Davian's wrists and ankles, securing him in case he falls ill and his body rejects the bites. Just because it hadn't happened yet, doesn't mean it won't. Kellan said everyone reacts differently.

I close the space to Davian, giving him a quick once-over, double checking to ensure he's as comfortable as he can possibly be, all things considered. Adam and Evander did their best to pad the cold floor with leaves and moss. The blankets Kellan brought help as well, but I don't think anything will ever be good enough.

Tristan groans, drawing my attention to him. He opens his eyes and tries to sit up but fails. I stride to him, kneeling on the blanket to get into view.

"Relax. It's going to take a bit for your body to heal from such a deep wound. Kellan said with his salve, you'll be better by tomorrow night as long as you take it easy." I scoot closer, keeping my voice calm. I was so scared seeing him bleeding out. The terrifying moment is forever imprinted on my mind.

Tristan licks his lips. "My gorgeous hero. How can I thank you?"

My heart lightens with his playful comment. "By behaving and not dying. Can I get you anything? Water? Something to eat?"

"I'm a bit cold. Lie with me?" He extends his hand to me.

I don't know if he's serious about being cold or just using it as an excuse, but I won't deny him such an easy request.

I ease myself down beside him and tuck my body against his, taking care not to touch my hand near the wound slicing across his torso. He rolls his shoulder, shifting slightly to meet my gaze. "What did I miss? Where is everyone?"

"They're getting a few things taken care of to help us for tomorrow." I try not to think about the hunt Kellan mentioned. He didn't get into detail, but I know shit will be going down tomorrow night.

"Did you guys get the boat?" he asks, reminding me of the reason he and the others had been in the forest in the first place.

I puff a breath of air through my lips and frown. "Not yet. But we will. We had nowhere to hide it, and Chase didn't think you could handle heading to sea in your condition."

His brows lower on his forehead. "Ah, fuck. You guys gave up on escaping because of me?"

"Not exactly." He doesn't know about Davian, and I'm not exactly sure if I should tell him. "I don't want you blaming yourself either. It just wasn't possible. Not yet at least."

"Why don't you sound so sure?" Tristan runs his fingers along my arm.

I roll to my side and face him. Linking my fingers through his, I hold his hands close to my chest. He already looks better. Color returns to his handsome face and he no longer appears as if he's on the verge of death. Being able to lie here with him, clutching his hands and gazing into his eyes fills me with relief.

It helps suppress the fear constantly rolling inside me, tangling up with my soul.

"Because I'm not. Things are changing here. I don't know what to expect. Kellan says that something has shifted within the packs and their rules no longer stand and the laws agreed upon by the alphas are being challenged. There's hostility. We're caught up in the middle of it." I lean forward and rest my head to his, wanting to just blur the world with him as my focus.

"This is all so unbelievable. You know I still can't accept that this island is full of werewolves. What is so great about me that they think I'm a good candidate to be one of them? I'm not exactly talented. I could barely keep a job. I was a damn beach-bum half the time. I have no motivation to do anything except be in the water and live my life without ties. Just me and my van." It's funny how easily I can imagine him living that lifestyle.

"I was squatting in a vacant house," I admit, whispering the words so close that my lips graze his. "I made money by being...I had a...let's call him my sugar daddy." This is the first time I've said the words out loud. My chest tightens, and I expect Tristan to pull away from me. I expect him to frown against my mouth and tell me that my former lifestyle is something he wants nothing to do with. Maybe he'll change his mind about me.

He surprises me with a chuckle. "A sugar daddy, huh?

How do I get one of those?"

A smile crosses my lips at his teasing. "The internet. I was desperate and apparently, it's a thing...Rocco was tolerable at first—smart, likable, okay-looking, and we had a pretty good arrangement. But then things became...difficult. We had different expectations." I squeeze my eyes shut, thinking about him and how my life went from blah to crazy.

It started out casual with Rocco. He was a businessman and single, just looking for companionship and someone to have on his arm for events. Sex wasn't part of our arrangement at first, but then I became more comfortable. He gave me more and more until I thought I'd be set. I was working toward getting my real estate license and had planned to do something more, which he didn't want. He wanted me to depend on him. And then his friends found out. Some of them offered me much more money for a moment of my time and I couldn't refuse. It pissed Rocco off. I was his girl. His piece of ass. He thought he could do whatever the hell he wanted with me.

He used my desperation against me, and it was nearly my downfall. I was to be taught a lesson by a supposed new client, but it was Rocco setting me up. When someone pays for your time like that, they think they own you. Rocco wanted me to think he was the good guy. He hired someone to prove his point, and it almost got me killed. It's how I ended up homeless. Because I preferred to live on the streets than have Rocco be my future.

"Let's just say he was a horrible man with even worse friends. Comparable to the monsters here," I add, shifting my jaw, not wanting to get into more detail with Tristan's sullen expression.

Tristan eases back, looking at me more clearly. "I can only imagine. I'm sorry you found yourself in that position. I hate that life has been hard on both of us." He doesn't ask for more details, which I appreciate. I'm not sure I'm ready to have this kind of conversation with him.

I shrug my shoulders. "You seem to be worse off, though. I mean, look at you. You nearly died. Now you're stuck here with me as your babysitter."

His face lights up with another smile, and he raises his arms a bit, wincing in pain but not letting it stop him from touching my cheek and pulling me closer. "I'm the lucky one. You have no idea."

I can't stop myself from closing the space completely to mold my lips to his, kissing him softly, sweetly, and just enjoying his closeness and how open we both are in this moment.

"I think I do. Because I feel it too. I have gone from no one and nothing to having people risk their lives for me. No one has ever cared about me like this, asking for nothing in exchange," I murmur against his mouth.

"It's only going to get better from here. It has to. We're going to get through this. Together." His fingers slide into my hair, and he draws me closer, kissing me deeper and sliding his tongue into my mouth.

I hum my agreement, gliding my tongue over his, tasting the sweet fruit flavor on his lips. Being so close to Tristan, all open and honest, allows me to relax and have a moment to just take everything in. My legs tangle through his, and he fills me with something indescribable. Hope, maybe. I can't be certain. It's been so long since I've had any.

We are so wrapped up in each other that it takes Davian coughing to remind me that we aren't alone. I ease away from Tristan, worry suddenly gripping me. I shift over and look at Davian across the cave. He meets me with his eyes, and they flash like an animal's.

A deep growl escapes his mouth, and he scowls, baring his teeth. I search over his body, expecting to see his skin rippling, but he still looks like a man. He doesn't shift nor does his body break on him. Bolting upright, he plants his hands to the floor and pushes to his knees. Davian growls again, whipping his attention at me.

"Davian, please. You need to rest. Don't get up. I can get you whatever you need." I pull myself away from Tristan and get to my feet. "Are you hungry? Thirsty? Cold?"

Davian doesn't respond with words. He growls again.

"What the fuck is wrong with him?" Tristan asks, groaning as he sits upright.

"He was bitten." My voice cracks with the words.

I don't get a chance to explain anything, because Davian

screams. His voice pierces the air and he startles me.

Tristan pushes to get to his feet and locks his hand around me. He moves me behind him protectively. It should be me protecting him. He was the one who was stabbed, after all. But I really doubt he's going to allow me as much.

So, I make him.

Sliding around him, I step a foot away and closer to Davian. I raise my hands in caution, trying not to panic as Davian screams at me again.

"Hey, take a deep breath. I know you're experiencing a lot of agony, but you're going to get through this." My voice quivers with my words. I feel like a liar. I feel like I'm giving hope where there shouldn't be any. I don't know whether or not he's going to get through it.

"I hear voices. They're gathering nearby." Davian smacks his hands over his ears. "They're fucking with me. Getting into my head."

My heart aches. I wish there was something I could do. Kellan didn't tell me about this part. He only warned me about the possibility of Davian's body rejecting his transformation. If that happens, he'll start shifting into a wolf and never complete the transition. We'll only know for certain with the full moon that will either bless him with life or finish him off unless we do it first. That's what happened with the others. That's why it was so fucked up that they had been bitten so soon. They would have remained in that half state until the full moon. I couldn't even imagine. That's utter torture and should be criminal. But the laws here are incomprehensible. Not like we have in civilization. This island is intended for the wild.

"I'll find Kellan. He shouldn't be too far." I shift on my feet and swivel to look at Tristan. "I need you to stay here. Make sure he doesn't hurt himself."

Tristan grimaces. "I don't think so, Eliana. I'm not letting you go out there alone. You stay here. I will see what I can do."

I open my mouth to argue, but Davian surprises us by hopping to his feet. He gives neither of us a chance to try to stop him before he charges toward the mouth of the cave.

And fuck. He's fast. I don't know if that's his normal speed or what, but this is going to be one hell of a time trying to get him. Because I'm not losing him. Not like this.

Tristan grabs my hand, as if he reads my thoughts, and he drags me with him until my feet and brain decide to team up and work together for once. If the forest wasn't so thick with overgrowth, Davian would already be gone. It's our luck that he trips over some tree roots sticking out from the ground.

He stumbles, pushing to his feet. I rip my hand away from Tristan and lunge forward. This might be a huge mistake, but I don't know what else to do.

I launch from the ground and onto Davian, tackling him. He crashes back to the dirt. I straddle him from behind, shoving all my weight against his body in attempt to keep him down. The bastard gets to his knees, and I screech and yank his hair, nearly losing my balance as he makes me ride him like a damn horse. But I refuse to let go. If I let go, he will start running again.

"Eliana! Grab his throat. Punch him. Wind him," Tristan calls from behind me.

Davian manages to get to his feet, and I squeeze his torso between my thighs, riding piggyback style. He bows forward again, his speed making it hard to shift my arm enough to lock it around his throat. If I loosen my hold even for a second, I'll land on my ass on the ground. I will lose him.

"Hurry, Eliana! He's going too deep into the woods. I heard a howl." Tristan groans from behind me, making all sorts of noises he tries to keep up.

A growl sounds from somewhere in front of us. Crossing my ankles, I lock my body to Davian's, freeing my hands long enough that I can swing my arm across his throat. I don't try to be gentle. I do it hard enough that he gasps and bounds forward. I fly off his back, landing with a thump on the ground before him. I'm so terrified that he will just jump over me and start running again, so I kick my leg up and strike him in the balls. Dropping to his knees, Davian curls in on himself with a yell. Tristan jumps on top of him, tackling Davian to ensure he doesn't get up again.

Neither of us have a chance to prepare as a wolf launches from between two trees in our direction.

I cover my face with my hands protectively. It's like they

just waited for us. Waited to see that we were unarmed and separated.

The white wolf sinks his teeth into my forearm and bites hard enough to send my eyes rolling. Tristan hollers my name. Another wolf darts from the trees and collides into him, stopping him from trying to intervene. It pins Tristian down with its giant paws and snarls in his face.

Teeth sink into my ankle next, and I scream in pain.

The white wolf shakes his head, treating me like a damn chew toy. Or prey.

I dig my nails into the ground, looking for anything to hold onto. But the wolf is too strong.

It drags me away.

CHAPTER 16

Eliana

WOLF WARS

VOICES MURMUR IN my ears, and I blink my eyes, trying to orient myself to everything going on. Firelight casts shadows around the forest. I peek through my lashes and see four men sitting around a campfire. They look far more civilized than I expected them to, fully dressed in shirts and shorts, and eating something off plates. It looks as if they're camping and not hunting in the wild like animals.

"I don't see why we just can't take her back. You know

staying here leaves us vulnerable for retaliation." One of the men leans forward and tosses another piece of wood onto their campfire.

"If you're worried about the Twilight Cove pack, then you can run back to Sunrise Pointe with your tail between your legs to tell Sean." The man beside him whacks him on the shoulder with the back of his hand. "It will be your neutering."

The man growls and flares his nostrils. "Shut the fuck up. I'm not worried. I just don't want to start shit before the full moon. We don't even know if she's going to make it. All of this will be pointless otherwise."

My stomach bunches with nerves, and I try to look around the campsite for anything I can use to my advantage. I need a weapon. I need a clear path to escape. They're so consumed with each other that they might not notice if I crawl out of here. I just need to get far enough away and to somewhere I can hide.

"She'll survive, Miles. Her bloodline was already chosen. She was fated for this. You know about Eleanor. That's why my pack has spent so many years looking for one of her descendants," a third man says, leaning back and resting his palms to the ground. "She hasn't reacted negatively already, which is a good sign."

"Whatever you say, Lou." Miles raises his hand, pointing in my direction. "I'll believe it when I see it."

"You don't have the same faith because you weren't

blessed as a pure lykoswulf, ya mutt." Lou smacks him on the back of the head. "Isn't that right, Gerry and Tim-boy?"

"You might be right. My ass has been cursed again and again. Why do you think I'm here? I'm tired of all this bullshit." The man, Miles, pushes to his feet. He scrubs his hands through his ratty beard and peers around the campsite. "I just hope Sean stays true to his word."

"Our alpha has never broken his vow. Not like yours. Not like Windshore or Twilight Cove. Sean knows what he's talking about. He knows what we want and knows what we need." Lou follows Miles's lead, getting to his feet. He stretches his arms over his head and turns in my direction.

I hold my breath, trying to remain utterly still. I don't want them to know I'm awake. It's hard enough as it is with the pain coursing through me. I want it to stop, but I don't want to blackout again.

"We need to do another sweep of the area. They'll know by now that we entered their territory and took one of their chosen. They'll be on high alert, especially because of her moonborne lineage." Lou grabs his shirt and tugs it over his head before kicking off his shorts. "Even if she wakes up, she'll be in too much pain to try to run. The restraints will help. No one needs to stay."

I've never been so thankful for someone being overly confident and cocky. I'm going to show them that they underestimate me. They probably think I'm some weak little girl who is scared out of her mind.

But I'm not scared. Not much, at least. I'm more pissed off than anything, and the second they turn their backs, I'm going to strike. I'll kill them for what they've done to me. I know what it means to have been bitten by a pack I don't belong to. Kellan said that if his bite doesn't take for Davian that he'll be cast out and killed. I don't know if that will be my fate because I'm a woman, but I don't want to find out. If that's the case, I need to find the boat. I need to get off this island even if I have to swim my way back to the human world.

The other men follow Lou's gesture. I relax the best I can with my eyes closed and try to keep my breathing even. I know they have super-hearing as wolves. Whichever one of them who bit me might even be able to get into my head telepathically. I just don't know to what extent yet. I don't think it'll be like it was with Kellan. He swears up and down that we're soulmates. These guys, on the other hand? No fucking way. I'd rather neuter them all and sacrifice them to their moon goddess before I ever consider bonding with them.

Something cracks beside me, and a cool nose touches the side of my cheek before a tongue slides across my skin. I nearly smack whoever does it, but I know that if I try, the wolf might bite me. I've already been bitten twice. The last thing I need is to have teeth marks on my face.

After a minute, one of the wolves barks. The four of them bolt away, the sound of their paws thumping on the dirt fading as they head deeper into the forest.

I slowly crack my eyelids, peeking around. I'm afraid that they could've set me up. I wouldn't put it past anybody to turn this into a trap of some sort. That's what I would do.

Luckily, these guys don't do what I would do and leave me alone. There's a rope knotted around one of my ankles and tied to a tree. It's the only thing keeping me here. Besides the pain, that is.

I dig my fingers into the thick knot, attempting to loosen it, but the rope is too tight. I look around the campsite and at the fire. If I can get close enough, maybe I can burn through the rope to free myself. I'm willing to risk it to break free. If I stay...I can't stay. I have to keep trying.

I manage to make it within three feet of the flames. My hand gets within reach of the fire, but it's not my wrists that need freeing. Burning my fingers won't do me any good, and there is no way I can get my foot or the rope within reach.

"Come on. Think. Think, Eliana. Think." I spot a branch next to where Miles was sitting, and I stretch as far as I can, pressing my stomach to the ground until I lock my fingers around it.

"Thank fuck," I whisper to myself, snapping my mouth closed. It's hard to think. It's hard to be quiet with the pain. I want so badly to scream for Kellan. I don't know exactly how big the island is, but I know that he's always nearby. Even though he went to meet with another pack, he still wouldn't have been that far. Maybe he's already searching for me.

Do I risk it? I don't think I should. Not until I get away from here.

Stretching out my arm again, I hang the tip of the branch over the fire, waiting for it to set ablaze. It takes longer than I expect it to, the wood just burning and smoking without any embers until finally I spot the tip smoldering.

I carefully bring the burning branch to the rope and press it against the binding, praying that it's enough to at least fray some of the thick strands. I don't care if I end up with a knot around my ankle. It's better than being trapped here. I can cut it off later. I just need to break away from the tree.

"Well, look at you, pretty girl. You sure know how to fake sleep." I recognize the voice belonging to the man named Gerry. And damn it. Faking sleep to avoid unwanted attention was supposed to be my specialty. "What do you think you're doing? Good girls don't disobey their superiors. Right now, you're not even considered close to any level that we are. Why don't you put the stick down and raise your arms?"

I don't respond to him, taking an extra moment to burn the rope. He'll have to rip the stick away from me.

He tries just that, rushing toward me. I take advantage of his closeness and swing the branch, smacking him in the shins. He howls in pain and swings his arm, reaching out to snatch me, but I manage to jerk the stick up between his legs. He tenses the second the hot, smoldering tip strikes his balls, and his holler turns into a high-pitched wail.

As he drops to his knees, I yank at the rope, using my strength to break it. But it's not quite burned all the way through. I'm still trapped. And now this man is livid. I swear his face turns red from rage and not from the pain I inflicted on him. He looks ready to retaliate, shoving his palm to the ground and forcing his body to comply.

I tighten my hold on the stick and swing it again, getting him to stay at a distance. He paces back and forth for a second, swearing at me and calling me names that I've heard at least a dozen times over my life. I don't care if he thinks I'm a bitch or cunt. I don't care if he thinks I'm a slut or a piece of trash. His opinion means absolutely nothing to me.

"Just stay the hell back and leave me alone." I grind my teeth and yank at the rope again, praying that with enough force, it'll snap.

"Leave you alone? After what the fuck you just did? No way. You're about to understand the consequences for your actions. The Sunrise Pointe pack doesn't give warnings." He fists his fingers, shaking them at me but still keeps his distance. He's afraid of me. His hesitation proves it.

I swing the branch again, lunging closer to give myself an extra foot. I manage to whip it across his thigh. He stumbles away and trips, falling backward. I cover my mouth with my hand as he lands in the fire, burning his ass in the process.

I never heard somebody scream so loudly. And it seems

I've heard so many people scream in pain recently.

As if the fear of his pain enhances my strength, I yank the rope hard enough to snap it. I don't wait to find out if he manages to pull himself from the campfire. I run in the opposite direction, limping from the pain but still managing to keep a steady pace. I don't know if it's my adrenaline or what, but half of my body feels numb. It could be my survival instincts kicking in. I know that if I don't hustle my ass, they'll catch me again. If what he says is true, they'll do something horrible to punish me.

As if this wasn't punishment enough. The savages. The world darkens around me the farther I get away from the campsite. I peer around, taking note of every shadow that crawls through the forest.

I don't hear the wolves. I don't see them either. I don't know what's happening, but they aren't chasing me. They either didn't hear the man's screams or they purposely ignored him. Maybe they're hunting and torturing me by giving me hope. I guess I'll find out soon enough.

"Eliana, where are you? I can sense you nearby but something's different." Kellan's voice comes through my mind. "Are you injured?"

I can't stop the sob from escaping my mouth. Relief floods through me at the sound of his voice in my mind. He must be nearby. He knows that I'm missing.

"They bit me. They bit me and kidnapped me." My voice

whimpers with my thoughts, the agony too much to keep me silent.

Kellan falls quiet, not responding to me.

"Kellan?" I tremble at his sudden absence in my mind. A part of me refuses to believe that he does it on purpose. Another part of me knows better than to trust him completely. "Kellan? Please. I need help. I don't know where I'm going."

Silence greets me again.

Sadness pours over me. I never expected to feel so hurt by the lack of response from a man I know is partially responsible for my state. The man who claimed that we were soulmates but now suddenly vanishes.

"Kellan!" I yell, limping forward, wishing with everything in me that I had some of the damn healing potion he gave me before. "Kellan, please! You promised. You said you'd never leave me. You'd always be near."

I trip over a tree root and fall to the ground. My arm screams in pain, and I hit my stomach to the ground. Why is this happening to me? I thought my luck was beginning to change. I realize now more than ever that I'm not a blessed chosen one. I'm cursed.

Closing my eyes, I listen to the world around me. If I can hear something apart from the pounding in my head, maybe I can make my way to the beach. It'll be easier and safer to navigate the shores rather than stumbling through the dark forest.

"Eliana, get up. Get up and run." Kellan's voice snaps

through my mind, dragging me from my delirium and pain. "I need you to describe the area. I'm struggling to feel you. I can't track you by your scent. It has changed."

I sniffle and scrub my face with my hand. "I thought you left me and that being bitten might've changed things with you. I was so scared."

Kellan groans in my mind, his voice softening. A wave of foreign emotions crashes through me. He's conflicted about me. About the situation. I was right. Things have changed with him, but I don't understand what or why.

"No, my love. Things are just a bit complicated. Now listen to me. I need you to get to your feet, channel my strength if you have to, and hide. I don't want you running to the beach. I don't want you trying to find me or the cave. Hide. It's important."

Hide? Where do I hide? I can barely see the forest in front of me. The wolves have more enhanced senses. They can hear me. Smell me. They probably already see me, watching and stalking me like a game of cat and mouse. Wolf and hare.

Then I remember what Kellan had me and Adam do. We climbed a tree. If I can get up high enough, the wolves will have to transform into humans to reach me. It will give me a fighting chance. I refuse to make this easy on them.

I stumble forward, looking at the trees. I find one with a low branch that I can swing my leg up and climb even with my throbbing wounds. I think through each move carefully, getting high enough to slide from one heavy branch to another in a different tree without the lower branches. Huge leaves unlike any I've seen before obscure my surroundings, and I carefully camouflage myself. Hopefully the earthy fragrance helps mask my scent. It's possible I spilled blood on the way up, but if they can only smell me and not see me, I'll have an advantage. I can keep them away with the branches. Try to knock them off if they get within reach.

I balance on a sturdy yet narrow branch, pressing my back into the tree trunk, facing the tree I managed to climb. Hopelessness courses through me. I hate feeling trapped. I hate feeling as if I'm just waiting for my end. Because what if the dickhead Miles was right? What if I don't turn into a lykoswulf?

Pushing the thought away, I concentrate on my breathing as I dig my nails into my palms. It doesn't help with the pain, but it does distract me enough that I manage to keep my shit together.

The forest comes alive the longer I focus on it. Birds rattle the branches of the trees, and I swear I hear a snake hissing somewhere overhead. I stare up, searching for the animal, but it never comes into view. Only the moon does, the bright white orb illuminating through the leaves. It's almost full, which means it's supposed to call to those worthy. If it does, this will be it. I'll be one of these beasts, blessed by their lunar goddess yet cursed by this island. Kellan said I'll be able to transform into a wolf by my own freewill except for the one night a month that forces us to succumb to the nature of the wolf.

Fuck. I wonder if it hurts as much as it does now. Bending and breaking, contorting and changing into a completely different species sounds fucking unpleasant. It does nothing to keep me calm. Just when my body and mind start to relax, the idea sets me off all over again.

Or maybe it's the wolves.

Low howls echo through the forest, bouncing around. I can't distinguish where they come from and can only tell that they draw nearer. I inhale and exhale softly, clutching onto the branch. I pray that I'm well hidden from below. I can't be certain, though.

A flash of white zooms across the ground beneath me, and I recognize the white wolf. It's the one who bit me. Anger rushes over me, and I narrow my eyes, wishing for the universe to give me a break and do something useful on my behalf like send a tree crashing into the asshole to take care of him for me.

Bowing forward, the white wolf stretches its body with a low rumble. I can't take my eyes off the naked man who now rests on his hands and knees in the wolf's place. I don't recognize him, yet I know he was the one who bit me. It's as if my body buzzes with the knowledge.

"She came through here," the man says, his voice husky and deep with annoyance. "You allowed her to get too far. I knew I shouldn't have trusted you with someone so precious."

My mouth trembles. It grows harder and harder to remain

quiet. I know if I move even an inch, I'll risk them realizing that I'm closer than they think.

Lou strides into view below. "I'm sorry, Ravi. It shouldn't have been possible. Gerry fucked up and let her take advantage of the situation, but I handled his stupidity."

The man, Ravi, doesn't look at Lou. Instead, he draws a line through the dirt and brings a palmful of soil to his nose to sniff. "You had better. Our pack was counting on this to push power into our territory. She's the closest human we can get to creating a pure bloodline. Sean has already grown too weak."

Creating a pure bloodline? Fuck. It sounds like they plan to breed me or some shit like an animal. No fucking way. I will destroy every damn cock in the pack if they think they can get away with that.

"We'll find her, Ravi. She couldn't have gone far. You bit her on her leg and arm. It's going to be hard for her to do anything." Lou strides a couple of feet away and spins on his feet. He inhales a deep breath as if he can catch a whiff of my scent.

I tense and close my eyes, saying a silent prayer.

"It had better be before the moon calls. You know she needs me to support her through it. She might die otherwise. Or the pain could become too unbearable where she does something drastic to make it stop. This is why it was so fucking important that you watched her for me." The concern lining his voice makes me open my eyes and shift. The leaves rustle, and I regret my gesture immediately. But I was just too nosy. I wanted to look down. And now Ravi looks up, his gray eyes light enough to look as if they capture the moon's ethereal beams. Luckily, our eyes don't meet. He searches the tree with the low branches instead of where I remain.

Pursing his full lips, he releases a light whistle. Lou stops moving and listens beside him. Another whistle cuts through the air, coming from somewhere in the distance. This must be how they communicate when they aren't in wolf form.

Ravi's long, light brown hair hangs over his shoulders, and he gathers it in his palm, tying it out of the way. "Go help Miles. He should be able to track her better than you can since they share a bloodline." Strolling next to the tree I hide in, he touches the bark and sniffs it.

My nerves get the best of me, and I release a small breath. Shit. It's growing harder and harder to be quiet. Kellan's taking too long, and I'm getting anxious. This beast of a man is bound to find me up here.

"Kellan?" I think, the thought hopefully reaching him wherever he is. "Please hurry."

Silence greets me.

Ravi whistles again. "Eliana, I know you're here. You don't have to be afraid of me. You're going to need me soon. Let's make things easy for you."

Fuck me. Did he hear my thoughts? Davian mentioned that the voices in his head were getting to him. Is it possible that more than Kellan will be able to hear me? I never thought to ask him how wolves communicate. Well, lykoswulves communicate.

"I'm sorry things had to be this way, but the Crystalrock pack and the Twilight Cove pack already have too much power. They don't need you like we do." Ravi takes a few steps away, returning to the tree that I climbed. He gets close, pressing his nose to the bark. "Your scent is all over. It ends here. Come on, Eliana. You don't want to make me climb into the trees, do you? You might get hurt when I carry you down."

I don't respond.

The leaves rustle below, and I stretch my neck and catch sight of Ravi swinging his leg over the low branch. No. He knows I'm here. He's going to try to snatch me from my hiding place.

I fist my hand, clutching one of the branches. I stretch it enough that it should ricochet and snap toward him if he gets near me, hopefully giving me a chance to fight him off. If I fall from this height, I know I'm going to break something. But he might also break something too. It'll be either him going down or the two of us together. Regardless, he's insane to think I'm going to accept this and make it easy.

"Kellan?" I think his name as desperation grabs hold of me. Where is he? I did what he asked. I hid. But it wasn't good enough. Now...

"Eliana, I can hear you breathing. You sound as if you're about to hyperventilate. Just take a deep breath. Like I said,

I'm not here to hurt you. I'm here to take you somewhere safe. I'll take care of you, but you have to let me. My name is Ravi. I'm the betaborne to Sean of the Sunset Pointe pack." Ravi lowers his voice, the words almost melodious as they caress my ears.

It takes everything in me not to yell at him for lying. For biting me in the first place. Had I not known what the hell was going on, I would've been so scared. Of course, I'm still terrified. I need to get away. I need to figure out how to jump from this tree without breaking my neck or something. I need to run. I know I'm supposed to stay away from the shore, but it might be the only way I'll be able to find the others. The thought of getting taken and never seeing them again ignites panic in my heart.

"Eliana. It doesn't have to be this way. If you just come out, we can act as civilized people. I won't have to drag you away and treat you like an unruly she-wolf. You can have some dignity. Just show yourself, don't try to fight, and we'll be okay. How does that sound?" Ravi continues to talk as if it's going to make a difference. He speaks to me, knowing that I listen even if I don't talk back.

It takes everything in me not to respond. I know he's trying to get me to say something so he can pinpoint my exact spot.

"You must be in pain. Hungry and cold. I'm used to it. I can stay here all night. It's your choice, Eliana." More branches snap and crack. Shit.

I finally break. "It's not my choice. It hasn't been my choice since the moment I fucking got here."

A hot hand grabs the back of my arm, squeezing tightly.

I can't do anything as Ravi yanks me from my spot.

I scream as I fall.

CHAPTER 17

Eliana

BETABORNE

RAVI CATCHES ME by my wrist, yanking me back to him. I know that I should thrash and fight, but my fear of falling overwhelms me and the only thing I can do is cling onto him.

He releases a soft moan in my ear, and I realize that he's butt-ass naked, and I can feel his body awaken as I unintentionally grind against him. As if things couldn't get any worse.

"That's a good girl. Don't worry. I won't let you fall. You can hold onto me as tightly as you'd like. I don't mind." Ravi presses his palm to the small of my back while grabbing onto the branch with his other hand, holding the two of us with just the strength of his one arm. I stare at his corded muscles, admiring his capability.

He lets go, and the world rushes around me. I can't stop the scream that escapes my mouth. I expect for him to drop me or something—maybe stumble and land on top of me—but he lands on his feet with a thump, bending his knees and steadying himself in a crouch.

As if the sudden stopping of the world kicks me in to action, I swing my arm and punch him in the face. He mistakenly let his guard down, thinking that I was just going to suddenly comply. Now I have the chance to escape.

I will escape.

I jab my fist into his throat next, and then knee him in the balls, using the force to push me away from him. I stumble to my feet and command my body to move, my fight or flight instincts battling for control over my actions.

I want to make him suffer, but I also want as much space as I can get between us. I limp for a couple steps until I manage to shove the pain away and pick up my pace. My body numbs and my skin cools but sweat prickles along my hairline and drips down my back. This is too much. If I stop, I might pass out. The only thing keeping me going is my need to survive and to get away.

"Kellan!" I yell, sending my voice through the forest. I

don't try to be quiet anymore. Being quiet will slow me down. I need to hustle my ass before Ravi snatches me with his jowls again. I know that he'll turn into a wolf to chase me.

Howls sound through the forest, a couple of them bouncing off the trees. I'm being surrounded. I know it. The other guys probably listen to Ravi's calls, and they'll trap me within their vicious circle.

"Eliana, don't run. It's taking everything in me not to chase you and pin you down. Be my good girl, and I'll make you my princess. You're only tormenting my deep-seated instincts as a lykoswulf now with your evasion. You don't want to do that. It doesn't help that some of my packmates are a bit pissed off at you right now. They'll expect you to be put in your place." Ravi speaks the words, and I realize they echo through my mind.

Oh no. Oh fucking no. This can't be happening. He can't have a mental link to me too. It was hard enough with Kellan.

Where is he anyway?

A white wolf jumps in front of me and snarls, charging in my direction. I fail to stop fast enough, and I trip over the beast, screaming in pain as I land on my hurt arm.

Hooking my arms around the wolf, I roll over and force him with me. I don't know if I catch Ravi off guard, but I manage to knock him away from me with my strength. But I'm too slow to get up. He comes at me again and latches his teeth to my shirt, tearing at the fabric.

He tries to bite the collar next, attempting to drag me away. I link my fingers to the sides of his furry head and keep the distance between his teeth and my clothing. I'm afraid he might bite me again just to teach me a lesson. I can barely handle the pain of the bites already.

His vibrant gray eyes sparkle, and he locks me in a gaze. It's as if he tries to intimidate me with just his wolfish glare. I smack him on the snout hard enough to get him to shake his head. I kick my feet into his chest, sending him sprawling across the ground. He only stays down for another second, preparing to charge me.

He doesn't make it.

A giant grey wolf launches through the air and crashes into the white wolf's side. It's Kellan. He found me, and now fights on my behalf, facing Ravi.

I gasp for breath, craving relief from the stress and anxiety, but it does nothing for my nerves. I use the nearest tree to pull myself to my feet, my knees and legs aching, threatening to send me sprawling back to the dirt.

"Eliana," Chase says, my name sounding so beautiful on his lips. I don't think I've ever heard anything so amazing in my life. "Hurry. Let me help you."

Another wolf materializes behind him, and I open my mouth to scream. A figure slams down a huge branch, knocking it against the wolf's head hard enough to send it to its belly. Adam stalks closer and joins Chase. I wish I could hug them. I wish I could stop the world and thank them for coming for me. But the fighting continues on behind me, and more wolves howl in the distance.

"Pick her up and carry her, doc. It'll be faster. I'll watch your back." Adam swings his branch, hitting the dirty, tan-colored wolf again. I think it might be either Miles or Lou. I can't be certain.

Chase hooks his arms behind my knees and around my back and lifts me up, cradling me like a small child. I press my face against his taut chest, trying my best not to break down before we even make it to safety. I just hurt so badly. My adrenaline wears off, and agony consumes me.

"You're going to be fine. I know you're in pain, but we'll get through this together." Chase kisses the top of my head, trying to keep me together as I fall apart in his arms.

"I don't think we will," I say, my voice hitching. "I was bitten. I know something has changed. I don't know what we're going to do. Kellan is acting weird now."

"He was just surprised. We'll be okay. You need to have faith," Adam murmurs under his breath.

Faith? That's the last thing I have. I'm hopeless.

The fight for survival has changed. The lack of rules does nothing for my sanity either. I wish I could manage to stay as calm as Chase and Adam, but all I feel is like I'm on the verge of dying.

"I can't. You don't understand. These men—they speak

of bloodlines and strengthening their packs. It sounded like they intend to breed with me or something." Tears burn my cheeks but the crisp air cools my body. "It's so messed up. I can't live like this. I refuse to."

Chase stiffens, his hold on me tightening. "Are you sure? Kellan mentioned that the packs get their strength from transforming humans. So few survive even a week here that only the strongest join the packs who bite them. They don't breed to pass on or create strength."

"Then Kellan didn't tell you everything." I sigh with my words. "Because I know I didn't imagine it."

"Damn, doc. I don't know about you, but I don't know how much I trust Kellan. He only said that some might find Eliana appealing because of her grandma and the fact that the odds are in her favor to change." Adam keeps up his pace, cutting away greenery that gets in our way.

"He's the lesser of two evils on the island. We need him." Chase glowers with his words. "He's helped us when he could've thrown us to the wolves already."

"He could be playing us. He's already managed to gain enough of our trust that we followed him here without much explanation and only that Eliana needed help. What if it's his way of manipulating us? Manipulating Eliana? I mean, he's already..." Adam snaps his mouth closed, not finishing his thought. Even without saying the words out loud, I know it's my moment of passion with Kellan he refers to. I was so caught up with him in the cave that I let my guard down. What if it was a mistake? Then again, what if it wasn't. What if it was fate like he claims?

"You can say it, Adam. I fucked him." My sharp tone surprises even me, and I try to shake away the negativity clinging to me at the thought. "I was stupid and gullible to think it was just some fun. It's possible he used me."

"But in hopes of knocking you up?" Chase rubs his lips together. "I'll perform an unmedicated vasectomy if that is the case."

"You can hold him down while I do it myself. Thank fucking God for my IUD." I shudder, thinking about how messed up that would be if any of us are right about Kellan.

I don't want to assume the worst, but I'd be idiotic if I didn't rebuild my protective wall around me to keep Kellan out.

"Remind me never to piss you off," Adam says, his breath gasping as he jogs, keeping pace with Chase. "And so you know...I don't want kids, so you don't have to worry about that kind of shit with me. I wrap up and pull the hell out when I can't."

My brows knit together, and I swing out my good arm and whack him in the back of the head. "I'll still worry about it. Your wants might align with mine but it doesn't prevent anything."

A wolf barks, the loud noise enough to snap my mouth

closed. Adam and Chase move in closer, no longer talking as we head...maybe toward the beach. I can't be sure.

"No more talking," Chase mutters, adjusting me. "They're too close. I don't know if Kellan's pack is even coming."

Chase picks up his speed, navigating the dark forest until we reach the beach. I spot Evander holding Tristan's weight. My heart sinks into my stomach because I don't see Davian with them. That means he wasn't found. He's somewhere out there still.

"Davian?" I ask, whispering the words.

Chase shakes his head. "We couldn't find him. Kellan lost his scent at the creek. We had to make you a priority, Eliana. Davian can take care of himself. He's experiencing the effects of the bite."

I want to argue with him, but there's no point. I know why they chose me. It doesn't make me feel less guilty about it though.

I'm glad for it.

Does that make me a bad person? Maybe. But it seems it takes a bad person to survive this island. I just hope that Davian is okay. I'm so terrified that he might die alone. Nobody deserves that. I wanted to be there for him with his transformation. Sadly, I don't know how much I can do now. Not like this.

"Don't worry, Elle. We're going to find him next."

Evander helps Tristan walk closer to me.

I wiggle until Chase sets me on my feet. I don't make it far because my legs decide to give out on me. Adam catches me and helps me upright, stopping me from hitting the ground. Evander and Tristan close the distance completely, rushing together toward me.

Flinging my arms out, I hug them both. I'm so glad Evander doesn't reject me after the cave incident and instead embraces my affection. I know it bothered him that I don't want to be with anyone exclusively, especially now after everything that has happened.

"Thank God you're safe. Both of you. Are you feeling any better, Tristan?" I ask, tilting my face to look at him.

He offers me a weak smile. I can tell that something dark lingers on his mind. "I'm more worried about you, Eliana. I was so scared. It should've never been you. It should've been me that they bit. If I could go back in time—"

I shut him up with a kiss. He shouldn't feel guilty over any of this. It wasn't his fault. It's not even his job to protect me. It was my job to protect both him and Davian and I failed. This is on me.

I ease away, grazing my fingers over his scruffy cheek. "I wouldn't change it. I'd rather it be me than you. Everyone seems to think that I'm going to survive. But you guys...fuck. We need to get off this island."

Evander massages his fingers into my shoulder, remaining

close despite the fact that I just kissed Tristan in front of him. Clearing his throat, he says, "You're right. We do. So we need to make some quick fucking decisions about what we do next. We can try to find Kellan, and then we can wait for the next boat to land on shore with more people. Or we can try to build our own raft. Maybe we can swim together. Risk the ocean. I know there's a couple of things that float pretty well. We can use what we have for freshwater and just hope that we reach the next island or another boat will find us. It might be better to risk that than risk anything else."

We all look at each other, weighing our options. If we do decide to just swim, it's nearly guaranteed that we would die. I can't imagine us surviving otherwise. If we wait it out, someone is bound to find us. We're being hunted by wolves, and they're masters at tracking, especially if what Kellan said about the bloodlines is true. It means that Ravi could track me because of the bite, and a member of the pack that turned my grandma could also track me. Fuck, probably anybody who came into contact with me and now knows my scent can find me. There are only so many places on this island that we can hide. And it's not guaranteed that the yacht will come back with more people. It might finish the round this time because of the coming full moon.

A collection of howls ricochet through the vegetation in front of us, and I squeeze Evander tighter. We need to move. We're too exposed on the beach. It's too dangerous in the forest.

"I think we need to hide. We need to be able to think everything through." Adam bounces on his bare feet, kicking sand with his nerves.

"Where? They're everywhere. Seems like there are more wolves than ever." Chase rubs his lips together and peers around the beach.

"We can try to find another cave," Evander responds, adjusting me into his arms, preparing to keep me within his embrace instead of setting me on my feet. I'm grateful for it. I'm so tired. I'm in pain. All I want to do is relax and go to sleep. I don't want to have to fight for my life tonight. I don't want to have to fight for my freedom either.

"This might sound crazy, but I have an idea. We should head into the water. We don't have to go far but just make it far enough from the beach that we can keep out of the way until we figure out a plan. I saw some big rocks just offshore. It's swimmable." Tristan motions down the beach.

"I don't think Eliana's going to be able to swim that far. We're going to need something to help us float." Chase turns and looks at Evander. "What do you suppose we use?"

"We can use our clothes," Adam says, tugging at his shorts. "They're not as good as pants, but we should be able to tie up the legs and inflate them. It was something my dad taught me. We just need to get them wet. And since we're already going into the water...who wants to volunteer? We don't need everyone naked."

The four of them look at each other, silently arguing with their eyes.

"Should we play Rock-Paper-Scissors?" Tristan asks, raising one of his eyebrows, clearly not amused about the possibility.

"Since it was Adam's idea..." Evander tries to keep a straight face.

"I'm not going to fucking expose my dick as fish bait." Adam throws out his hands.

"You're right. Some damn guppy will mistake your junk for a tiny worm or some shit." Chase punches him in the arm.

I can't help laughing. "Don't be ridiculous. They'll definitely mistake it for an eel. But if you guys are too concerned, somebody can squeeze into my shorts, and I'll go naked. I just don't think these are big enough to use."

Evander groans and shakes his head. "That's not necessary, Eliana. I'm not going to be a little bitch about swimming naked. It's not the most dangerous thing I've ever done. I'll volunteer."

I smile at him and surprise him with a kiss. He relaxes and molds his lips to mine, acting as if he's starving for my affection.

It makes me feel a bit better about how he acted earlier. Maybe he's not as upset as I thought. Maybe it was something else. I don't know. It doesn't matter right now. We have more important things to worry about.

"Damn. I volunteer if I can kiss you next," Adam says, playing with the strands of my messy hair.

Evander spins toward the water, yanking down his shorts in the process. He kicks them at Adam and manages to smack him in the face with them.

"Too late, asshole. I'm also going to swim with her. Make the device. I don't want to wait much longer." Evander marches toward the water, his heart beating loudly enough for me to hear.

His action gets everyone else to follow his lead, and I hug him tighter as we enter the waves. The water feels colder than before, less tropical. I can't help shivering as Evander heads deeper and deeper.

Adam swims up next to us, his weird flotation device surprising me. The wet fabric manages to hold the air in the shorts. I'm pretty impressed. I had no idea such a thing was possible, but I guess I should be more open, all things considered.

"Everyone stay close. You don't need to swim fast. Try to save your energy." This comes from Tristan. He treads water beside us, and I bob in Evander's arms as he kicks to keep us afloat.

"Eliana, can you hold onto my back? It'll be easier with both arms free." Evander rests his forehead to my temple, brushing my skin with his lips.

I nod my head, letting Chase help me swim in place as Evander spins around. I slide my arms around his neck and hold on using one leg to help him kick. My other one hurts too badly to move.

He swims forward, following Adam, and Chase remains by Tristan's side, ensuring that he can handle the stress of swimming as he heals.

I don't know how much time passes, but it feels like forever. The longer I hold onto Evander the colder I get. Out here, I can't hear the wolves, but the roar of the sea is just as intimidating.

Tristan points his hand, and I look in the direction he motions to. I expect to see the rocks, but fear tightens my chest and what appears before us. It's not the rocks or land.

"It's the yacht," Adam says, swimming ahead. "Do you think they'll see us? The rocks are over there."

I flick my gaze to where Adam points next. The rocks look a lot bigger than I expected them to. And thankfully, they're not that far.

Chase splashes up next to us. "I don't think we should go to the rocks. We need to go to the fucking boat. If they don't know we're here, we might be able to fight them."

"They're probably armed." Tristan frowns with his comment.

"If you're not willing to risk it, you can take Eliana and wait on the rocks. I'm going. This might be our only chance.

It's dark out and all the wolves seem to be hunting on the island, looking for us. They won't be looking in the water." Chase heaves a breath, swiping the water from his face.

"I'm in. We don't have much to lose," Evander says.

"Fucking fine. It's better if we stay together." Adam adjusts his bag. "We still have a knife. We can use it."

Tristan groans. "If Eliana is willing, then I'll do whatever you guys want to do. We need to agree though. All of us."

The four of them look at me. All I can think about is how I need to get away from here. I need far, far away from the packs who either want to breed with me, capture me and cage me, or control me. I need to go home.

"We can always come back for Davian," Chase adds.

"No, man. He wouldn't want that." Tristan crinkles his nose with his words.

I nod my head, inhaling and exhaling slowly. "He's right. As much as I hate the idea of leaving him behind, we don't know what's happening. And if I start to change, you need to..." I let my words trail off.

"We're going to handle it. But first, we need to take that boat." Evander takes the initiative and swims, moving in the direction of the yacht.

"Hell yeah, we do." Adam swims up next to us, offering me a smile. "Eliana is going to kick some fucking ass. You've seen her."

I roll my eyes. "I'll just flash my boobs, and you can do all the hard work."

He chuckles. "That's what I'm talking about. These fuck-ing wolves are going down, and they're not taking us with them."

CHAPTER 18

Adam

KILL OR BE KILLED

I DIDN'T KNOW being a wolf man was such a lucrative business, because I'd never be able to afford a million-dollar yacht in my lifetime. It makes me curious to know what they do. Because this is definitely one made in the human world. I've only seen one like it in the old boating magazines my dad used to store in our bunker.

I wish I had paid more attention to the surviving in nature shit compared to the city survival guides. I wasn't much for camping in the woods and lived in a couple different places in different cities along the coast. I was more prepared for the fucking zombie apocalypse than Monster Wolf Island or whatever the fuck this place is. I'm more of a scavenger compared to a hunter.

"There's a swimming deck around the back. It will be easy to climb aboard there. I didn't see anyone looking out, and the yacht is anchored. It's possible no one's even on it." Tristan treads water next to me. He's a far better swimmer and fisherman than any of us. He was a nature photographer back in the human world, but paying gigs were hard for him to come by. And I get it. We're all hard on luck, which is supposedly just one of the reasons why we were chosen for this bullshit. As for other things? I have no idea. We all have our strengths and weaknesses.

"I'll go first and make sure things are clear before you board," I say, reaching into the small bag with only a couple things left in it. Not like we'll be able to use the matches now. The water canister is still good, and so is a knife.

"I'll go with you." Evander helps Eliana off his back and Chase takes over, helping her hug him from behind.

The five of us swim together toward the stern of the boat, and I grab on to the first rung of the ladder leading to the swimming platform where a garage remains locked. I wonder if that's where they keep the dinghy or some jet skis. I wouldn't be surprised. This massive yacht is equipped for basically anything.

I sit on the platform and grab the shorts from Chase, untying the leg holes to let the air out. I doubt Evander wants to stroll around the boat butt-ass naked, and Chase and Tristan can hold on to Eliana, keeping her secure and safe here.

Reaching down, I offer my hand to Evander and help him up. The guy was brave to swim with his cock out. He's both a grower and a shower and makes me feel a bit inferior. At least it's not obvious now that I'm dressed.

Fuck. I never thought I'd be putting this much thought into someone else's dick.

I look at Eliana, watching her drink in the sight of Evander. Raising my eyebrows, I smirk. She's so damn hot that I don't even care if she flirts with all of us. I don't mind her giving each of us attention. I'm just happy that she never rejected me, and there's still a chance to create something between us. Who fucking knew I'd be so open to the idea? A part of me hopes that the other guys will back off eventually. I figure if I wait it out, they'll get too jealous to deal with it. Me? I've never been a jealous guy. What's the point when Eliana has been clear about things?

Evander smacks my back, pulling my attention from my thoughts. I shake my head, flinging the water off. Excitement courses through me. This yacht is the fucking shit. I can already imagine exploring the seas or finding a less savage island to live out my days without the dumb shit laws and ways of life the civilized world forces on us. It shouldn't be so damn expensive just to exist.

"If you guys see anything, whistle." I look at Chase and dip my chin. "If I call out panda, it's safe to board. If I yell raccoon, get the hell away from the boat." I don't know why the animals come to me, but I once saw pandas at the zoo, and they were dope, rollie-pollie bears and my kindred spirit creature. Raccoons, on the other hand, are mean as shit. Far from deserving the name of trash panda. More like asshole bandits.

No one comments on my word choices, and Evander searches the in-seat compartments of the swimming platform and yanks out a chain. He winds it around his fist while I keep the knife, and we stay close, though I lead the way.

I focus on our surroundings, keeping a lookout for any signs of someone on the yacht. The pathway wrapping around the deck doesn't allow much of a visual. We reach the grand entrance of the main salon at the stern. Lights illuminate the luxurious living area. Sleek metal and dark woods accent a room bigger than any apartment I've ever lived in. It's fucking awesome.

"Damn. How in the hell do these bastards own this?" Evander mutters, strolling past me. He heads to the sectional couch in front of the fireplace and grabs a decorative sword from above the mantle. He unsheathes it and grins at me.

I shrug my shoulders. I don't know how to use a sword. Hopefully, he does or I might lose my head. A hand or some shit. Things I like having around.

Stepping back, I put some space between us. "Let's start with the bridge and then the master stateroom."

Evander nods his head and searches around, spotting a staircase leading up next to the elevator. There's no way I'm getting trapped in a box, so I take the stairs two at a time, trying to hustle my ass.

Evander cuts in front of me, preparing to stab anybody who gets in our way with the sword.

In any other circumstances, I'd hesitate. But not now. I don't care who it is. Anyone on this yacht is our captor and an enemy. I thought killing would be hard—it should be hard—but when fuckers keep coming at us with teeth and shit, I'm going to do what I have to for our survival. Kill or be killed. My dad prepared me for this my whole life as if he knew I'd find myself in this situation. Of course, he only thought it'd be a wasteland of dickhead humans fighting for resources after some natural disaster or plague or whatever. He'd shit his pants knowing that werewolves exist.

I was lucky I didn't have pants. Or not. I need to focus. I'm way too distracted to be preparing to head into battle. There's no way this boat is empty.

"There." Evander points the sword toward a closed door.

I shake out my nerves and clutch my knife tighter. I'm a bit thankful that Evander has the sword. He can rush whoever, impaling them. The little bit of space between us will give me the chance to take a fucker down.

"Take that side of the door. I'll be on this side. We're not going in and getting trapped." Evander steps toward the side where the door swings in.

I stand on the opposite side, ready and waiting. If anyone's in there, I'm sure they'll come running out. As long as we can get to them first, we'll get through this.

I raise my hand to knock on the door, but Evander stops me. He's a fucking smart guy, and I realize that if we knock, they won't come running. They'll have a chance to change into their beast forms. To get out, they're going to need to be in human form to open the door to rush us.

I clear my throat. "Hey, fuckers? This is a hostile takeover. Come out with your hands up."

My muscles bunch as I say the words, waiting for the door to crack open. But nothing happens. I don't hear anybody either.

Evander waits another moment, motioning me to stay in my spot with his index finger. We stare at each other and then look at the stairwell and the elevator, half-expecting somebody to come rushing from those spots. But it remains silent. If someone's on this yacht, they're either not in this area or super fucking heavy sleepers. It wouldn't be the first time someone slept on the job. I can imagine whoever is the captain of this yacht might be kicking back in his chair and taking a fucking nap.

"Kick the door open, and I'll charge in." Evander readjusts the sword, trying to get a good feel of it to hold properly.

I nod and move in front of the door. I wish I could rely on myself to kick it hard enough from the side, but I need to be right in front of it. I'm fucking barefooted. I swear I better not break something.

Instead of trying to be a hard ass like a movie hero, I touch my fingers to the doorknob to check if it's unlocked first. I can open it and kick just as good, if not better, than if I were to try to break the damn door down like a raging badass. I'm not exactly that. But I'm trying. Eliana is more fierce than I am.

I touch my fingers to the handle, and it easily clicks open. My heart races as I kick the door with my barefoot and it swings open hitting the wall. Evander rushes in only to be greeted by no one. Maybe the captain and crew are sleeping. They are anchored, after all. There are no storms coming either. They wouldn't have very much to do. Not this late at night.

"Damn it. Maybe one of us should stay here so we can tell the others to come aboard. If they're sleeping, we can all take them out and just leave. Do you know how to drive a yacht? I have no boating experience." Evander peers around the cockpit, staring at all the buttons and levers. I spot a radio, and rush to it.

He locks his fingers to my shoulder and stops me before I have a chance to look at it.

"They could have other boats around here. I wouldn't try to call for help just yet." Again, I realize Evander is far more strategic than I am. My dad would be fucking ashamed. He had drilled it into my head that I have to think first before acting, especially in moments that I need to fight for survival. Oh well. Shit has changed. I'm not dealing with people...sort of.

"I can pilot this bad girl. I think. If not me, I think Tristan knows how. He's done a lot of traveling. I think he can even fly a plane. You should ask the asshole sometime. He was a nature photographer." It's one of the few things I really know about anyone here is what they were doing before.

"All right. Let's hurry up. I don't like how quiet it is. But if they haven't heard us by now, then we might be okay. The staterooms are on the opposite side, I believe." Evander motions for me to follow him, and we head back toward the stairs.

Holding my breath, I listen to the world around us, half-expecting to hear howls and fighting or some shit. I don't like how eerily quiet it is.

Evander heads to the stairs, and I remain right behind him.

Neither of us spots the wolf waiting in the salon. The beast doesn't growl or warn us or anything. It might have been stalking us this entire time.

Evander shouts, swinging the sword at the wolf. It darts around him, dodging out of the way. I kick my leg, managing to strike it in the side, but I'm not strong enough to send it sprawling.

"Run! Run to the others!" I shout, tensing and preparing to be devoured.

Evander doesn't hesitate, using me as a distraction to head toward the pathway leading to the swimming platform.

The wolf paces and releases a growl that strikes me in the gut.

"Change back into a fucking man and face me. You're only in wolf form because you know that I'll kick your ass otherwise." Am I stupid for this kind of threat? Maybe. I just need him to hesitate to buy time. I know if he bites me, shit will get even more real. I don't think I'm strong enough to survive this crap.

My words must dig under the werewolf's skin, because the man shifts, standing before me completely naked.

"Put your weapon down," he says, his deep voice still sounding a bit animalistic. "You're not going anywhere, so there's no point in fighting me. Even if you take this boat, you will never be free of Shadow Moon Island. That I promise you."

Anger rushes through me. The edges of my vision shadow with my rage, and I rush the man. I'm not going to give him the time to strategize how to overpower me.

He surprises me, transforming into a wolf as I tighten my arms around him. I don't get a chance to restrain him completely. Whipping his head, he locks his teeth to my shoulder.

I see stars from the pain.

Fuck. I'm a dead man.

Punching the wolf in the snout, I get him to release me. I jab my knife, stabbing him in the side. He screeches and transforms back into a man. I don't stay to fight though. Fuck that noise. His groans are enough to know that if he catches me, he'll destroy me. Fuck me up. Ensure I feel the same pain I caused him. Spinning, I rush toward the pathway leading out. Another wolf growls in the walkway, blocking my path. Fuck me.

"Adam, jump!" Eliana screams from somewhere in the water. "Jump!"

I swivel and grab onto the metal-rung barrier, looking over the side. Shit. It's still a good drop to the water. If I didn't see Eliana treading by herself, I would consider fighting the wolf.

"Hurry!" she calls, baring her teeth. "There's another boat coming."

The wolf charges toward me, understanding Eliana, and I suck up my fear and summon my courage to throw myself over the side.

I squeeze my eyes shut as the world blurs around me and my stomach flies into my throat.

I hit the water and sink under. I kick to the surface only to have Eliana throw her arms around me and squeeze me fiercely. I realize it's because she's swimming. I don't know how this beautiful bombshell of a woman knows to keep going even after being bitten, but here she is, trying to save my ass.

"The others are still on the boat. Evander needed help. He said that you were following behind him, so here I am. They told me to go." Eliana gasps a breath, kicking only one of her legs, but she now wears a life vest stolen from the boat. "I don't think we should leave though. We should fight."

I kick my legs, trying my best not to use her too much as a floaty, but I need her support. "You're right. I don't have anything to lose. I was fucking bit."

"What?" Eliana asks, her voice ringing through the air.

"Yeah, a fucker on the boat. I guess we'll find out if I'm worthy of the damn change or not." I grind my teeth and roll my shoulder, showing her the teeth marks on my skin, the blood washing away in the water.

Fuck. I hope I don't attract sharks or something.

"Shit," she breathes, huffing in my ear and making me shiver.

"Tell me about it." I lick my lips, tasting the salt of the sea. "This is fucking hell."

She blinks a few times and cranes her neck, trying to look around. I realize she's not focusing on me at all. "It might get worse. Kellan called to me. His pack is coming. They're the ones on the raft."

I don't know whether or not I should be thankful that someone who might be on her side comes or if I should freak the fuck out because Eliana no longer trusts the wolf man. I don't even know what to think. We're trapped. There's no way we're ever going to get out of here by stealing a boat. I also don't want to think about the fact that if Kellan's pack is coming now...who was on the boat? I've been bitten by someone from another pack.

"I won't let anyone hurt you. I'll die first," I say, snaking my hand around her waist and into the life vest, sharing it.

"Adam, no. Your life is not worth less than mine." She peers around again.

"You're wrong. It is on this island. And I don't mind. I'll protect you, Eliana. You don't deserve this kind of fate. You don't deserve to bow to a fucking wild man or their twisted desires. It's fucked up. Disgusting." I clench my teeth with the words. I could never imagine what it's like to be her. All I can do is try my best to ensure she's safe. "Like I said. I don't think I have much to lose. I'll either die or transform. I'm not sure about the second. I'd rather make sure you get away from here instead."

I don't get a chance to say anymore, because a blinding light illuminates around us as the motor of a boat hums in my ears.

"We got two over here. One's the female," a man shouts. "Net them. They might put up a fight."

I kick my legs, trying to swim with Eliana away from their boat, but I'm too slow. The pain's too much and I'm exhausted.

A net cascades over us and drags us through the water. Eliana struggles and clings onto me as a couple of men yank us into the small, motorized raft.

I don't see the others with them. Chase, Tristan, and Evander must still be on the yacht. I can't see much through my blurry eyes.

"Stay down. Don't try to fight. It's time you meet our alpha," a familiar voice says. "This can be easy or hard, but I know you're a smart group."

I shudder as I spot Kellan sitting next to Eliana, helping to pull the net away from her.

He was screwing with us and was never on our side. This was probably his plan all along, getting close only to betray us.

"Fucking traitor," I snap, trying to yank the net off. Something hits me in the back of the head, igniting pain in me. I fall forward and sprawl across the small seat.

Another man ties me up.

I guess it's time to find out who this alpha really is. And when I do, I'm going to fuck him up. He's going to realize that no one messes with me. I've been training my whole life for this.

I have nothing to lose. I will take them down, even if it's the last thing I do.

CHAPTER 19

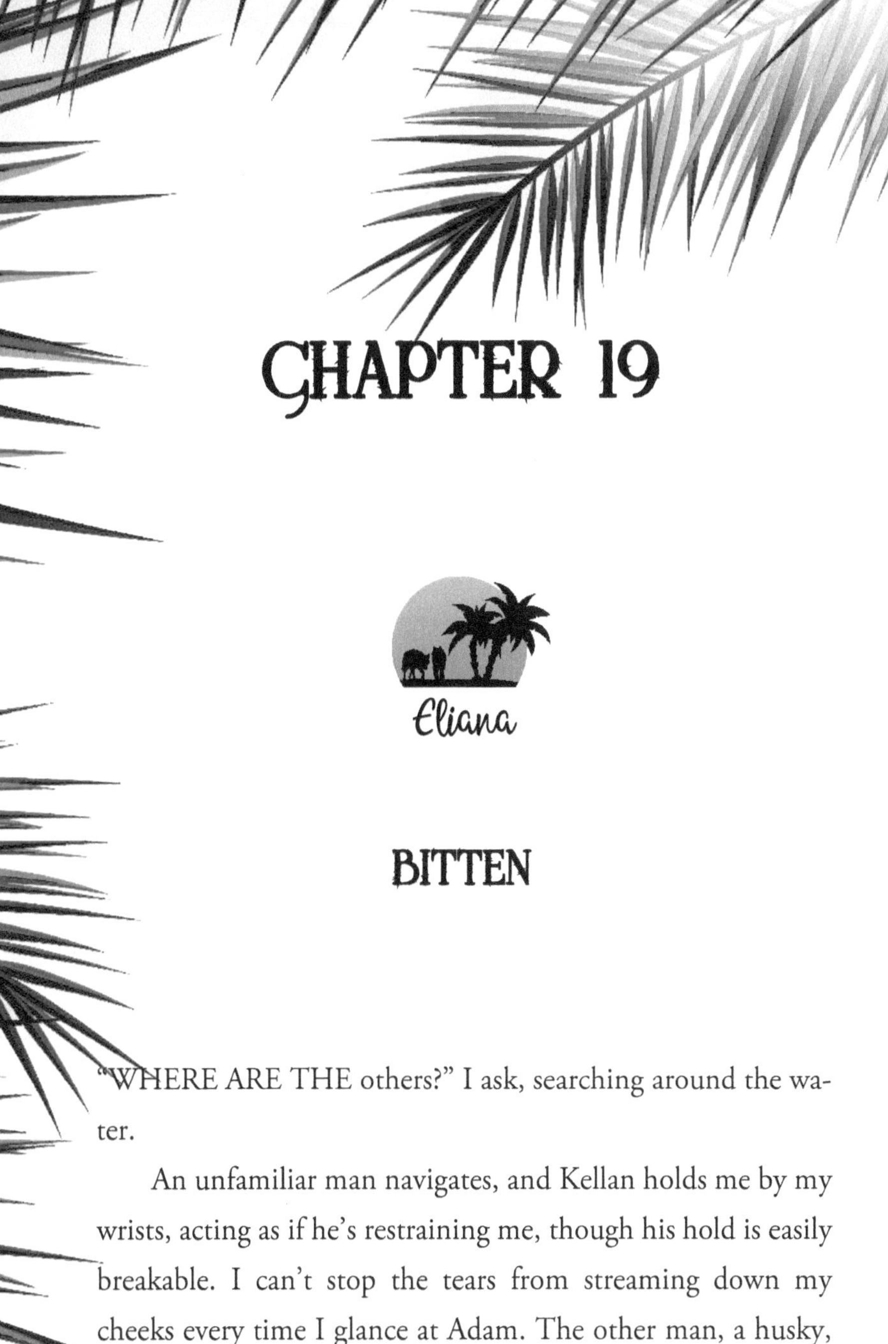

BITTEN

"WHERE ARE THE others?" I ask, searching around the water.

An unfamiliar man navigates, and Kellan holds me by my wrists, acting as if he's restraining me, though his hold is easily breakable. I can't stop the tears from streaming down my cheeks every time I glance at Adam. The other man, a husky, bald asshole hit him over the back of the head, and now he just lays there. I know he's awake, but he looks defeated.

"They're not important nor worth our time." Baldy whacks Adam on the back. "This bitch is lucky he was with you, though we might just drop him halfway to shore. He's not one of us."

"Don't you dare!" I scream, breaking away from Kellan's hold. "Don't you fucking dare!"

"Then he can learn his new place right here. He can earn the spot to serve me if he gives me what I want." The man grabs at the waistband of his shorts.

Shock and horror cools my blood, only to have rage blast through me. Kellan tightens his hold, but I punch him in the thigh, startling him. His grip loosens, and I launch at the man, shoving my hands into his back. He trips and falls off the side of the boat, splashing into the water.

"Fuck, you little bitch!" the other man shouts.

Adam bolts upright as if he was faking his injury and stabs the other man in the gut. I hadn't realized he was still armed. The blood pouring from the man surprises Kellan, and he tries to snatch me. Something dark comes over me. He's with these men. If he's with them, that means he's not with us. I'm going to be sick. My mind whirls as his voice tangles with my thoughts. He begs me to calm down telepathically, but I can't. All I can think about is knocking him off the boat. We need to get away.

Kellan focuses on me, not realizing that Adam tenses. He swings his fist, punching Kellan in the jaw hard enough to send him flailing back. Kellan transforms, trying to keep his balance on the boat, but it's no use. The boat rises and lowers on a wave, and Adam starts the motor, sending us flying forward.

"Eliana!" Kellan yells in my mind. His shouts fade on the wind.

I clutch onto the small handle, my heart racing and my stomach twisting. The cool air stings my eyes. I can't believe we got the boat.

"Adam, we have to go back," I say, blinking through the stinging wind. I screech as we hit a wave and fly a few feet into the air.

"We can't. Look," he calls, motioning behind us.

Shit. My heart sinks to my knees, leaving me weak. I couldn't stand even if I wanted to. I watch as a few men stand on the swimming platform of the yacht, forcing Chase, Evander, and Tristan into another motorized raft.

"Let's get out of the water and hide. We can camouflage the raft and wait it out. We'll keep an eye out to know which direction they head to go after them later. They wouldn't want us to risk our lives on their behalf by chasing them without a plan. It'll make things worse. You know this." Adam tightens his jaw. "I'd agree with them. You're the one needing protection. What they plan..." He shakes his head, forcing the thought from his mind.

"Doesn't mean I have to like it. I was so pissed when Evander came without you and said you were—" I snap my mouth shut, suppressing the memory threatening to break me open.

"I'm sorry, little badass. I wanted to give you time." Adam steers the boat, heading along the coast without going to shore. I almost ask him to kill the engine and set us adrift for a while.

It doesn't look like anyone is coming after us in the water, and Kellan and his cruel and disgusting packmates could never swim fast enough to catch up with us.

A part of me aches inside. How could Kellan go along with this? I expected him to help and not just act like an obedient minion. I don't know much about wolfpacks or how they work, and I don't think I want to find out. Not now.

"I didn't need time. I've been bitten, Adam. You weren't until now. I hate thinking about how this could all be for nothing. If that's the case, I just want to be with the others and you. I want to spend the last of our time just living instead of fighting." I lick my lips and swallow, tasting the saltiness of the ocean on my mouth. My stomach growls. I try to ignore the discomfort caused by my aching bite wounds.

"Please don't think like that," he murmurs, slowing down as we near the rocky shore.

I don't know exactly how far we are from where we were hiding, but now that I can see the outline of the island bathed in moonlight, it's far bigger than I realize.

"Eliana? Did you hear me?" Adam asks, scooting close enough to reach for me. I let him guide me closer until our legs rest against each other's.

I squeeze my eyes shut and nod. "I'm just trying to be real, Adam."

"So am I. We can't think as if our lives are over." Adam cuts the engine, letting us drift toward the beach. He jumps onto one of the black rocks and guides the boat through the surf. No one will follow us by boat in this area. Adam struggles to pull me close enough to where he ties the raft to a low arching palm tree over the still rocky beach.

Offering his hand, Adam helps me from the raft and kicks it a few times, testing to see if it's stable. He tears down a couple palm fronds and covers the raft the best he can.

"We should stick to the trees. We'll get a better view of the water and the forest. It looks like those assholes are heading west. You can see a light. They're camped on shore." Adam jumps, grabbing onto a lush tree, permeating the area with a floral scent. Thankfully, he drops our previous conversation, drinking in our surroundings with me. The flower blooms remain closed for the night, but I'm sure the morning sun will awaken them and create a breathtaking tropical view.

Dangling his leg down, he waits for me to cling onto him before using his strength to pull me high enough to grab onto me.

"Look, the yacht's pulling up the anchor. They're moving." Adam guides my head, directing me to look in the distance of the glowing yacht. I hadn't realized how far we traveled, but I'm relieved to see the distance between us.

"Maybe they've given up on us." It's a stupid thought, but I need to think of something to give me hope. Because right now, I feel despairingly hopeless. How did we go from so many to just me and Adam? What will the packs do with the others? What if they assault and torture them? What if—

"Eliana, hey. Look at me. You're hyperventilating." Adam touches my chin, and it takes everything in me to shut down the dark thoughts consuming me.

I gasp a few breaths, my heart feeling as if it'll collide from my chest and explode across Adam. He cups my cheeks and leans in, trying to fill my view with his handsome face.

"Doc would have you do some refocusing shit, wouldn't he? The whole sensory thing I've read about." Adam searches my eyes. "But I don't remember that shit. So I want to play a game. It's easy. Will you try?"

I open and close my mouth, unable to form my words. I nod the best I can. I hate how my body and mind shut down. It shouldn't be like this. I'm stronger than this.

"I'm going to ask you one-word answer questions. Answer the best you can without thinking." Adam smooths his fingers through my wild, damp hair. "Then you can ask me anything you want. Got it?"

"Yes," I manage to say.

He graces me with a smile that lights his hazel eyes in the silvery moonlight. "Good. Question one..." He taps his finger to his chin. "Favorite color?"

"Blue." The word barely sounds like a whisper coming from my mouth.

"Mine too." He gives me a little shake. "What's your body count?"

I frown for a second. "Sex or kills?"

His eyes widen for a second and he covers his mouth to muffle his howl of a laugh. "Fuck. Works either way. Just say a number. I'll ask which later."

I lick my lips. "Twenty-three and a half...twenty-four and a half."

"A half? How can you have a half?" He lifts an eyebrow. Shaking his head, he adds, "Never mind. I'm not sure I want to know how you measure."

"You?" My chest loosens, my heartbeat finally chilling out.

"Don't judge me...two...times. One woman. I lived a sheltered life. My dad's best friend's niece. We were teens." He groans, rubbing his scruffy face. "Damn it. I talk too much."

I laugh and shake my head. The direction of the conversation helps far more than I realized it could. "Sounds like you need a little corrupting."

Shifting beside me, he squirms on the branch, his body clearly hardening through his wet shorts.

He clears his throat. "Moving on—"

I laugh again and swat his hand. "No. I'm not ready. Let's

talk more about this corrupting deal."

"Whose cock would win a beauty pageant?" He chuckles at my reaction.

"Seriously? Dicks aren't cute unless they have smiley faces, glitter, and come from an artist." I crinkle my nose. "I'd have to see what kind of talent each of you possesses. Can yours dance? Sword fight? Play the drums?"

"I could use it to paint for you. No brush necessary." He rocks his hips, pretending to draw a circle with his obvious hard-on.

I practically cackle, slapping my hand over my mouth to keep quiet. "What about offering a good pounding? I can lead."

He groans at the thought, snaking his hand around my back and up to my neck. "Careful, Eliana. I would love for you to demonstrate your teaching capabilities. I could use a pain-killer, and the thought of fucking you seems like the perfect relief."

I smirk and meet his raised eyebrows with my own. "Sex does release endorphins. I'm in a bit of pain myself. Though..." I motion around us. "This isn't ideal. Someone might hear. Are you willing to risk it?"

He scrunches his nose, his expression adorable as if my comment is the most ridiculous thing in the world. "What kind of question is that?"

"A reasonable one." I lean in closer, only allowing an inch of space between our mouths. "Though if somebody is close enough to hear us, we're probably screwed anyways. Might as well be screwing each other."

Releasing a soft moan under his breath, he meets his lips to mine, kissing me softly. "True. You're absolutely worth the risk, little badass. I'd do anything for this moment."

The sensation of his mouth sets me off, and I kiss him more fervently, sliding my tongue between his lips, tasting the salt of the sea. He's an amazing kisser, soft and sensual yet passionate. He takes his time to explore my mouth with his tongue, gliding it over mine in a way that turns me on. His hand traces down my spine and to my ass. He uses one hand and lifts me up enough to where I shift onto his lap. He braces his back on the tree trunk, resting his legs on the tree while holding the branch with his ankles. This is going to be tricky, but I'm all in. I had no idea how much I wanted or needed this. A distraction. The chance to forget while the world falls apart.

This will truly test my capabilities, but this whole experience proves to me that I'm strong and crazy enough to get through mostly anything. And sex in a tree? At least it's not my ass risking getting splinters.

I grin with my thought and rub my hand over Adam's hard-on, feeling the length of his shaft. He moans softly under his breath, keeping his voice low, and I reach into his shorts and pull his cock out, rubbing it slowly at first, feeling him flex it in my fingers.

"You're so sexy." Adam drags his hand down my stomach, sliding his fingers along my pelvis until he can touch between my legs.

He shifts my shorts out of the way, playing with my body and strumming my clit in a way that tests my ability to remain quiet. His even strokes numb my mind from anything except for the sensation. I'm so turned on that I can hardly wait to align our bodies. I never knew I needed this so badly. The ache from the bites fade, and I squirm on his lap, trying my best not to knock us over.

Should we be doing this? No. Sex is the last thing I should do. But I was never that great at making the best decisions.

"You're so wet for me. I want to taste you." He brings his finger up to his mouth and pops it between his lips. "I hope you know how amazing I think you are."

"Not as incredible as you. You have no idea what your companionship and protection means to me. I've never had anyone really on my side. And here you are. Even when you don't have to be. Even when it could mean something horrible could happen." My emotions get the best of me, and I kiss him, shutting myself up before I say something I might regret later. Because this isn't the time for wearing my heart pinned outside my chest. It's a time for me to embrace my wild, feral, innate need as a woman. As a possible lykoswulf.

Adam doesn't lift me up right away, continuing rubbing my clit until tingles burst between my legs, and I feel on the verge of an orgasm. I kiss him harder, using his mouth as a way to keep quiet even though all I want to do is moan. I want him to hear my voice and to know exactly how he makes me feel and what he does to me.

I gasp as my muscles tighten and spasm. If he wasn't holding onto me, I might throw myself back, my body no longer aligning with my mind. It feels as if I've separated, experiencing a wave of ecstasy despite the pain clinging to me.

I brace onto Adam until the sensation goes away, and I crave more. He locks his fingers to my hips, easing me up and allowing me to align his dick to my body. He slowly lowers me, taking control of our movements. I can't do much in this position, my legs dangling as I straddle him. He eases up and lowers me, making me gasp. He groans and kisses me, keeping the two of us quiet as he picks up his speed, thrusting his hips just enough to hit me in the right place. I lose myself to Adam, pushing away the world and the circumstances. I'm not going to let it ruin my possible last days. I will the connection to Adam to give me the willpower to fight, to survive. Maybe it'll do the same for him.

What am I thinking? I know better than to feel this way. If I like him too much, I'll get hurt. Or he will. We don't know what's going to happen. He picks up his pace, pounding me harder and faster, making the leaves rustle. But I don't care. We're high up enough that we'll have a warning if somebody tries to attack. The rocks will make it more difficult as well. For the first time in a while, even in this tree, even as exposed as I am, I feel safe. Adam makes me feel safe. He makes me feel capable.

I comb my fingers through his hair, memorizing how hot he is, how his muscles flex, and how his body feels in mine. He kisses me again, more desperately, nipping and sucking my bottom lip between his teeth. He digs his fingers into my ass cheeks with a grunt and breaks away from my mouth. He comes, thrusting a few more times, his breathing as hard as mine.

"Fuck, I wish we were somewhere else. I want to cuddle the fuck out of you and go at it again for the rest of the night. I think I'm addicted." Adam murmurs the words in my ear, kissing the skin right below. I shiver and smile, resting my head on his shoulder. Clean up is going to be a bitch. I didn't really think things through. But I guess it's whatever now. It's not like we have the luxury of showering.

"You can use my shorts as a cumrag if you want." It's like Adam can read my mind. His face softens, and he cocks his head. "Holy shit. I can."

I blink my eyes and lean back, meeting his gaze. "What are you talking about?"

He tightens his mouth and cups my cheek with his hand. "Eliana, can you hear this?"

I tense, hearing the words but his mouth never moves. It's just like with Kellan. And holy fucking shit is right. What does this mean?

"Whoa. I don't understand. Kellan claimed that he was my soulmate, and we were connected, which left me open for him. Wolves communicate telepathically a lot of times, but he was able to do so while I was human because his wolf picked me. He claimed that I was his." My heart races, and I can't help capturing Adam with my eyes. I stare into his hazel irises, trying to decipher the confusion washing between us. It's a blend of his emotions and mine, wrapped up with lust and something else. Something sweet yet terrifying.

"Do you think this means we've been moon chosen?" he asks, searching my face. He darts his gaze away from mine and stares at the water behind me as the moon crawls across the sky, nearly full.

I ease myself off him, needing to step into the moonlight. I don't know what it is about this moment, but he might be right. I feel as if my body can heal under the light of the moon. Especially with him by my side.

He swings down, dropping back to the rocks. Extending his arms, he waits for me to slide down. He catches me and steadies me on my feet, my knees weak from the night and our passion. Just from everything happening around me.

Reaching up, I grab the sleeve of Adam's shirt and pull it out of the way, looking at his bite mark. It's the strangest thing, seeing the spiderwebs of color crawl over his skin, but he doesn't transform yet.

I twist to look at my leg, seeing the same thing. Our bites are nearly identical. "I don't know exactly what this means, or what we are going to go through, but I don't think we're going to die."

"I think you're right, Eliana. I hear something. Someone. It's another voice in my head. Can you hear it?" Adam rubs his hands against his ears and shakes his head. "There's a lot. More and more keep adding to the mix."

I close my eyes and try to listen, trying to hear what he hears. Nothing breaks through. Only Adam questioning what the hell is going on. He shifts on his feet and peers around. A howl cuts through the night, striking me to my very soul.

"Fuck. They're getting ready. We need to hurry and get to the others." Adam pulls me along the rocks and back to our raft. "I don't see any boats. I think we should head down the coast and see if we can spot anything. They won't be able to move fast enough to get us in the water."

I help him move the palm fronds out of the way. "What if we're too late? What if somebody catches us?"

"We have to do this, Eliana. If we are transforming, we need to heed to the call of the moon. I don't think we're going to have a choice." He frowns with his words as if he hates saying them.

I can't blame him.

"We've never had one. Maybe things can change." I know it's wishful thinking, but something about this night feels as if more possibilities have opened. It's hard to explain.

"I'm willing to try. But I think we need a pack to survive this." He pulls the boat along until the waves swell around our ankles.

"Then we will make our own. I'm not going with any of these assholes, especially not the one who bit me." I peer again at the moon.

"Fuck yeah. That's what I want to hear. You can be our leader. Maybe we can still get off this island." He leans in and kisses me.

Like my grandma.

I don't want any other fate.

I want to return to human civilization.

I'll never accept my place among the lykoswulf packs. They'll never have us.

CHAPTER 20

SAVAGE

I CLUTCH ONTO Adam's hand, staring at the beach full of writhing humans, half-changed and experiencing utter agony. Not a single one of them looks to have accepted the bite of the lykoswulf. The fact that whoever did this to them has just left them here to suffer...it's cruel.

"Fuck," Adam mutters, turning off the engine. "We need to do something."

I hold on tight to the side of the raft as he hops out into

the waves, guiding the boat into the sand. "They're danger-ous."

"They're in pain." Adam tugs the raft the rest of the way into the sand, ensuring that the waves can't take it away. We team up and drag it toward the nearest cluster of trees, picking up the palm fronds. Apart from the cries of agony from those left here, silence fills the air. I don't think the wolves stay where they discard those unworthy of the moon. It's disgusting. Inhumane.

"I don't know if I can handle killing so many." My voice shakes with the words.

"I'll do it. I just need you to show me exactly where to stab. I didn't watch doc." Adam pulls out the small knife from his pocket. "I know he did something with the neck."

I shudder at the memory. "He was severing their spinal cord to damage the nervous system. Right at the base of the skull."

Adam groans and releases a growl. And holy shit. I didn't think a man could make a noise like that. He sounds almost like one of the wolves. It shouldn't excite me so much, especially in this situation but damn.

"I'll try so you don't have to." I heave a deep breath, the briny air filling my lungs. A hint of something more rancid taints the sea breeze. Something more human and dirty. "I just...I'm scared. This sucks. But we can't leave them. You're right. It would be even more cruel than the fate they face now."

"Then we can take turns. We'll carry the burden of this shit show together." Adam pulls me close and kisses me. "Let's promise each other that no matter what, we'll be our own pack. We're in this together. Every decision we make will be together."

His words touch me deeply, and I nod my head and kiss him harder. "Together."

The promise itself helps give me the strength to turn back to the madness. To the humans trapped in a half state between wolf and monster. I couldn't imagine what it feels like, and I feel terrible. Even if these people came after us or some shit, they don't deserve that kind of fate. No one does. What the wolfpacks of Shadow Moon Island do is horrendous and unthinkable. It makes me sick. I don't want to turn into them. I want to be nothing like them.

"You can restrain the first one. I'll sever the spinal cord. We have to work fast. There's so many of them." I try to suppress my thoughts about them being human. The longer I look at them in their grotesque deformity, the easier it is for me to consider them more animal. More alien even. Is it fucked up? Yes. But everything about this whole situation is messed up.

Adam straightens his shoulders and guides me along the pebbly beach. A man with fur sprouting from his hand snarls and reaches out, trying to snatch my leg. But he can't move. His legs look to be broken, twisted monstrosities. The best he can do is drag himself closer inch by inch.

"Pick someone more...placid to start. We'll save the fighters for last." I crinkle my nose, sweeping my gaze over the beach.

"Do you want me to pick?" Adam tightens his jaw and looks around. "Fuck. What about that one? Looks like a chupacabra or something. Can't even tell it was ever a human. It's like a fucking demon here to drag us to hell."

He's right about that. If I shut off the idea that these people are still human, it'll make it easier. Though I can't think of them as animals either. It's a bit harder for me. I've always liked animals except for if they're trying to maul me to death or, you know, if they change into asshole men who want to basically make me their breeding bitch.

"Hell's probably more pleasant than this. It's where all the fun people go. At least, some of the fun people. There are the psychos too. I like to think that the fun people get to be the ones who torture the horrible ones." I raise and drop my shoulders. I don't know why I say it. I've never really been religious, but I need to refocus my thoughts.

Adam chuckles. "Let's leave this discussion for twenty questions. I'd like to know more about your ideas. But right now...that thing has to go. Banish it to the bowels of hell, little badass."

Adam releases my hand, and my palm feels cold without his touch. He hands me the knife and rubs his palms together, standing over the beast. It doesn't move much, but a strange whimper escapes its elongated jowls with a mixture of human and canine teeth. It's freaky as fuck, and I try not to look at it too much.

Adam says every swear word I've ever heard and some I haven't as he grabs the shoulders of the beast and steps on its back, using his hand to press its head down. It's easier with it on its belly, and it doesn't have fingers anymore. I try not to look at the human feet, half deformed with claws instead of toenails.

I hold my breath and position the knife at the base of the creature's skull. "I'm so sorry. Fate should've never brought you to an end like this. I hope you find peace." I jam the blade into the spine, killing the creature quickly and hopefully with as little pain as possible.

"Amen," Adam says, dropping the beast. "Rest in peace, Chupa."

We move on to the next one and quickly work our way through the writhing bodies. There are still five more after we've hit a dozen, and I can't believe that we manage to do this in only a minute or two. Once we got through the first one, each one after was easier and easier. I was able to shut myself down and not think about it.

"Here. I'll do the last five. You've done plenty." Adam holds his hand out, silently asking for the knife.

I smirk at him. "I've done them all."

He scrunches his face, peering around. "Sorry about that.

You just worked so fast."

"It wasn't as bad as I thought. Terrible, right?" I rub my hand up and down my forearm, silently trying to comfort myself.

"No. We're showing them mercy. Don't forget that. We didn't kill them. Not really. The assholes who bit them were the executioners." Adam tightens his fingers into a fist.

I suppress my emotions the best I can. If I think any more about this, I might lose my shit. "Let's just finish up. It's been too quiet."

It feels like an eternity has passed even though I know it's only been minutes.

"Because I'm impressed with what you're doing." The voice enters my mind, startling me. I reach out and clutch onto Adam.

I open my mouth to say something to him. "Adam—"

"I wouldn't tell him, princess. He'll try to either run with you or fight. If he tries to fight, I will have to put him in his place and make him submit to me. Do you really want that?" I recognize the voice. It's the man from the woods. The man who bit me. Ravi.

"No." The word comes out a whisper of a breath, and I realize Adam stares at me, his brows furrowed.

"Shit. Is that...?" Adam mistakes my reaction for something on the ground. Not something, someone. I recognize Ian. I didn't know what happened to him, but it looks like he has been abandoned. "It is. Tiffany was supposed to give him up. What if she did and this is what Kellan's pack did?"

"I'm sure that's exactly what happened." I swallow my nerves and try to push Ravi out of my head. I nod and glance from Adam and to Ian. "Let's hurry and finish so we can find the others."

Without another word, I follow Adam and he restrains the remaining half-humans. Ian stares at us with familiar eyes, his mouth opening and closing without words coming out. Only growls and what sounds like a plea. He doesn't want to die. He wants to live. He wants to wait.

I close my eyes and jab my knife into the back of his neck. I know that he won't complete the transformation. Kellan told me as much. I hate that I had to do this. I hate that I had to end the life of anyone, but especially someone that I sort of knew, even if it was only for a little bit.

"The fuckers are going to pay." Adam uncurls his fingers, taking the knife from me, and jabs it into the sand a couple times to clean it off instead of going back to the water.

"I hope so. If anything happens to Evander, Chase, Tristan, or Davian, I will do whatever it takes to get justice for them. I swear. These lykoswulves think they're in charge, but they're going to learn otherwise. All they've done by biting us is give us a better chance to destroy them." I raise my voice a bit, hoping that Ravi hears my words.

"I not only hear your words; I can also feel them. You

don't believe that's true. I will work on your confidence though. A mate of the Sunset Pointe pack will always be capable of great things." Ravi thinks the words to me, sending goosebumps over my skin. My body reacts to his words in a way I never expected. How could I like what he says to me? He bit me. He stalked me. And now he's here, hiding and waiting for the chance to attack.

"Unlike the bastard from Twilight Cove, I'm not. I'm here to claim you. I'm here, waiting for the moon to rise and for you to call my name, princess." Ravi hums in my mind, his voice seeming to twine around my very soul, squeezing me tight and stealing my breath. But it isn't in a bad way. It's confusing and unbidden. "I know you'll realize you like being a good girl, especially my good girl."

Adam squeezes my hand, giving me a little shake. "Eliana? Are you okay? Are you in shock? Talk to me." Bending forward, he closes the space and meets my eyes. "You look as if your mind is somewhere else."

My mouth dries, and I try to moisten my lips. The salt from the ocean doesn't help. I can't even remember the last time I drank any water. "Sorry, I'm just trying to think. How are we going to find the others?"

"We know that someone came to this area. We just need to find the signs. No one can go anywhere without leaving a trail. If we find someone, we can get the answers out of them." Adam frowns at his words. Our plan sucks. There is no raft here, but it was the only place that a boat could have entered the island because everything past this is rocks and cliffside. We saw the light on the beach from their campsite.

We are grasping at air, falling through a world of nothingness.

"If you try such a thing, you'll put my mate at risk. That will only piss off our pack." Ravi steps from the trees naked, raising his hands in surrender. He might be trying to look as if he's not a threat, but the fact that he so confidently strolls out here, proves he is.

Adam grabs me and gets in front, clutching the knife and pointing it at Ravi. "Stay back. If you come any closer, I will gut you. Don't think I won't."

Instead of glowering, Ravi smiles. "I know you will, little pup. You're now on the Twilight Cove shit list. The man you stabbed on the raft didn't survive. You'll be thankful once the moon calls that it was one of my packmates to bite you. I was."

Anger rushes over me and I dodge past Adam. He yells my name, but I need to confront this bastard. I need to kick him in the balls. I need to make him feel pain. Something. Anything. I can't just let him stand there and act as if we're beneath him. Like Adam might be beneath him.

My mind catches up to my body, and I slow down only to grab what looks like a makeshift spear from the ground. If I didn't know any better, I'd think it belonged to one of the guys. I don't have time to inspect it. I know that Evander had carved his initials into his.

Swinging it, I aim for Ravi's legs, trying to drop him to his knees. The bastard jumps into the air, transforming into a wolf, not giving me a chance to even brace myself as he collides into me. He growls, the sound vibrating to my core, but it's not at me. His eyes look above my head at Adam.

And then he drags his tongue across my cheek from my jaw all the way to my temple.

He transforms on top of me, caging me in with his body, but he doesn't pin me down. He kneels, straddling my legs, and points at Adam.

"If you take another step closer or try to hurt me, I'll leave your ass here for the call of the moon. You're going to give me a couple minutes to talk. Eliana is mine. She has accepted my bite, and once the moon calls, she'll be my official mate. My alpha has promised her to me as long as I get the other packs in line. Who she chooses to spend more time with is up to her. The rules on this island vastly differ from the human world. But it seems like you already know that. Eliana knows that. I can smell her all over you. Be thankful that I have far better restraint from killing unnecessarily than most here. If I were Sean, you'd be dead for laying a hand on my mate before me."

Annoyance and rage explode through me, and I swing my hand out, attempting to slap him across the face. Ravi catches my wrist and yanks it over my head, leaning in far enough to make me stiffen. He inhales a deep breath near my ear, and his lips brush my lobe.

"Be a good girl now, princess. I'm doing you a favor. If you behave, I might let you see what happened to your friends." Ravi releases his grip on me and slides off, getting to his feet. Extending his hand, he holds it out to me.

I ignore him and hold my hands out to Adam instead. Adam hesitates for only a second before getting the nerve to help me up. It's the strangest thing. It's almost as if he was waiting to see if Ravi would allow him.

"You know where they are? It was you, wasn't it? Your pack?" I reach for the knife Adam clutches, and he lets me take it without saying a word. I point it at Ravi. "You fucking monsters. How could you do this? How can you assume that being nice to me now is going to change anything? I shouldn't be on this island. None of us should. What you're doing is horrific. It's inhumane. You can't just bite a bunch of humans and leave them to suffer."

Ravi flares his nostrils and bares his teeth at me. His eyes flash with a reflective light. "Do not put my pack in the same category as those who kidnapped you. This—" He waves around the beach. "This is not Sunset Pointe's doing. There are many other packs. We all have different beliefs on how things work here. If we were all working together, there wouldn't have been so many casualties already. I wouldn't have had to fight for you until the full moon. But I had to ensure your place."

"My place? My place is back in civilization." Shadows crowd my vision. My breath quickens, and I struggle to keep my shit together. I want so badly to charge him again in an attempt to attack him, but I know it won't get me anywhere. He's expecting it. I need to surprise him somehow.

"It's not. Now, come on. We don't have a lot of time. If you want to see the rest of your group and say goodbye in case, let me take you. We had to snatch them or Twilight Cove would have." Ravi steps closer and offers his hand to me, acting as if the knife I hold isn't a threat.

"I think we should go with him, Eliana. We don't really know what else to do. If he can take us to—"

Ravi charges forward, snatching me off my feet and swinging me over his shoulder. He locks his other arm on Adam and drags him, forcing him to run beside us. I stare at the ground, my heart racing.

The knife falls from my fingers before I can even defend myself.

"Don't scream, princess. Someone's coming." Ravi's voice hums through my mind. "You need to trust me. I'm your mate now. I will not allow anything to happen to you."

I don't respond to him.

I don't think I'll ever trust a lykoswulf. Not now. Not ever. Ravi seems like he's trying to help, but so did Kellan. I won't be fooled again.

The second I get a chance, I'll make him regret biting me.

I'll make the whole island regret ever bringing me here, even if I must become as feral as them. My humanity will die with the moon. I know it. Now I must embrace it. It's the only way I'll ever have the future I want.

CHAPTER 21

Eliana

WILD WOLVES

A RIDICULOUSLY BUFF man struts from the trees with his dick swinging between his legs. Ravi keeps his hand across the back of my legs, not setting me on my feet as we remain hidden. But I can see the guy upside down. He tips his head back and inhales a deep breath before taking in the surroundings.

"There are two packs through here and the girl. They can't be that far." The man says the words out loud, twisting on the balls of his feet.

My heart sinks into my stomach at the site of Kellan and another man closing in. What is he doing? I knew I should've never trusted him. I'm not his supposed soulmate. I can't believe I fucked the guy, and here he is either hunting me or torturing these people alongside the other men.

"I'll keep looking. They can't have our recruits or our female." The other man rubs his hand on the back of his neck and glances at Kellan. "Head south. Call your connections and see if they've seen anything."

Kellan swivels on the balls of his feet and stares at all the dead bodies. "Yes, sir."

I scrunch my face at how formal he sounds when addressing the other man. In this moment, Kellan looks less threatening. He almost looks as if he lacks any power at all.

"Because he does. That wolf is so low in his pack that he might as well be...human. He is here to serve his pack and nothing else. We refer to him as infraborne." Ravi thinks the words to me.

"So like an omega?" I know some things about animal hierarchy but not much. I know wolves in the human world act more as a family but this whole thing—lykoswulves—is different.

"Not quite, princess. That's what you will be to me." Ravi smirks with his words, enjoying the thought.

"And what am I going to be?" Adam's voice rings through

my mind next. Ravi was talking to both of us telepathically. It's the strangest thing.

"You're a pup. You'll learn your place soon enough. I'll teach you how to be a good boy." Ravi's smile widens, though he doesn't say the words out loud. And the way he says it? I don't even know how to take it. Is he joking? He has to be joking.

"I'm only joking if you stop thinking about the idea of this man being a good boy. You like it. I can sense it. You want him to be your good boy, princess. Don't you?" Ravi's words prod into my mind, but Adam doesn't react, so I know that they were intended just for me.

Blush crawls up my chest, warming my neck and cheeks. The way he says it? What is wrong with me? I shouldn't even humor his banter. He bit me. He forced a fate onto me that I did not want. He's my enemy.

Or is he?

"Far from it, Eliana. You've met our true enemies. Those men prefer to see the destruction of you as you are considered weaker than them. Just wait until they realize who put a claim on you." Ravi adjusts me in his arms, taking me off his shoulder but he doesn't set me on my feet and instead cradles me. Looking into my eyes, he adds, "If only I had found you sooner and before the infraborne. He put thoughts in your head. He has nearly ruined your ability to trust me. And for that, he will pay."

I shouldn't feel the sudden fear at the idea of Ravi hurting Kellan, but I can't control it. He was there for me and the rest of us. He gave us necessities. He protected me.

"He did the bare minimum. He should've done more. You shouldn't have needed protection. You should've had necessities the moment you arrived and had not been left to the fates." Ravi's anger rushes through me, and I can feel his emotions as if they're my own.

I gasp and jerk in his arms, bucking my body with my head rush. He remains steady as I flail, keeping a grip on me, ensuring I don't fall.

Clearing his throat, he whispers, "I'm sorry. You're not quite ready for the intensity of our mate connection. It's hard to keep it to myself."

I whack him. "We don't have a mate connect—"

Ravi covers my mouth and steps back, moving from tree to tree, remaining hidden. He motions for Adam to keep his pace a moment before surprising me by handing me over like I'm some doll they can throw back and forth.

He growls and transforms into a wolf, spinning around and leaping past us. Adam doesn't follow him, picking up his pace, running in the direction Ravi was originally heading. I cling onto Adam. Staring over his shoulder, I search the forest. A white beast crashes into a grey wolf, and the two of them snarl and roll. It's Kellan and Ravi. They fight each other, snapping their teeth, trying to incapacitate one another.

A third wolf launches from the trees, crashing into the both of them. Fur flies and the snarls grow louder, increasing off my fear. This is absolutely nuts. I should be thankful that they go after each other instead of us. I should pray that they take care of each other. But a small part of me fears that sort of outcome. What will happen to me if they do? Is it weird that I'm afraid we can't survive without them no matter their true intentions? Maybe not.

"Help me keep a lookout. Ravi said we must turn and head northeast when we come to the waterfall. Remember how Kellan said not to go that way? Well, that's where we're going." Adam once again speaks to me telepathically as if it's the most natural thing.

I nod my head in response, wiggling until he slows to re-position me. I hop onto his back and lock my ankles together around his waist. Pain shoots through my calf, but I force myself to hang on. Our lives depend on it. Everything I thought I knew might be wrong. I don't even know what to believe any-more.

I lose myself to my thoughts, listening to Adam's deep breathing. The noise of the fighting wolves suddenly silences. My body chills, my mind getting the best of me. Did Kellan and the unfamiliar wolf kill Ravi? Did they give up? Should we even be running this way?

"If you don't think we should follow Ravi's directions, we won't. We can head back to the beach and grab the raft." Adam slows as the sound of rushing water hums through the air. He navigates the thick landscape until we break through the trees to see a breathtaking waterfall cascading into the bluest pool I've ever seen. "If we follow the creek, we might find the place where we originally started. I don't think the raft would be that far. Or we could just give it up and hide until the moon. I wouldn't mind staying in a tree with you for a while."

An image flashes through my mind of me on top of him in the trees. Heat flourishes across my body. As quickly as that image arises, it disappears. I don't have a chance to respond to him. A man covered from head to toe with mud runs from the trees.

Adam takes an automatic step back, bumping my back into the trunk of one of the twisted trees behind us. My hair tangles in the branches, and I thrash as I try to pull myself free. Positioning his legs, Adam gets into a fighting stance. He holds his fists up protectively.

"Elle." The man gasps and clutches his side, my name faint on his lips. But his voice? I know it. It rises relief inside me. It's Davian. I can't believe he found us. I'm so thankful that he's alive. He isn't one of those half-beast things.

"Holy fucking shit." Adam rushes forward, grabbing Davian by the shoulders and staring him in the eyes. "Where the fuck have you been? We tried looking for you, and then shit got bad. Eliana and I were both bitten. We think Kellan was double crossing us. The others have been taken. And...we found a lot of bodies."

Davian doesn't respond right away, his dirty face cracking with his frown. The dried mud flakes and I reach out over Adam's shoulder and run my fingers across Davian's cheek.

"I had to disguise my scent the best I could. They're hunting me. I could hear them in my head. I feel like I'm going crazy." Davian scrubs his cheeks, sending more dried mud dusting around him.

Adam throws his arms around Davian and hugs him, not even caring that he's filthy. "You're not. Those voices are because the lykoswulf speak telepathically. They're probably fucking with you while they track you, waiting for the moon. Whatever pack that bit you has a claim."

His eyes widen. "We have to get off this fucking island. I can't be a part of that pack. The voices...they're monsters. The things they claim they're going to do...I won't ever survive that."

My heart aches, hearing the shaking of his voice. I can't even imagine what he's been threatened with especially with what I found out about it in regard to me. It makes it even worse. The strange hierarchy. The way these wolves treat each other within their pack is just as bad.

"We will. I won't let them have you, Davian. Even if I have to murder them all. We're going to get through this. You're not part of their pack. You are now part of my pack." My pack. The sound of it feels so amazing coming from my mouth. Just the idea of joining together with Davian and Adam...Evander, Chase, and Tristan. We can make this work. If we stand together, we can fight. At least, once the moon comes.

Suddenly, I look forward to it. Ravi unintentionally gave me hope because he thinks I'll survive. If I survive, then I know the guys will. None of them have turned into that nasty half-beast thing. Maybe this was fate. Maybe it's because my lineage gave me an advantage and that affects things. But I don't think I'll ever know. I don't want to hang around with those on the island to find out.

"I wouldn't want to be with anyone else, but we have to hurry and hide. They're going to be coming. I hear them." Davian spins around and searches the trees. "Do you?"

I close my eyes and listen. I don't hear anything. I wonder if he only hears the pack that cursed him.

"I think you're right, little badass," Adam thinks to me. "We're not receptive to them."

"I don't know," I respond to Davian, trying to keep my voice steady. I don't want him to freak out.

"We hear some voices, but they're still fighting each other and not tracking us yet. I trust you when you say that someone is after you, though, so let's go. We'll stick to the creek for a clean path. Everyone keep a lookout." Adam takes charge of the situation, and I hold on tightly to his back, thankful that he still carries me. I don't think I would be able to keep up with the bite to my leg. It's still tender and throbbing. My arm doesn't fare any better.

Davian sticks close to our side, clutching a spear. I'm thankful he has a weapon. It's not very sharp, but it's enough to at least keep some space around us if a wolf tries to attack us. I don't know what would happen if the wolves after him find us or if the wolves after me find him. Ravi said that Adam was bitten by someone on his pack, so he's supposedly on our side.

I inhale and exhale slow breaths, trying to keep my racing heart in control. We only make it a couple dozen feet before a howl sounds through the air. It's impossible to hide from wolves. They're masters at tracking us.

A grey wolf jumps into our path, and I recognize Kellan's bright blue eyes. Davian yells and swings his spear, not even hesitating. He clocks Kellan's wolf form on the side of his head, sending them sprawling into the creek. Kellan growls, the sound guttural and scary as hell, and he snaps his teeth as he tries to charge us.

Davian scrambles away, and Adam steals his spear and aims it at Kellan.

"You son of a bitch. Stay the hell back. You're a lying asshole. We know you've been playing with us." Adam jabs the spear, trying to knock Kellan back.

Kellan surprises me by transforming into his human form. He fists his hands, his muscles rippling and his eyes sparkling.

"What the fuck are you talking about? I'm trying to help you. Come on. This way."

None of us moves. None of us talks either. I don't know who to believe or how to feel. I don't trust any of the wolves.

Kellan strides closer, holding his hands up. "Please. The packs are out for a hunt, grabbing and biting anyone they can. If you've already been bitten by another pack, they'll kill you. They don't want their enemies to grow stronger in numbers." Kellan looks at me as he says the words. "Eliana, please. It kills me inside to think that you could ever belong to another. You're my soulmate, even bitten by someone else. I'll learn to accept that. But right now, we have to go. I have a place we can stay until the full moon passes."

I heave a couple deep breaths, my whole body buzzing and tingling. His words swirl through my mind, and panic tightens my chest. So not only do we have to face the viciousness of getting bitten, but we also now have to face the possibility of being mauled and killed by others in an attempt to prevent us from changing. I didn't think things could get any worse. But damn it.

What about Ravi? He was going to help us too. He has the rest of the guys. Even if Kellan is telling the truth, a part of me wants to risk denying him and following Ravi for the fact that at least I can reunite with Tristan, Evander, and Chase. We need each other more than ever.

"Get out of our way. Eliana doesn't want to go with you,

and you need to accept it. We live in a world where you'll respect her decision. Do you understand? You will not guilt her or pressure her into anything else otherwise." Adam growls with his words, sounding more beast than man, and the noise is incredibly sexy. Protective is so hot on him.

"I can't allow it. You'll get her killed. You don't understand anything." Kellan changes his stance, his muscles rippling with his flexing fingers. I hear the thought cross his mind about tackling us and just dragging me away. It freaks me out.

Adam must hear my thoughts, because he doesn't give Kellan the opportunity. He swings the stick, whacking him in the legs and knocking his feet out from under him. Shoving Davian, he gets him to rush in the other direction. We're going to head up the creek after all.

"Run. Don't stop. We need to pass the waterfall and keep going. We're going to get the others. We're not going to just submit to anyone." Adam's voice deepens with his words. I didn't know that he could take charge so easily, and I'm ready to do whatever he says. I trust him. Davian does too.

"He's still a pup, princess. But I respect his ability to make quick decisions. If only you would behave for me. I told you where you were supposed to go. I wouldn't have to fight anyone else had you just been a good girl for me." Ravi's words slap me in the mind, jerking my attention away from the forest around us.

Surprise washes over me. I thought maybe Kellan had

won. I don't even know what to think or how to feel anymore. I just know that his voice brings me relief.

"That's our mate bond, Eliana. You know that I'll always take care of you. You're my girl. You just need to accept it. Once the moon calls..." He hums without finishing his thoughts.

"Shit. They're coming for me." Davian gasps with the words, picking up his pace and moving ahead. "They said if I grab you, Eliana, they wouldn't beat me into submission. They're fucking crazy."

Many people would take advantage of the offer. Especially for someone they've just met. Especially me. But Davian only encourages us to move faster. He has chosen me and Adam, trusting that we will stand by his side through anything. I won't break my promise. We'll be a pack. I don't care who these assholes think they are. If we stand together, we can fight a lot better than if we just give in and do as they say.

Adam picks up his pace until we cut back in front of Davian to lead the way. I realize it's because he wants to shield me between their bodies. With me on his back and Davian behind, I'm not as exposed. Wolves can't attack me from behind. They'll have to go through Davian first. Or Adam.

More howls sound through the air, and goosebumps prickle over my skin. I feel like we've been running forever. My anxiety makes it hard to breathe and think. I brace myself to be attacked at any second. I expect it. We're at a disadvantage for those who know this island. For those who control everything on it.

"You're coming up to our camp. Sean is expecting you, but you need to be a good little girl and don't do anything stupid. Wait for me." Ravi's voice prods at my attention.

"How will we know it's them?" My words sound out loud, my mind struggling to keep everything inside me.

"You will see your group. Now, Adam, let Eliana down. She will go first." Ravi speaks to both of us telepathically.

Adam slows, shifting me down his back and gently setting me on my feet. Davian grabs my hand. He didn't hear Ravi and stares at me in confusion. Then we hear voices sounding through the trees. I catch the scent of burning wood. Somebody has a fire going. My stomach growls, the scent of something cooking stirring my hunger.

"Shit. Where do we go?" Davian asks.

"Just stay behind me." I know I should tell him more, but I don't. "They're supposed to be on our side...sort of. The wolf that bit me sent us here. It's where they are keeping Chase, Tristan, and Evander."

"Maybe I should hide." Davian tugs away from me, moving toward the tree. "I don't belong here. I don't belong anywhere. I'm sorry, Eliana."

I turn to Adam. "Go with him. Just listen for me, okay? I need to get closer.

"We can't separate. That's fucking insane." Adam tightens

his jaw, looking as Davian ducks beneath a low tree branch. His fear makes him reckless, but I can't really blame him. He's been taunted by assholes for who knows how long.

I start after Davian, afraid he'll vanish. Grabbing Adam's hand, I tug him along, knowing he won't leave me. I won't let Davian leave either. We just found him. "Davian, wait!"

A yell sounds through the air, and I tense and yank Adam harder. Davian appears in the trees again, cocking his head to the side. It wasn't him who yelled. It was someone else.

"You fuckers! We'll kill you!" I gawk at Davian and Adam and then whip my attention to where the voice came from. It's Chase.

He yells again.

A wolf snarls, the sound vicious and feral. Wild.

Silence fills the air.

CHAPTER 22

Tristan

HUNTED

"STOP! THAT'S FUCKING enough!" Anger rushes through me, and I yank against the ropes binding me to the tree. A wolf growls and pins Chase to the ground, getting in his face and looking as if he's going to maul it off.

"Easy, Miles. That's not how we do things around here. You might treat the pups in the Crystalrock pack as such, but we are more civilized." A tall, hairy as fuck man grabs the wolf by the scruff of his neck and yanks him off, pinning him to the ground. The wolf submits and exposes his stomach, releasing a whimper like a little puppy. How he can go from vicious to complacent is weird as fuck.

The wolf transforms into a man, and I scowl at him. "They can bring the girl to you. Isn't that what you want? You don't truly think Ravi deserves her, do you?"

The man straightens his shoulders. I think he's the leader of this pack. "Mind your place. You are not a part of the Sunset Pointe pack yet. The arrangement I have with my betaborne is none of your concern."

He flicks his eyes down to where Chase hangs his head. "But—"

Blood squirts from Miles as his words gurgle. A small dagger lodges in his neck. I have no clue where it came from, and from the shock crossing the alpha's face, neither does he. Chaos breaks out as our captors transform into wolves. I rub my palms together, trying to roll the ropes down my hands. If I work at it long enough, I might be able to free myself.

"Shit, Tristan. Brace yourself." Evander's voice cuts through the air, and he bucks, trying to block a tan wolf charging us. Another wolf crashes into it, and the two wolves roll and snarl, sending tufts of fur through the air as they tear into each other's coats.

I release a breath, peering around the small camp. At least ten wolves fight each other. Our only saving grace is that they consider each other the bigger threat. Clenching my jaw, I rub my hands together harder, loosening the ropes as they slide lower on my wrists. Evander groans, startling beside me. A wolf gets within biting reach, snatching his ankles. The thick rope blocks the wolf's teeth, and Evander kicks his legs up, knocking the wolf away.

Snarling, the wolf lunges again. It dodges Evander's kick and whips its head at me, sinking its teeth into my shin. I holler and thrash, the movement enough to drop the rope from my wrists. The wolf grabs the rope around my ankles, attempting to drag me. I clutch onto Evander, using him to hold on and fight the wolf as it tries to play tug-of-war.

A long spear whacks the wolf across its snout, and it whimpers and shakes its head, backing off. Someone throws a rock next, the baseball-sized stone enough to get the wolf to back up. My mind whirls. Fiery agony crawls up my leg.

"Tristan, hey. Tristan, look at me." Eliana's voice prods at my attention, but shadows crowd my vision. I think I black out from the pain. One second, I'm sitting on the ground, tied up by my ankles, and in the next, Davian hoists me up, holding my weight. Fuck, he's strong.

"Hustle your cute ass, Eliana. We gotta move. More wolves are coming." Adam's familiar voice hums in my ear. I blink a few times, trying to figure out what the hell happened. "You good, Davian?"

"Yeah, man. He's putting weight on his feet." Davian

adjusts his hand around my side. "You're doing good, Trist. The fucker bit your leg to make it easier to grab you. Suck up the pain and try to walk. They'll hunt us next."

Davian guides me forward, getting my legs to move. It's as if my body and mind finally connect and realize if I don't do as Davian asks, I'm a dead man. But fuck. I already might be one. I was bitten. Surviving a stabbing just couldn't be enough. Now this godforsaken island is testing me with a curse. I could turn into one of those beast things at any minute. I could turn on Davian and hurt him.

"One step at a time, Tristan. You got this." Davian practically carries me along.

"Fuck, incoming," Adam says, stepping in front of us. "Evander, the fuckers are out to bite. Use this. Keep them back from you and Chase."

"I've been bitten," Chase responds, coughing. "A white wolf."

Shit.

"Goddamnit!" Evander groans with his words. "What the fuck!"

I lose my footing, stumbling toward a tree. I try to brace on the trunk, but my leg gives out on me. I can't focus. I don't think I'm going to make it. I don't know if I should be terrified or relieved. Being one of these lykoswulves? What kind of life is that? Trapped on this island forever. Fuck that.

Several deep, guttural growls strike me to the core. I use

the tree trunk, trying to pull myself to my feet. A white wolf darts through the trees, blurring past me. I tighten my jaw, bracing for the beast to crash into one of the others. It skids past Eliana and circles her, its hackles rising on its back. Evander swings his makeshift spear, missing the wolf by inches. The gesture leaves him open, and a black wolf launches toward Evander, locking his jowls to Evander's arm. He flails, knocking the wolf away. Eliana screams out and jerks her arm. A blade sparkles on the ground in the soft sunlight bursting through the thinning trees. We're closer to shore than I realized. If we can make it to the beach, we can escape.

We have to. It's the only way.

Pushing away from the tree, I stumble toward Eliana and Adam. Davian catches me, locking his arms around my waist. Neither of us sees the wolf darting from the tree. A grey wolf lands on top of me. It growls in my ear, the vicious sound cooling my blood.

"Take his throat, Lou!" someone shouts. "Don't let Windshore get another asshole."

Windshore? That's the pack that had gotten to the others—who was supposed to take Tiffany.

"No!" Eliana screams. "Tristan!"

The wolf pounces harder on my chest winding me. My vision blurs, and a snarl cuts deeply through me. Pain shoots from my throat, zinging through the rest of my body as fangs sink into my flesh. Eliana screams again.

"Stand down! Go after Lagoon Hollow and Windshore. Don't let the bastards leave the territory," a deep, raspy voice snaps. It's the leader guy. "Ravi, get them to the border. All of them."

Someone steps over me. "You got it, brother."

My head swims with unfamiliar voices, but Eliana's soft prayer trickles through the discordant roar of growls, shouts, and my head pounding.

"Help your friend up, pup. You heard Sean. Now's the time to find your place." The man nudges me with his foot. "Looks like he might be okay but watch yourself. The rejection happens fast."

Adam shoves his hands under me, lifting me up. He meets my gaze, tightening his jaw. "Hey, man. It's going to be okay." Golden light flashes across his hazel eyes. Something's different. He looks as if at any minute, a wolf will burst free.

"Everyone move. Don't do anything stupid," Ravi says, coming into my view. "Tell them, princess." He grabs Eliana's hand, yanking her closer. She doesn't resist.

Her mouth quivers as she flicks her gaze to me. "Listen to him, okay? We're going to be okay."

If only she didn't sound unsure.

I don't think anything will ever be okay now.

The lykoswulves have won.

I can't move. Every muscle on my body aches. I don't know where I am, only that I'm not alone. Evander and Adam whisper from somewhere to my right. I can't understand them, but I hear them mention Kellan. Eliana, too.

"Tristan?" Eliana murmurs my name, her breath tickling my ear. I hadn't realized she was so close. "Tristan, here. Your lips are so dry. You need something to drink. I need you to keep your strength."

My strength? What do I need my strength for? I've already been captured. We all have. Now, we just have to wait to find out what the fuck they plan to do with us.

I don't argue though, because Eliana is right. I'm so parched that my lips crack when I open them. Her gentle hand coaxes me to sit up, and she offers me a glass of water. It's weird seeing her with one. She's changed her clothes as well, clean and free of any signs of the sandy beach shore. I flare my nostrils, catching the scent of her damp hair. It smells like pineapples and something warmer like vanilla. I don't think I've ever smelled something so incredible in my life.

She releases a breathy laugh. "Are you sniffing me?" Holding up the glass again, she waits for me to take a sip.

I try not to chug the whole thing, but the cool water is utter bliss to my mouth. Her golden eyes lock onto mine, and

I force myself to stop before I drink the entire thing and make myself sick. "Hell yeah, I'm sniffing you. You smell delicious."

She laughs again and pats my cheek. "I think you're going to be fine. Do you think you can get up? We don't have much, but there is a shower. I can help you."

"Unless you prefer me to scrub your smelly ass down," Evander says, sitting up from on the other side of Eliana.

It's now that I really look around.

I flick my gaze to Evander. "I knew you wanted to do that bullshit with me. What did it? Not seeing my cock all the time? You miss it?"

He tips his head back and laughs. "I'm just tired of your stench and figured I'd save Eliana from that nasty task."

Eliana shakes her head with a smile. "It's really okay. I don't mind. You need to rest as well. I think I'll be a bit more gentle."

"And when she's finished with you, I'll bandage your throat again." Chase shifts in the edge of my vision, and I spot him sitting by Adam and Davian.

We are in an actual room of some sort. Not a cave. Not some makeshift camp. This is a real bedroom with the bathroom and everything. There's even a window, and orange light glows from the crack in the curtain like the world outside might have been set on fire.

I clear my throat, trying to find my voice. "Where are we, anyway? What happened? Are we with Kellan's pack?"

Because if we're with Kellan, I want to kill him for taking Eliana and leaving us behind. He made it seem as if we could stay together and help each other, because apparently you need a female or some shit, but then he went and kidnapped her. It's when another boat came for us at the yacht.

"We are with the Sunset Pointe pack. They have taken us in temporarily to wait out the evening until the full moon." Eliana offers me her hand, but my body aches too much, and I don't want her to have to pick up my heavy ass.

She knits her brows together and shifts her hands under my arms, dragging me up to my feet, forcing me to put weight down on my legs. She's a lot stronger now. I'm nearly certain she wouldn't have been able to do that before. It must be the golden sheen flickering in her eyes. She was bitten too, after all.

My need to take care of myself outweighs my pain, and I tighten my jaw and limp across the small room into the bathroom. Eliana squeezes past me and flicks on the shower, setting the temperature hot enough to send steam through the air. She looks behind me and then quietly clicks the door closed. The second we are alone, she throws her arms around me and hugs me, not even caring that she buries her face into my dirty shirt.

"I'm so sorry, Tristan," she says, tilting her head back.

I furrow my brows, confusion swelling in me. "You don't need to be sorry for anything."

Her mouth trembles and tears sheen over her gaze. "I

misjudged Kellan. I thought we could trust him."

"How were you supposed to know? He was helping us." I reach up and push strands of her damp hair behind her ear. I want so badly to kiss her, but a part of me hesitates. I don't know where we stand. I might cross a line if I try.

She lifts and drops her shoulders, easing away from me and turning to the shower. Training her gaze to the stream of water, she adjusts the showerhead to my height and doesn't look at me when she says, "I don't know. I just...I don't know what we should do anymore. Everything is so complicated. I know that when the moon rises tonight, we're going to learn whether or not our bodies will accept the transformation."

"So some of us are fucked all over again." It's not a question. I know the answer. I close my eyes and inhale a slow breath, filling my lungs with the steamy air. It does nothing for my nerves. A part of me doesn't want to risk getting into the shower, leaving me exposed and vulnerable especially when I don't know exactly who this pack is. Another part of me knows that this might be my only chance, and I've missed taking hot showers. Missed soap.

Eliana closes the space again and hooks her fingers to the band of my filthy salt-crusted shirt. She helps lift it over my head and I wince as I shift my shoulder. My neck throbs, and I reach up and touch the bandages sticking to the wound.

"I thought the bastard was going to tear your throat out. I was so scared." Eliana grazes her fingers over my jaw, standing up on her tiptoes to get a better look at me. "This whole situation has been so fucked up. We need to figure it out. If we stay..." Her words trail off, and she busies herself by playing with the hem of my shorts. "We can't stay. What I have gathered so far is that whoever bites you has a claim on you. I don't know anything beyond that."

Realization hits me, and I stand utterly still as she slides my shorts down, careful not to rub them against the bite on my shin. "We've been bitten by different packs, haven't we?"

She motions for me to get in the shower, and I use her arm to help myself step in. "I think so. It's why that wolf tried to kill you. He didn't want another pack to gain a member. I don't think they procreate like humans do. At least, not completely."

"Because of the lack of females." I heard Kellan speak of it. Other wolves too. That's why he said we needed to have a female if we were going to make it through this. I guess it's some sort of test or some bullshit.

"Yeah, something like that. I'm sure we're going to learn shit soon enough. Ravi is only giving me another hour with you before I have to meet with him. It's why we're all here. I promised I'd give him a chance if he'd help all of us through the call of the moon. His pack leader wanted to abandon the rest of you guys." She reaches down and lifts up a bottle of soap, squirting it into her hand. I guess she is planning to take washing me seriously, and I can't stop the lust pouring through me despite her revelation. Ignoring my growing boner, she shifts me to face the shower stream, massaging her fingers into my hair and soaping up my dirty strands.

"I don't like it, Eliana. What if he tries something? We're going to be stuck in this room, aren't we? I don't think you should go. No answers are worth jeopardizing your safety." I turn around to face her, needing to see her face to gauge her feelings.

She meets my stare and touches my shoulder, carefully peeling away the bandage to look at the bite. "I'll be okay. Ravi won't hurt me. He thinks I'm his mate. We can use this to our advantage. It wouldn't be the first time I used my sex appeal for something. Don't worry about me. I've already decided that you guys are going to be part of my pack. You have to let me do whatever I can to ensure our safety and that we get off this fucking island."

Damn.

She does nothing to help kill my boner. Her words turn me on unexpectedly. I should be the one promising that. She dares me with her eyes to argue, her expression tight and prepared to argue right back. She's feisty, and I love it. I'm not afraid to submit to her.

If she wants to be my leader and control the situation, I'll gladly lie beneath her.

The thoughts send a shiver through me, and I bob my head, trying to ignore the pain flourishing across my throat. I turn back around without saying anything and stick my face in the water, rinsing off the blood and dirt and filth from being exposed to the elements then being bit.

Eliana gently uses her hands to massage soap into my skin, traveling over my shoulders and down my back. She rubs her hands over my arms and turns me around to wash my chest.

I've never experienced such bliss without returning anything, but she doesn't let me finish cleaning myself. She takes her time rubbing soap over every inch of me, including my fucking hard-on, teasing the hell out of me. She smiles as she does it, knowing exactly what she's doing, making it impossible for me to stand still.

I grab her before she gets to her knees and tug her up, meeting her for a kiss. Our lips brush each other's, and she smiles against my mouth, sliding her hands over my slippery body.

"If I didn't know any better, I'd think you'd like torturing me," I murmur, getting her clean clothes wet. She doesn't complain, entering the shower with me instead of making me stand in the cold air.

"Torture? I'm just taking good care of you." She bites her bottom lip, leaning up to kiss me again. If I couldn't hear someone arguing outside the door, I'd let myself get carried away on the emotions she elicits in me.

She sighs against my mouth and pulls herself away. Swiveling, she looks at the door and shakes her head. "He's here. Let me help you rinse off and get dressed."

I want so desperately to argue and stop her from putting herself in danger, but she looks ready to throw down if I try. It gives me the confidence to know that whoever this Ravi guy is will have one hell of a time trying to do anything she doesn't like. She looks ready to gut everyone against us.

Without another word, I finish rinsing off and allow her to join me, savoring the closeness and how this is the first time someone other than my family has put effort into ensuring I was okay.

"I want you to come up with a plan with the others. As soon as the full moon rises, and we face our fate, we need to be prepared." Eliana whispers the words into my ear, kissing me one more time.

"We'll figure this out." If only I had more faith in myself. Because right now, I'm lost. I'm lost and have no clue what will happen next.

A knock sounds on the door, drawing Eliana's attention away from me. "Princess, I've given you extra time."

Eliana squeezes her eyes shut. "Coming."

Ice blooms across my skin, watching her exit the small bathroom. The man, Ravi, gives me a long once-over without a word.

"You better fucking keep her safe," I say, clenching my fingers into fists.

He chuckles and shakes his head. "Worry about yourself, pup. I only promised my mate to help her through the transformation. I need you to prove yourself worthy."

He quickly closes the door, not letting me respond. The bang resonates through me, stealing my breath. I have to figure this shit out. The bastard is right. I'm doomed otherwise.

CHAPTER 23

Eliana

MOONBORNE

THE BRILLIANT SUNSET ignites the sky aglow with fiery colors. Ravi motions for me to join him on the ground, looking over a cliff where ocean stretches out endlessly. With the bright sun, the usual turquoise water appears gray, but it isn't any less beautiful.

"Tonight will be the hardest one for you. The full moon forces the change on everyone. It's the only time we don't have control to shift between wolf and human." Ravi stares at the side of my face, but I don't look at him.

I keep my gaze trained on the horizon, trying to figure out if what I see toward the east is land. Another island maybe.

"What you're looking at is Starrise Island. It doesn't belong to us." Ravi touches my leg, getting me to look at him. It's easy to forget that he can hear my thoughts as if they're his own. "But that is information for another time, princess. What's important is that you know what to prepare for tonight."

A dozen thoughts swirl through my mind. If it doesn't belong to the wolfpacks, then who does it belong to? I hate this. I hate not knowing. Fuck me. I don't even want to think about it.

"It's better if you do. You don't need to think about all of the other bullshit right now. Let's focus on you. On us and what to expect. The change will begin in a couple of hours when the moon rises high in the sky." Ravi traces his finger over my knee and works his way down until he reaches for my hand, my palm flat on the ground. I let him take my hand in his, the heat of his palm keeping the chill away.

"It's going to hurt, right?" I swallow with my question. Of course, It's going to hurt. I'm already hurting.

"I wish it didn't, but it won't last forever. The first forced change next month will be easier. You'll get used to it and perhaps even look forward to it." Ravi laces our fingers together, moving to get a better look at me since I keep staring at the horizon. I should feel better that he gives me answers without having to beg, but a part of me still hurts, feeling betrayed because Kellan made it sound far more complicated.

"Fucking great. I just don't understand why. Why did the packs kidnap us? I know you claim that you need more power or whatever, but I can guarantee that if you just asked people, I bet you could get a bunch of volunteers for this bullshit. Don't you think it'd be easier if they were willing?" Anger rushes through me at the thought, and I wonder what it would be like if I had been given the choice.

"The willing often fail. They are not as...creative. They don't know how to work together. They have too many weaknesses. We need those who are willing to fight to survive." Ravi tightens his jaw. "You can tell the difference. Look at those who survived your original group. There is one female left. The others perished. Those who took the easy way died."

I lift my eyebrows. "So Tiffany is alive?"

"You know she had originally made a deal with Windshore. I wanted to offer as much to you, but you made things rather difficult, princess." Ravi smirks with his words, not answering my question. "But I suppose it was proof enough, seeing as I still managed to claim you as mine."

He keeps stating that—that I'm his—as if I'm a piece of property to be owned. It reminds me of one client from my past. The one who thought that because he paid for many of my things that he could do what he wanted. It doesn't work like that though. Not for me, at least.

"There is a difference, Eliana. My claim on you lies on a different level. You're not my property, nor are you my slave. You're my mate. There is a difference." His voice deepens with his words, his response feeling more intimate.

I tilt my head and look at him. How can he be so certain? He feels a bond. I know it. I sense it myself. But I refuse to believe that one bite could just tie us together as mates. My brain would never allow such a thing. Relationships must be cultivated. They must be equal. And honestly, with how things are on this island, they must be earned.

"That is true in a sense. At least for the young pups you've seemed to collect. Originally, the packs had agreed to bring humans here and allow them to form their own alliances. But things are now complicated. There are many hungry for power and control. Our numbers are dwindling too quickly. Females stopped being born. Now it seems as if they only can be blessed by the moon if they're bitten. Except for you. Your lineage with Eleanor changes everything. You might not be able to shift yet, because Eleanor didn't mate with a lykoswulf, but it's in your blood. You were meant for this. You are meant for great things as my mate." Ravi leans closer to me, his eyes flicking toward my lips. The thought of kissing me crosses his mind. It awakens desire inside of me, but I try to ignore it. Now is not the time to let these unbidden emotions control me. I will not give him the satisfaction of seducing me. Not here. Not now.

I put space between us, shifting my body until I use his arm to rest against. He wraps it around my shoulder and pulls me closer, unfazed by my silent rejection.

"I think you have too many expectations for me. I don't want anything to do with your pack or you for that matter. I'm only here because you seem to be the lesser of all the evil on this island. I just want to make that clear." I shudder with my words.

"That might be the case now, but we will see where your ideas fall after the moon claims you. You need someone strong. You need someone who knows the ways of the lykoswulf. Because once the change happens, you're going to need me to not only protect you but teach you. You're going to need me to help those pups. You do realize that those who are not bitten by our pack cannot join us easily. They will be called upon by the alphas. And once they're in their wolf forms, they won't be able to resist." Ravi's words shock my heart, stealing my breath away. I never thought about how he offers refuge from the other packs control. If it's on a mental level, and strong enough to fuck with them already in their human forms, I'm afraid to find out what happens next.

"What are your expectations from me? I can't let that happen. I made them a promise I intend to keep." My heart raps in my chest, knocking against my ribcage and threatening to crack my bones in an attempt to throw itself free. Desperation makes my mind spin, and I blink my eyes, trying to stay calm.

"That's the thing. Sean has his ways, and he commands I follow through. Only Adam will be able to fight for a spot. But if you submit, I can challenge him. It will give me the strength to claim my rightful place. Your decision to be my omega and mate by choice will change everything. No other female can. Not with the impurities of being human-born." Ravi remains expressionless, turning his gaze to the horizon.

"That sounds weird. Why hasn't Sean kidnapped me and forced me to be...his omega?" It sounds so twisted, the idea churning my stomach. I can't help thinking about what the hell all of it even means.

"Lykoswulf alphas can't force an omega into submission. Such an act is a gift from the goddess, and you, as a chosen, can reject such a bond. Sean thought giving you to me would help him in the end. Me as your captor and he as your savior...because he wants to ensure you have no one left." Ravi grazes his thumb over the side of my hand. "He doesn't understand your connection to the pups. They're not worthy of you in his eyes and only worthy to serve."

I don't respond, letting the information sink in.

"If you agree to my terms, I'll ensure you never regret it. Those pups will have a place where other packs couldn't annihilate them. As your true and rightful mate, I will ensure they survive the night," he continues.

Again, I can't get my mouth to work to respond.

"Everything you do moving forward will be with me in

mind first. And when it's time to mate, you will allow me the honor." Ravi groans in his throat, his stipulations exciting him. "We will bear strong children. You will have protectors in the pups. But you have to agree and submit. Accept your place and embrace this offering."

I stare at the horizon in shock. He lost me at mating. He did not just say what I think he said. He will only help if I let him mate with me? What the actual fuck?

I shove him with my shoulder, pushing him away enough that I can get to my feet. I'm not humoring any sort of deal like that. Just a thought...I'm not a thing to be bred. I'm a fucking person and there's no way I'm going to bring a new life to this twisted world.

Ravi doesn't get up from the ground, letting me go. I hug myself, shaking the thought from my mind. As much as I want to help the guys, I can't agree to this. They would never agree to this either. There has to be another way.

"There is no other way. If you reject me, Eliana, my pack will not stand beside you. I will give Sean his way. You'll be on your own for the night. I must ask that you reconsider." His words swirl through my mind as he responds to my thoughts.

I peer at him from over my shoulder and raise my hand, flipping him off. I refuse to be manipulated like this. If his pack doesn't stand beside me, then they're against me. He's against me. If he truly thought that I'm his mate, he would try to help me regardless.

With a thought, I wonder about Kellan. He did help me regardless of things. And if Ravi was right about his stance in his pack, about being an infraborne, then maybe I should think things a little differently.

"That's not an 'if,' Ravi. I'm rejecting you. You can go fuck yourself." My voice shakes with my words. This is it. He was a safety net, but the force of my will is too strong, and I ripped through it, and now I freefall. I need to find something else to grab onto. Either that, or I need to learn to fly.

I need the power of the moon. The power of the men who will be part of my pack.

It's the only way.

Please, goddess. Don't let us down.

I peek through the crack in the curtain, staring at the empty meadow with thick trees acting as a barrier. I expected Ravi to chase me, but he let me go.

"We can't stay here. We need to figure out where else we can go. If we stay, someone will come for us and we'll be trapped." I bounce on my feet and close the curtain. Spinning around, I look at each of the guys. They look exhausted, frowning in pain, and as if they just want this all to be over. I can't blame them. So do I.

"We don't even know where we are. We could barricade

the door," Evander says, grabbing the small twin bed by the frame.

Chase stops him. "That's not going to work. They will just wait it out."

"Yeah, man. I don't want to make it easy on these fuckers. Anywhere is better than here. If we're about to go beastly, let's go somewhere open where no one can sneak up on us." Adam shuffles forward to me and peeks out the window next. "How much time did the asshole say we have?"

"Until the moon rises high in the sky." I shift and look toward the others. "He warned that it'll be painful and that whatever pack that bit us will call to us, which is something hard to ignore."

Davian scrubs his hands over his cheeks. "I'd rather die. You didn't hear them."

My chest clenches at the fear shaking his voice. I close the space to him, holding open my arms until he gives in and hugs me. He inhales a breath of my hair, nuzzling his nose to the crook of my neck. "I won't let that happen."

"Neither will I. We're going to get the fuck through this. Together." Tristan slings his arms around both of us, sandwiching Davian in the middle.

"Make some room. I need your guys' love too," Adam says, engulfing me from behind.

I laugh as Chase and Evander join our hug, and we just stand together, savoring the closeness of our new bond born from the need to survive and cultivated by time and companionship.

Tears burn my eyes, and I blink them away. "I want to make a pact. Whatever happens, we will do whatever is necessary to stay together. They can't win."

"They won't win," Chase corrects, easing away to allow us to separate.

"Damn straight. Just imagine the real doggy piles we can create as fucking wolves. Fucking wolves!" Adam ruffles his fingers through his hair. "It sounds a lot cooler when it's us turning rather than being hunted."

"As long as you don't sniff my ass," Evander mutters.

I tip my head back and laugh harder, watching the two of them playfully punch each other's arms. It helps ease the heaviness of what's to come. Just talking about things gives me enough hope to think we might actually get through this. I don't need Ravi. Nor do I need Kellan. All I need are these guys—my pack—who treat me as their equal but also with care.

"All right. The sun dipped into the horizon. Grab whatever you can carry. Anything can be a weapon with enough creativity." Adam rubs his palms together, looking around the room. "Same goes for sex toys." He winks at me with a huge-ass grin. The cute bastard. "And speaking of sex, want to help me break the bed, little badass?" Flicking his gaze to me, he wags his eyebrows. "We can practice for next time."

"We have to be quick, and if I'm getting on that bed with you—" I snap my mouth shut at the sound of the howls echoing outside.

Davian rushes past me and into the bathroom. Glass shatters and he holds a few shards in a towel. "We're out of time. Here. Grab something to hold these with until we can add them to branches. I want them to hurt."

"We all do." Evander uses a piece of glass to cut the towel enough to pull it into strips.

He hands each of us a piece while Davian passes them out.

Chase struts to the door first, cracking it open. I look outside over his shoulder, seeing the land surrounding the small building empty. I don't know exactly where this place is or what the Sunset Pointe pack uses it for, but they're not here now. Ravi had mentioned something about the moon forcing all of the lykoswulves to change. Maybe they have already gone into the forest, and now they lie in wait.

Ravi said he wouldn't help me through this, yet I know he hasn't gone too far. I doubt he will risk something happening to me with the moon. He just refuses to help the guys unless I give him what he desires. Which isn't happening...because fuck that.

"We need to follow the cliff's edge. It should lead to the beach." Adam scopes the area, sliding past Chase to exit the building first.

"If anyone feels any sort of pain besides what we already

experience, tell us immediately." Chase holds his hand to me, quietly asking me to stay by his side. I give in to his need, linking our fingers together. "It'll at least give us a small warning before things get real."

Tristan shakes out his hands and whips his messy hair back and forth. "I'm not looking forward to this shit. I already feel like death. I can't imagine it getting even worse."

I frown, popping out my bottom lip. "It's one night. We can do it." It sounds as if I'm convincing myself more than anyone else. Maybe I am. I'm scared. I don't want my body to break and crack and turn into a monstrous beast.

Evander comes up to my other side and takes my hand. We still haven't had the chance to talk after whatever happened with him in the cave, but I'm glad he doesn't ignore me now. I guess coming close to death gives people a reason to forgive or at least realize that there are more important things than a little jealousy.

"We need to protect Eliana at all costs. If the wolves get her, her fate will be far worse than any of ours. She is the most important." Evander squeezes my fingers, offering me a tight smile. He's trying to resonate bravery, but I can sense the fear working through him. It's strange, cold and palpable, almost as if it's my own.

I inhale a deep breath, pushing it away. "My life is no more important than yours. Don't do anything rash. I don't want you sacrificing yourselves on my behalf. Like I said before, we are in this together. We are going to be a pack."

Davian rests his hands on my shoulders, kissing my cheek from behind. "Our fearless leader."

If only I felt like it.

Without another word, we walk toward the cliff, keeping our distance from the edge yet traveling alongside it. The vast ocean, even though it's dark and foreboding, is really beautiful. A halo of light illuminates the island Ravi pointed out, making it look as if it glows in the dark. Starrise Island. It probably has even worse monsters than Shadow Moon.

"Everyone hold onto each other. It's time to start a bad bromance." Adam wiggles his fingers at Chase. "Come on, doc. You promised to protect me too. Consider this me putting out."

I can't stop the giggle escaping my lips. How Adam manages to joke despite everything? I wish I had that ability.

The eerie silence of the night kicks my heart into overdrive. It's too quiet. The wolves stop howling until we're left with the roar of the ocean and the pounding of our hearts.

"Eliana," two familiar voices say in unison, invading my mind.

"Brace yourself. Females feel the call first," Kellan says, his voice separating from Ravi's.

"Last chance." Ravi's warning resonates through me, overpowering Kellan's attempt to stay connected with my mind.

Muscle spasms rip through me, stiffening my body. My

legs give out on me, and if Chase and Evander weren't holding my hands, I'd hit the ground. The agony coursing through me makes it impossible to speak. I can't think. All I can do is cry.

"Fuck. It's happening. We need to move as fast as we can." Chase picks me up in his arms, cradling me. He whispers in my ear, his breath panting as he risks jogging down the steep terrain.

"The moon isn't even high yet. The asshole lied to her." Tristan growls with his words. "He probably set us up."

Adam clears his throat. "He didn't know it would claim her so suddenly. Their bond just alerted him. Pheromones or some shit. It's a wolf thing."

"It could be her lineage with the Crystalrock pack." Davian's voice pushes through the pounding in my head.

"How the hell do either of you know this?" Tristan asks.

The world shakes as Chase keeps his speed and his movements even out. I blink through my tears, my body spasming as imaginary fire licks across my flesh. I think we've made it to the beach, but I can't be sure.

Chase inhales and exhales, his heartbeat steady against my shoulder. "Ravi told us. He's in my mind. I think because one of his packmates bit me."

"Kellan told me," Davian adds, popping into view as he stands next to Chase.

"Damn it. This must mean I'm going to be hunted by a different pack, huh? What about you, Tristan? Do you hear anything yet?" Evander touches my cheek, moving my hair from my face.

"Nothing but silence. What if that means…?" He doesn't finish his question, and I realize he might be thinking if he doesn't hear what the others hear that maybe he won't transform.

The thought intensifies the pain rolling through me. I wish I could speak. I wish I could do anything other than just cry through the pain.

"Don't think about it. You haven't turned into one of those half-beast creatures. You're going to be fine. We're going to be a pack. Now, let's set up. We need to get close to the water. That should be the only thing we place our backs to." Adam disappears from view, and Chase lowers me to the sand.

"Eliana, can you hear me?" Chase asks, pulling me into his lap. He presses his fingers to my pulse point on my neck, counting in silence. I realize I can hear him in my thoughts too. I didn't think he was bitten by one of the Sunset Pointe pack-mates but he was.

"He shouldn't have been." Ravi's voice hums in my mind, and I do my best to shove it away. I don't want anything to do with him in this moment. "Don't be stubborn, princess. I know you're in pain. I will help you if you let me. I said I wouldn't help the pups. I'm here for you."

I ignore his words and rest my cheek against Chase's chest. I close my eyes, trying to concentrate on it. If I can think about something else, anything else, it might help with the pain.

"Do you remember what we did when we first met?" Chase asks, rubbing his warm palm over my arm, smoothing away my trembles the best he can.

The others move around the beach, but I can't see them. I can't open my eyes anymore. I don't have the strength. I can't even move my head to respond silently to Chase.

"You don't have to respond to me physically. I can hear your voice in my head now. It's as if a door has been open between us. I guess that's what happens when an alpha bites you." Chase uses telepathy to communicate with me.

"Did he say an alpha? Sean bit him?" Ravi tries to sneak back into my thoughts. Once again, I shove his voice away.

"I want you to listen to my voice, Eliana. Feel the connection we share. I want you to inhale and exhale with me. On my count. Inhale. One. Two. Three. Exhale. One. Two. Three." Chase breathes with his counting, encouraging me to join him.

I do, sucking in a long breath only to blow it out.

"Now, I want you to try to open your eyes. I want you to look at me. Focus on me." Chase touches his fingers to my eyelids, smoothing my pinched brow.

It takes everything in me to do as he asks, and I flutter my eyes open, gazing into the beautiful depths of his dark eyes. He offers me a smile and leans in, nuzzling his nose to mine. He's close enough to kiss me, but he doesn't. Instead, he just takes up my view of the world, so he's the only thing I can see.

"Tell them to move, my love. My pack is nearing you. Please, you can't fight them. You have to run." Kellan's voice snaps through me, and I startle at the desperation cascading through me, his emotions feeling as if they're my own.

I don't get a chance to do anything. Chase tenses, lifting me back up into his arms.

"You fucker! You're a traitor!" Davian shouts, his words ringing through the air. "You said we had a minute. Your pack is here."

Confusion rushes through me. I think he is talking to Kellan.

"Those pups better prove themselves worthy, princess. That's not Twilight Cove. It's Crystalrock. They don't know about their traitor. They think you still belong to them because of Eleanor." Ravi's words flood my mind, but I can't push them away this time.

A wolf snarls and charges in our direction.

My head spins, and I feel as if I'm going to be sick.

I hang limply in Chase's arms, watching as Evander and Davian go after the wolf.

Another wave of agony blurs my vision.

Another wolf barrels from the tree line.

This is it. This is the fight we've been waiting for.

CHAPTER 24

Eliana

SUBMIT

"OPEN YOUR MIND to me, Eliana. Let me give you my strength." Kellan growls in my mind, yet he doesn't show himself. "I'm coming."

As if I can't resist him, my body relaxes and the edges of my vision clear. The pain doesn't subside but it feels as if I manage to disconnect enough to focus on something else. A wolf screeches, and I spot Tristan jabbing his makeshift spear into its side.

Blood stains the sand, yet the wolf doesn't give up. It snaps its teeth, locking its jaws onto Tristan's spear. Evander takes advantage of the situation and stabs the wolf again, dropping it to the sand.

"We'll kill all of you! Leave us alone. Eliana is ours!" Adam yells, swinging his branch, knocking the other wolf back. "She has been claimed by Sunset Pointe. Any act against us is an act against their pack."

"Smart little bastard." Ravi mutters, his voice growing louder in my mind. That, or I'm growing weaker.

The wolf responds to Adam with a long, low howl. Another wolf howls from the trees, and the wolf vanishes. I can't believe they backed off.

"Not for long. They're just regrouping and talking to their alliances." Ravi refuses to get out of my head. I wish he would speak to someone else instead. I can't communicate with the guys. I can't do much of anything as another bout of pain crashes through me.

I think I black out.

One second, I was in Chase's arms, and in the next, Tristan cradles me. Fear clenches my chest, and I thrash, my mind refusing to cooperate with my body. Cracks sound through the air, and I feel something inside me pop. I scream, the agony intensifying. And then I see it. My fingers curl in, cracking and breaking, the transformation deforming my body. Horror leaves me reeling. I can't believe this is really happening. The moon calls to my very being, forcing my body into a beastly state. Fur sprouts along my forearms, and a guttural, wet noise escapes my mouth. I can see my nose changing, my face aching as if someone punches me.

"Shit. Shit. Shit." Tristan chants the words, locking his arms around my writhing body tighter. "What do I do? She's changing."

"Just keep holding her. Watch her teeth. She might try to devour you or some shit. We don't know if she'll keep her humanity as a wolf." Adam stays out of my view, and I listen to the world around me, trying to focus on anything else to distract me as I turn into the strange creature. The last thing I expected in my life was to be kidnapped and brought to an island. But turning into a lykoswulf? It's unthinkable.

"Davian? Davian, can you hear me?" Chase's voice swirls through the air, and I realize that he handed me to Tristan because Davian now lays flat on his stomach in the sand. His back arches, and I spot coppery fur tearing through his clothes.

"We're not going to fucking make it out alive." Evander growls with his words, his voice stabbing me right in my soul.

More howls call through the air, the cacophonous sound the most terrifying melody I've ever heard. It's even worse than the screams of the unlucky. It's worse than the cries for mercy. Because the howls come from those out to get us. Those hunting us in an attempt to stop the other packs from claiming new packmates.

Tristan groans deep in his throat, and the world drops out from under me. I crash to the sand, landing on my belly, and I stare at the two mahogany-colored paws burying in the sand. Holy fucking shit. That's me. These two appendages were once my arms, but now they're part of some freaky-ass monstrous beast.

I wish I had a mirror to see my reflection. I can't get over how long my nose has become. The world shifts in color, the dark sky brightening and the ocean turning from gray to blue as if the sun rises. I see colors unlike anything I've ever experienced, the ethereal sight leaving me senseless.

I'd continue to stare at the beauty of the world around me if Adam didn't holler. His voice whips through me, lashing my spirit, and I jerk my attention to where he kneels in the sand, transforming before my eyes.

"You better get your ass up, princess. It's time to run." Ravi's voice sounds as if he sits next to me, but he's not here. He's nearby though, being a complete asshole and refusing to help the rest of my group. He's out of his mind if he thinks I'm going to just leave them.

"Fuck you. Leave me alone. If you're going to stand by like an infraborne, you're not worthy of making such demands of me." My words resonate through me.

Ravi growls, his voice reverberating through my bones. He materializes in the tree line, staring at me from a couple feet away. I knew he was a stalking asshole. His white wolf form glides forward like a phantom in the night. His eyes shine golden, and he bares his teeth. I expect him to pounce on me and try to force me into submission, but he watches over me instead and crashes into another wolf, trying to sneak up on me from behind.

The two wolves roll, snarling and biting, sending fur flying through the air. I force myself up, my new form stupid-complicated to get used to as I try to stand on two legs, the task impossible. It feels awkward as hell being this low to the ground. My wolf body trembles, but at least the agony subsides, leaving an annoying ache in its place.

I stumble forward, landing on my belly again. I need to figure this shit out and fast. The others need me. They all remain in various states of transformation, the process taking longer than I had expected. It may be my lineage that gave me an advantage. But is that enough to make up for the bullshit that comes along with my grandmother's bloodline? Absolutely not. Too many of these assholes think that my sole purpose in life is to breed power. All I feel like doing is destroying it. I want to sink my teeth into anyone who tries to get in my way.

I'm nobody's omega. I'm nobody's supposed mate.

A whimper catches my attention, and I crawl closer to Chase and Davian as they wriggle through the pain. I press my pink nose into Davian's coppery fur, nudging him from his back and onto his side. Pain explodes at my backside, and something drags me a couple feet by my—Fuck. I have a tail.

This is some other bullshit.

Jerking around, my wolf form releases an automatic growl, and I snap my teeth at a hulking grey wolf twice the size of Kellan. The wolf snaps back, grabbing onto the scruff of my neck and swinging me away. I don't even know how to use my legs. I roll a couple times until a wave crashes over me, and I find myself floundering in the ocean.

"Rocco! Stop! Don't do this." Kellan's words whirl through my mind, but I can't see him anywhere.

Teeth lock onto the back of my neck, and the wolf drags me from the waves. I blow out water through my nostrils, unable to orient myself. I can't think, let alone fight, and it gives this giant grey wolf an advantage.

"She was supposed to be mine. I cannot have a she-wolf tainted by the bite of the Sunset Pointe pack. They took her from me, so I will take her from them." The snarly voice ignites panic inside me. This is Kellan's alpha. He's the one that Kellan has been disobeying when he was helping me.

"Please, Rocco. She's my soulmate." Kellan's desperation ties around my heart, squeezing it.

"Infraborne don't have soulmates! They don't have mates at all." Heavy paws slam into my side, pinning me down. My survival instincts kick on, and I thrash, trying to roll out from beneath this monster wolf.

"Rocco—" Kellan's voice cuts off at the same time another grey wolf appears.

The weight of his alpha vanishes off me, and I force my paws to work, lifting myself up in the sand. Pain radiates through me, but it's not my own. Kellan's alpha and another wolf go after him, snarling and ripping at his fur, trying to force him into submission and to back down.

I spot more wolves coming from the trees and heading in the direction of Evander and Tristan. I think they might belong to the packs that bit them, and now they're coming to take them away.

I can't let it happen.

It takes everything in me to pad my way forward, moving through the sand. It slows me down, doing nothing to help my wobbly legs. A tan wolf grabs onto Tristan, biting him on the back of the neck. He's not even done transforming yet, and I see blood seep from the wound.

Rage rises through me, pushing me forward, and I surprise the tan wolf by jumping into his side. He growls and snaps his jowls, biting onto my front leg.

I screech, my wolf releasing a high-pitch, pathetic noise. I feel a disconnection to my body. I know this wolf is me, and I'm her, but it's as if my humanity refuses to accept that I'm now moon chosen. I'm a damn wolf shifter. Lykoswulf.

But I'm not a female to be bred.

I will be my own leader.

A deep, vicious snarl echoes through the world, and the tan wolf doesn't see Davian's coppery form. He's completed his transformation, his new wolf body incredibly stunning. I've never seen anything his color, his fur sparkling in the strange light created from the moon. Latching his teeth onto the tan wolf, Davian shoves him into the ground, trying to pin him. The wolf fights back, and I push to my paws and join Davian, using my weight to keep him down so Davian can tear out his throat. I never thought I'd be such a savage. I never expected to be capable of ending a life. But here I am, my body count stacking up. I can't even recall how many people I have killed since arriving here. I wish this was it. I wish this would just stop.

"Davian. Eliana. He's dead. Come on. We need to run." Chase nudges his black nose into the side of my face. "Wolves took Evander."

Fear resonates through me, and I whip my attention around, staring at the beach. Adam and Ravi team up and chase off another wolf. It's the strangest thing seeing them work together. I don't know if it's because Adam is considered part of the pack or what, but I don't like it. I don't like seeing him with Ravi.

A screech booms through the air, and I swivel and catch sight of Rocco crashing into Kellan again. My wolf whimpers, my whole body turning cold. I thought I hated him. I want to hate him for not giving me answers and for keeping things from me. But a part of me doesn't believe that he did it with ill intentions as I previously thought. I realize that because of his position in the pack, he was afraid. Because they obviously don't believe that infrabornes deserve to pass on their genes or some shit.

And now this bastard alpha plans to kill who he considers the weakest member of his pack.

"Go after Evander. I need to help Kellan." The command comes easily enough, and shock rolls through me as Chase and Tristan obey.

"Restrain her for me, my pup. You're now Twilight Cove's infraborne." Rocco's rumbly voice shocks me. His words aren't intended for me though. They're intended for Davian.

It's now that I realize why he hasn't left or obeyed me.

Davian bares his fangs, releasing a low growl. His body trembles, and he slowly steps forward. I can't do anything as he bows in his wolf form, giving in to the alpha without a fight. And holy shit. The strange disconnect cuts through me, and whatever I felt from Davian before vanishes. With his bow, he will no longer be able to resist the command of his pack alpha. Not now. Not like this. I'm no longer of influence.

Jerking around, Davian crashes into me, planting his big paws on my chest. I snarl and whip my body, biting into the fur on his chest, trying to break away.

"Davian. Davian, get a hold of yourself. Don't do this. This isn't you. We are part of a pack, remember?" I think the words, trying to send them to Davian through a mental link.

He doesn't respond. He doesn't move.

I don't want to hurt him, but I don't want to die either. And the Twilight Cove alpha plans to kill me. That's his way of getting back at the Sunset Pointe pack for stealing me out from under them. I was promised to Twilight Cove by the Crystalrock pack after all.

"Bring her here. She will watch as you kill this traitorous bastard," Rocco says, the dark eyes of his wolf staring at me as if I'm his prey.

"I'm sorry, Eliana." The softness of Davian's voice hurts me more than his teeth grabbing me by my neck.

I buck my body, trying to break free of his hold. I feel like a small puppy getting carried around. His wolf frame is twice the size of mine, and he easily drags me forward no matter how much I fight. I can't swing my body close enough to bite him.

Davian only releases me when Rocco grabs me with his teeth next, slamming me to the ground and pouncing on my side, pinning me in place.

I meet Kellan's bright blue eyes, his wolf whimpering with blood staining the white parts of his coat.

"Davian, please. Please don't do this. Remember who you are. You're not some feral animal. You're a human. You are from the human world. Don't give in to your beast. You don't have to do this. Please." I whimper with my words, my wolf crying with my deep distraught. It's as if a part of me dies even though I continue to live.

"Do it. Do it now," Rocco snaps, pounding his paws

against my ribs.

I howl in pain, struggling to breathe in my new form with the weight of his body crushing me. I expect Ravi to come rushing to my side, but he doesn't. I don't know where he is. I don't know where the others have gone chasing after Evander. They didn't know that Davian would fall victim to the call of his alpha so suddenly. I didn't know that either.

Rocco snarls. "Now!"

"Davian, no!" The words whip from me with a bark, the noise wild enough to strike strength into Kellan. He manages to shift his body, but he can't get to his feet. I bark again, thrashing, putting up a fight. I will not submit to this beast. I will not allow him to treat me like this or let him hurt Kellan. "You need to fight with me, Kellan. Davian is lost. You need to fight. You need to turn your back on the Twilight Cove pack. I will take you as my own. But you have to fight. Prove to me you're worthy of a bond. Fight!"

Rocco swings his big head down, locking his teeth to my neck. Pain seers across my body, but instead of incapacitating me, it jolts me into action. I whip my head and snarl, snapping my teeth, trying to bite him anywhere I can. He stumbles, my movements knocking his big paws away, and he automatically releases me. I manage to snag his front paw with my teeth, and I bite as hard as I can. I won't let go. Someone is going to have to pry me away or kill me. This alpha is not in control. I'm not a thing for him to claim or discard. I'm moon blessed and goddess chosen. I accept the call of the moon. I accept this fate.

Growls sound around us as Kellan and Davian fight, and Kellan manages to get to his feet. He locks his jaw onto Davian's neck, tearing at his flesh. But he isn't intent on killing him. He's trying to slow him down.

Rocco drags me around, thrashing his body while snarling and sinking his teeth into my side. I still refuse to let go. I know if I do, I'm a dead wolf. I will never be able to escape this island. I will have let my guys down. My pack. I will have wasted my grandma's efforts, and I will prove that I'm not worthy of her lineage.

I refuse to believe it. If she could do this, so can I.

Kellan breaks away from Davian, charging toward us. Rocco whips his attention to Kellan, leaving himself open to me. He grabs Kellan by the throat and bites down hard enough to silence the growls escaping his mouth. My vision crowds with pain. Kellan's pain.

It's enough to get me to release Rocco's paw, but I don't let him get far. I knock into him, sending both him and Kellan rolling. I do the only thing I can think of. I bite down on his back leg, sinking my teeth not only into his thigh but also into his balls.

He yelps, his wolf wailing with a screech. He spins around, snarling at me, but he freezes. He doesn't attack. Instead, he rushes away and runs toward the trees. I sink to the ground, exhaustion grabbing hold of me. I know I need to get up. I know I need to keep fighting.

"Little badass, fuck." Adam's voice trickles into my mind, wrapping around me.

"Let me through." Ravi's giant form stands over me, and he nuzzles his wolf snout into my neck, he glides his tongue over my fur, licking my wounds as if he can suddenly heal me. He releases a deep growl. "Get the traitor."

Fear clenches my heart, and I whimper, peering at Davian and Kellan. "Please. Don't."

As if my words ignite something inside Davian, he launches to his feet and runs toward the trees. I stare at the empty spot where he was, seeing the blood staining the sand.

"Adam, you have to go after him. We promised." I think the words to Adam, trying to see him past Ravi, but Ravi blocks his way.

"He has made his decision. You must let him go. You're too young to face the Twilight Cove pack alone." This comes from another guy. I think it's Sean. It's strange how I can sense it.

A couple of new voices sound through my mind as the quiet murmurs of the men circle around me. It wasn't only Adam and Ravi to scare off Rocco. It was the entire Sunset Pointe pack. They only interfered because they had to. They weren't going to let me die.

But it's kind of late for that. A part of me already has. I don't think that part of me, the human part of me, will ever be revived again.

"We need to take care of the infraborne. He is of no use to us," Sean says, his muscular wolf form stepping over me as if I'm just some sort of obstacle in his way.

I whimper, my whole body aching. "Please, don't."

Sean snarls at my pleas.

He ignores me completely.

Ravi drags me by the scruff of my neck, pulling me away as the Sunset Pointe pack surrounds Kellan.

My heart breaks.

Even Adam and Chase join them.

I guess I was stupid to think I'd have a pack.

I have no one.

And I realize now that being alone just isn't enough. I'll never be enough.

CHAPTER 25

Eliana

MANIPULATION

"IF YOU EVER want me to consider you as a mate, stop them. Please. He helped me." I struggle beneath Ravi as he pins me, not taking me far. "He rejected his pack…for me. Please. Don't let them do this."

"You know my terms, princess." Ravi releases me, towering over me with his hulking frame.

I'm going to kill him. I've never wanted someone's blood

so badly on my hands. He could help but instead he tries to manipulate me into doing something unthinkable.

Kellan shrieks in his wolf form, his human voice yelling through my mind. I gasp with his pain. He might have been right all along about our soul bond. Everything he feels, I feel. It's as if I experience what he does.

Jerking my head, I snap my teeth, catching Ravi's leg. He growls and leans down, nipping my ear. I shake my head, using my body weight to yank his paws out from under him. We roll together, and I break free and rush the circle of wolves, taunting and torturing Kellan, taking their time to end him.

"Chase! Adam! You need to resist!" I shout, projecting my thoughts. "Stop! You're better than this!"

I bound forward, my fear for Kellan boosting my energy. I feel stronger with my desperation. More vicious. I'll rip Sean to pieces if I have to. I'll destroy them all. Jumping with my hind legs, I crash into him. My world spins as he whips around and locks his teeth to my fur, flipping me onto my back before I can react.

Ravi growls, snapping his fangs at Sean, threatening him. "Handle the pack. I will remind her of her place."

Sean bows, snarling in my face. "I will handle both."

My heart races at his words. "Ravi, please! Please! Make them stop. I'll be your mate. I'll do what you want. Please, just make them stop. Call them off."

A loud laugh echoes through my mind, the creepy noise

coming from Sean. He bares his fangs, the gesture terrifying. He ignores Ravi's warning growl, peering into my eyes. Panic ignites inside me. I can't fight. I can't think. All I can do is lie docile beneath him, praying to the universe that he doesn't destroy me.

"I think you're mistaken about who you need to beg," Sean says, his grumbly voice striking me as if he bites my soul. "I'm your alpha."

I heave a breath through my nostrils, my heart thudding in overdrive. His comment feels more like a command as if his very being wants to put me in my place even though he hasn't done anything yet. Ravi had mentioned that Sean was growing weak. He had a plan because only alphas can claim omegas. He doesn't think Sean is worthy of his position any longer, but he needs me. He needs me to bow and to bear power with him in the form of offspring.

Sean doesn't notice.

Maybe this is what I need. I can bow to Ravi and offer him empty promises. It might cause enough tension to give me a chance to fight. It could give me a chance to get Adam and Chase to snap out of whatever hold Sean has on them. It could help me save Kellan.

I never thought I would bow. I never thought I would hit my breaking point.

But as my body breaks and changes, I realize that it isn't the end. Broken things can be fixed. Broken things can create even better more beautiful possibilities. I might be broken, but I can rebuild myself stronger than ever. Something that wouldn't have been possible had I never fallen apart.

"You are not my alpha." I think the words to Sean, channeling my strength and anger from this fucked up situation. "You won't grant me mercy. You have nothing to offer me. But Ravi? He is an alpha. My body and soul recognize his strength over yours. This is why I accept you, Ravi. I will exist for you as your intended mate. I will bow and acknowledge that you are my alpha. I offer my life and future to you."

Sean snarls, baring his teeth and jerking his head down. I brace for him to bite me. I brace for him to tear my throat out. But Ravi expects it. Sean doesn't even get within an inch of my exposed body. Ravi launches at him, knocking him off of me. I scramble up, darting around the two wolves fighting. Fur flies through the air, and the rest of the pack grows restless, growling and barking and howling. They turn their attention away from Kellan.

This is my chance.

I might have offered my loyalty and my future to Ravi, but he's going to have to catch me first.

Dodging around the wolves, I rush to Kellan and shove my snout beneath him, forcing him to get to his paws.

The two wolves crash past me, and I watch as Ravi tears into the throat of Sean. Blood soaks his white snout, staining it red. Sean stumbles in his wolf form, trying to drag himself away, but Ravi doesn't let him.

"I don't want to kill you, Sean, but you're no longer fit to be our alpha. You do not see things as clearly anymore." Ravi growls and snatches Sean by the scruff of his neck again.

"You will fail. You are not worthy." Sean's voice resonates through my mind as he projects it to the pack. "If you bow to him, it will be your undoing. He is not your intended alpha. I a—"

Snarling, Ravi sinks his teeth into Sean's throat, biting down so hard that it cuts off the guttural noises escaping the alpha. And he doesn't release him. Sean's body stops fighting, going placid. This is the end. He's going to kill him.

This is my last opportunity.

I need to get the others and run. This might be our only chance. I have to take it. I have to risk it.

"Chase. Adam. Come on," I think to them, barking in their direction. The sound of my voice weirds me out, but it feels so natural. I feel natural in this form now that my limbs finally cooperate, and my body, mind, and soul align in harmony.

Chase and Adam don't respond to me. They don't even look at me. Their gazes remain focused on Ravi fighting against their alpha. One of them will have to win, but I don't want to find out who will rise.

Kellan nudges his head into my side, pushing me away. "We'll have to come back for them after the moon sets. They won't be of any use right now."

I think he's right. I hate that he is. I don't know what I was expecting, but a deep ache cuts through me, knowing that Chase and Adam might be lost to me. Davian, Evander, and Tristan too. I have failed them. We were supposed to fight together. Stay together. Get off this fucking island together. But now? It feels as if this island will never let us go. The packs will never stop hunting us. I will never be able to create my own pack and future to my liking.

"My love, don't give up hope just yet. I'm your mate, and I will help get our pack together as you desire." Kellan whimpers with his words, nudging me again, getting my paws to cooperate.

"I want to believe you. You have no idea how badly I do, but I don't trust you anymore, Kellan. You have had so many chances to give me answers. We wouldn't be in this position if we had the chance to be better prepared." It hurts to say the words, but I need to be honest. I can't just run with him, allowing him to think that because I saved his life that it means I have forgiven him. I haven't. I don't even know if I can.

"I understand, Eliana. The way of the wolves leaves a lot for you to long for. I can't promise that I can change overnight, but I will prove myself worthy of you." Kellan's words touch me deeply, and that I do believe.

I know he has it in him. I know that people can change, but only if they want to change themselves. No one else will do it for them. And whether or not I can stand by to watch the metamorphosis of him learning how to be on a team is another story. I guess we have to survive the rest of the night first.

"That's all I ask of you. Give me a chance," Kellan adds, herding me with his body, getting me to navigate between two trees.

Neither of us sees the wolf coming until it's only feet away. Kellan snarls and lunges, but the black wolf lands on top of me. I wiggle my body, rolling and kicking. Snapping my teeth. Doing whatever I can to get this fucker off me.

Kellan charges the wolf, knocking him away. Anger rushes through me. Without thinking, I give into my wild instincts to protect Kellan and lock my teeth onto the black wolf's back leg. It growls with a shriek, trying to whip around to bite me, exposing its throat to Kellan.

He bites the wolf hard, pinning him to the ground. Something dark and fatal grabs a hold of me, and I sink my teeth into the wolf's neck, now out for blood. I want nothing more than to kill him. It's as if I crave murder. It's dark and twisted and tangles around my very being, stealing whatever humanity and light and goodness I have left in me. But it takes a monster to survive Shadow Moon Island. It takes someone wild and feral to be a wolf. To accept the gift given by the lunar goddess. It takes someone vicious and strong to be a lykoswulf. To be an alpha. And I realize that's what I want to be. I crave the power. I deserve it. Maybe that's the reason my grandmother was able to escape the island. She knew she had a better purpose. A bigger purpose.

I just need to fight for it. I need to win.

"Stand down, princess. Release the Blackshell's betaborne. He will be mine to destroy." Ravi's voice shocks sense into me, and I automatically ease away from the wolf.

Something strange comes over me, and I back off and comply.

What the actual fuck?

The need is unreal. It's as if his closeness awakens a part of me that I never knew existed. The previous fight I had diminishes, and now all I can think about is how I want to give Ravi whatever he wants. Whatever he needs.

Oh fuck.

It's the call of the alpha. Of my alpha

It's because I submitted to him.

My wolf form decides to obey him, to fall into line. Except my mind refuses. I'm better than this. But why won't I fight?

"Eliana, I will come back for you, but I can't stay. Your soul bond weakens to me." Kellan's words stab me in the heart, sending my mind reeling. "I didn't know that you had already had a strong enough bond to Ravi to accept your place as his omega. And it seems...he is now the new pack leader of Sunset Pointe. You won't be able to come with me. I'm sorry I failed you. I'm sorry I was too weak to fight and you found yourself in this position. But I thank you. You saved my life, my love. I promise I will save yours."

Growls resonate through my bones, and I turn my attention toward the forest, spotting the rest of the Sunset Pointe pack lurking and stalking their way in our direction.

"Kellan, you have to go. Go now!" I scream, my voice echoing through my mind. Because this fight with the Sunset Pointe pack isn't over. They don't truly know their place yet, just as I don't know mine. They want Kellan dead. Even though I bowed to Ravi, and even though it was in exchange for Kellan's life, I don't trust anyone anymore. I feel safer with him away.

"Be brave, Eliana. Things will become more clear." Kellan nudges me with his snout and spins around, darting away and into the trees. He is now packless and alone, and my soul weeps for him. I feel all over the place, my body and mind at war, yet this is only the first battle. And right now? My body wins. My wolf wins. The moon and the curse, and the Sunset Pointe pack win.

"Everyone stand down and let him go. He won't wander far, and I need to decide whether he's worthy of Sunset Pointe." Ravi's words lace around me, pulling my attention away from the last place I saw Kellan.

The wolves relax, turning their attention away from the forest and back to Ravi. I remain in my place, watching him as he watches me, and it feels as if everything fades away to where it's just me and him and his steely gray eyes. Eyes that suddenly penetrate my soul. Eyes that capture me in a way I will never be able to escape.

"Come closer, Eliana. Let me get a good look at you to make sure you're okay." Ravi doesn't move from his spot, demanding that I come to him instead.

My legs move automatically, my paws thumping the dirt with each of my steps. The wolves spread out, circling us, caging me in as if they think I'll try to escape again. But I'm not going anywhere. It's as if my very soul clings onto Ravi, and he's the one that will never be able to escape me.

Ravi inhales a breath, sniffing his way from my neck and down the side of my body, inch by inch, inspecting me in my wolf form.

I automatically lie on the ground and roll over, exposing my stomach to him. My body hums, a strange wave of energy crashing through me. The longer he shows me attention, the better I feel. I catch a hint of his scent, the sweet yet warm fragrance igniting something hot inside me.

Fuck me.

I shouldn't be so compliant. I shouldn't like the attention he gives me. But I can't separate myself from the nature of my wolf or the bond I created from bowing.

"My beautiful she-wolf. I will ensure we have an incredible life together. I know you still cling to your humanity, and a part of you might resent me right now, but it won't last forever. You will see. Now come on. The moon will set soon, and I want to take you home." Ravi nudges me with his big head, getting me to flip back to my belly. He herds me, getting me to stroll with him until he takes the lead.

"Bring our fallen alpha. We will spend the day mourning our loss," Ravi says, tipping his wolf head back and releasing a low howl.

He's fucking crazy, acting as if he truly cares. He murdered Sean for power.

Ravi whips his attention and looks at me. "I didn't kill him. He failed us as alpha and he refused to accept any other place. I did it for you. I did it for the pack. Don't try to make me the enemy, Eliana. It's because of me that Kellan is alive."

He puffs a breath of air through his nostrils, turning back to the forest. I hang my head, my wolf form refusing to respond back. I give in to the call of the moon and the call of my new alpha.

Shadow Moon Island might have taken my humanity, but it hasn't taken my strength. It hasn't taken my will to escape.

And this isn't the end.

The lunar goddess has blessed me, giving me more power than I could ever imagine. I will prove my worth. I just might have to bide my time.

My life starts here and now.

I will get the guys back and create my own pack. I won't be this omega forever. Ravi hasn't proven anything. He hasn't proved his worth as my alpha.

But I have proved it to myself.

I will lead.

I will rise like the morning sun, banishing the moon and the night.

My wolf will break free.

EPILOGUE

Eliana

TRUE ALPHA

PAIN RADIATES THROUGH me, and I roll to my side and stare at the empty meadow in front of me. I'm nearly certain this is what it would feel like getting hit by a bus. Every inch of me feels bruised though my skin remains smooth and even in tone. My muscles burn as if I've been working out. I'm also completely naked. Fuck. Where is everyone? The last thing I remember is the moon setting. I remember Ravi circling me and encouraging me as my body shifted and transformed back into a human.

I remember swearing at him and sending him away. I remember watching him leave, thinking that it must've been a joke, but he listened to me. And I guess I fell asleep.

"Eliana..." the familiar voice whispers my name, and I peer around the meadow to see Chase sitting on the ground a couple feet away.

He's dressed in clean clothes, looking hotter than ever. If I hadn't known any better, I'd think he was never a part of this. I'd think maybe we were in some sort of weird-ass dream.

Chase combs his fingers through his soft hair, the strands sparkling in the sunlight bursting through the thinning trees. Colorful flowers bloom in bunches around the green grass, and I spy the turquoise ocean, sprawling into the horizon.

"Here, let me help you. I've been tasked with watching you while our pack handles a couple things. I would have covered you, but Ravi didn't want me touching you while you slept." Chase clears his throat and grabs the folded blanket from beside him. He crawls closer as if he's already used to being on his hands and knees from his wolf form, and he wraps a blanket over me, covering me up.

I shiver at his closeness, a strange scent wafting through the air like an intoxicating cologne. Notes of citrus and sugar mingle with the freshness of the sea, and I inhale a deep breath.

"You smell incredible," I murmur.

Chase chuckles and touches my cheek. "So do you."

I tip my head back and laugh. "Yeah, right. I'm filthy."

"A little dirt never bothered me." Chase helps me up, smiling at me.

It feels as if last night never happened. If I close my eyes, I can forget the night happened and that I'm naked because of something else, not that I transformed into a wolf. Holy fuck. I'm a wolf.

"And the most beautiful woman I've ever seen," Chase thinks to me, his voice mingling in my mind. "If only I hadn't let you down. I'm sorry, Eliana. I tried to resist. It was as if I couldn't do anything by my own freewill."

Tears burn my eyes, but I don't let them fall. Instead, I throw my arms around Chase and bury my face into the crook of his neck. I can't help myself from kissing his throat, needing desperately to distract myself. Fear crashes through me, and there's nothing I can do about it. I can't just go running into the forest without a plan in search of the others. Fuck. Evander, Davian, and Tristan are out there somewhere. They could be experiencing complete and utter torture.

"Stop. They are strong, and they will be okay, just as we are. We will find them. We just need to figure shit out here. Adam is currently with Ravi. He is going to learn everything he can for us. Anything we can use." Chase groans next to my ear, tilting his head to meet my eyes.

I dart my gaze to his lips, the sudden intensity flowing between us igniting more than just relief inside me. I've never wanted to be so close to him. I can't stop my rising desire, bursting because of his certainty in getting through this.

He lifts me off my feet, keeping the blanket snug around me, and I press my lips to his, kissing him softly and sensually, just reminding myself that I'm human and my life isn't over. I remind myself that I'm not alone.

"Never. I would never abandon you. I don't care what I have to do, but you're important to me, Eliana. You have no idea how much it kills me to know that Ravi put a claim on you. I always imagined that you would be mine." Chase swallows with his words, his soft breath tickling my skin.

I meet his gaze, staring into his beautiful caramel eyes. "He doesn't own me or control me. I might have bowed to him, but you're my real packmate. My mate. You, Adam, Evander, Davian, and Tristan. I know that it's been weird and complicated, but I—"

"You don't have to explain yourself, Eliana. I don't care if you feel connected to the others. All I care about is that you so amazingly share yourself with me." Chase kisses me again with his words, carrying me inside a small cabin, the open floor plan like a studio apartment. A dozen unfamiliar scents wrap around me, and I can tell the other wolves have been here. It's the strangest thing. I have so many questions, but Chase's sudden desperation to distract me tosses everything away along with the blanket covering my body.

I should be embarrassed by the state of my body and how

dirt smears over my skin and leaves and twigs tangle in my hair, but it's as if none of that matters. All that matters is that I'm with Chase in this moment, and he treats me as if I am everything to him.

"Because you are," he murmurs, carrying me all the way to the bathroom as if he knows that a shower would make me feel so much better.

He blindly turns on the water, sending steam through the air. Kicking out of his clothes, he holds me by my ass with one arm. I moan at the sensation of the water cascading over us, washing away the memory of the night and all of the heartache and fear that came with it.

I wiggle from Chase's arms, lowering myself to my knees, kneeling as I lace my fingers around his hard cock. He massages shampoo in my hair, moaning as I suck his dick into my mouth as he tries to take care of me, but all I want to do is take care of him. I lick him, rubbing my fingers over his balls and explore him in a way that sends a wave of lust through me. Our emotions tangle, and I swear I can feel the pleasure I bring him. It blooms wetness between my legs, and I shift and squirm, needing some sort of relief.

He hears my desires and pulls me up, only to drop down and position my leg on his shoulder. I clutch his hair and gasp as his mouth caresses over my body, his tongue gliding across my clit in even strokes, sending my head spinning with bliss. It feels so incredible. All I can think about is how I want more.

How I need more. Chase brings me more than just protection. He brings me love and companionship. He is everything I want in a man. Everything I never knew I truly needed.

My body spasms, the intensity of my orgasm making me scream out in pleasure. Chase lifts me back up and grabs a towel, wrapping it around us only to move us from the shower to the small bed. He drops me down, bowing to kiss me again, the scent of our passion so fragrant and intoxicating that all I can do is whimper.

The need to be with him overwhelms me, and I reach between us and grab his cock, aligning it to my body. Chase groans as he teases me with his tip, and he stretches both of my legs over my head, exposing my clit to him and giving him the view he wants as he enters me.

The pressure of his cock sliding into me makes my eyes roll in pleasure, and I grip the blankets, moaning as he thrusts, his passion as feral as his wolf and as wild as my free spirit begging to take control to steal my reserve away.

"You're so sexy, Eliana. So smart and fierce. You're my perfect mate. I want you to be mine," Chase murmurs the words, bracing on my legs as he kneels and thrusts inside of me over and over, stretching my body in ways that I know I won't forget as the ache will linger.

He strokes his finger over my exposed clit, strumming my body as he brings me to my peak again, making me come. His body tenses as mine tightens around his, and a more intense pressure steals my breath away. It surprises the both of us, and Chase bows forward, inhaling a breath by my ear.

I whimper as he tries to slide out of me, but the pressure increases even more. Fear clenches my chest, and my eyes widen. We stare at each other in shock, realizing that we are wolf-shifters, and we might have similarities to wolves, even in our human states.

I never even considered that things could be different, and obviously, neither had he.

"Fuck, Eliana..." Chase lets his voice fade as his mind turns to how wolves mate. It's the last thing I want to think about in this moment, but now that it's in my mind, I know that we're fucked. There's only one way we can break apart.

I did bow as an omega after all, but that means that Chase is...

"I was changed by an alpha. It was a way to give me more strength in an attempt to create more power." Chase shakes his head, slowly trying to ease his body away, but all it does is intensify the pressure.

I gasp and cling onto him, digging my fingers into his ass. "Don't. It hurts."

His face scrunches in worry. "I'm so sorry."

I'm sorry too. I don't say the words out loud though. Instead, I inhale a deep breath and pinch Chase by his chin, getting him to meet my eyes.

"You have to finish. It's going to be okay. I have my IUD.

But I think that's the only way. Just...let's just try to forget this is a thing." My voice shakes as I say the words, and I bring Chase closer and kiss again, trying to lose myself to our passion once more.

It works. I concentrate on the scent of his skin and how amazing he feels inside me. I devour his affection, helping him relax, and he thrusts slowly and evenly, not too hard but enough to bring me pleasure instead of pain.

Reaching between us, he plays with my clit again, moaning with his pleasure tingling in his body with mine, and I imagine what life will be like and how I know things will work out. I know that Chase will help bring our pack together, and we won't be in this position for long.

I orgasm again, my body tensing, and I moan and suck Chase's shoulder.

He grunts as he comes, his body reacting to mine, but he doesn't pull out. He continues to kiss me, showering me with his affection.

"I think I'm falling in love with you, Eliana. I wasn't going to say anything, but I need you to know. You don't have to say anything back. But I do love you. I want you as my mate, and I will do anything to ensure it." He smiles at me and kisses me, not allowing me to speak.

I couldn't find my voice even if I wanted to, because my body still hums, and the scent wafting from him keeps my body buzzing and turned on so that all I can think about is wanting more. Needing more.

The pressure between my legs subsides, and Chase groans as he finally manages to slide out.

He rolls over only to pull me on top of him, and I straddle his waist and plant my hands to his chest, feeling his heart beating seemingly just for me.

We stare at each other in silence, our hearts pounding and his body still ready and waiting. Chase arches up and kisses me again, lifting me to carry me back to the shower. Thoughts of caring for me twirl through my mind, his need to bathe me and feed me and cuddle me more prominent than his own desire to fuck me over and over again.

I savor his affection and love, realizing just how true it is. I've never felt an emotion like it, so raw and open and honest. I've never been in love before, but it's as if my very being recognizes it. My soul returns it.

His love for me isn't unrequited. It's everything I needed to realize that he is my perfect mate. Our pack will be stronger because of him.

A howl sounds through the air, drawing our attention. Chase cocks his head and listens, but I can't hear any voices or anything besides the howl. And it rises fear inside me.

"Come on, let's get dressed." Chase guides me from the shower again, helping me dry off and change into a summery dress. I wish he gave me pants, but I'm not sure there are any here. Wherever we are is intended to treat me like what some men define as the epitome of femininity. Whoever picked out the clothing thinks I need to be a stereotypical human female, but those times are long gone. I'm not human anymore. I'm a she-wolf. And I will bite.

Chase rushes the door, yanking an actual spear from the place where it hangs. It's the strangest thing, seeing him grab a weapon, and it also freaks me the fuck out.

"I'm still learning to transform. It'll take too long for me to try, and whoever just howled is not part of our pack. I don't recognize him." Chase remains even in tone as he tells me. How he manages to stay calm is beyond me.

"What? Where is Ravi?" I ask, looking around the room in search of my own weapon.

"He's coming. Our whole pack will be here any minute. We just need to hang tight." Chase leans close to the window, trying to peer through the curtain without opening it.

The glass explodes, startling me, and Chase lands on his back as fire licks across the floor, burning everything so quickly that I don't even get a chance to scream before the door swings open.

A man rushes toward me, his face covered with a bandanna, and he snatches me off my feet. It all happens so fast that I can't even fight before I find my hands bound behind my back.

Chase hollers, his voice filling with pain.

"Take the pup out. It'll send him a message. Eliana never

belonged to them." The deep voice is like a punch to my stomach, and I gasp, but I can't move. I can't break free.

The scent of woods, moss, and something greener like fragrance of grass permeates around me. It scares me instead of bringing me comfort.

The man tugs a bag over my head, cutting off my view of the world.

"Head east. Take anyone out that tries to get in our way." The man picks up his pace, jogging and bouncing the world around me. "And put out a call to our alliances. We have a she-wolf, and she's going to need to be claimed by an alpha. She'll need to be broken to bow. We must hurry."

My soul aches as the man puts distance between me and Chase, and Chase screams in agony, his pain hot and intense.

Then it vanishes.

A part of me dies.

To be continued...

Eliana and her wolfpack's story isn't over yet! Get lost in the wilds of Savage Wolves, book two in the Wolfpacks of Shadow Moon Island series.

OTHER REVERSE HAREM NOVELS BY GINNA MORAN

THE WOLFPACKS OF SHADOW MOON ISLAND:
Wild Wolves
Savage Wolves

THE VAMPIRE HEIRS WORLD

La Vega Vampire Showstoppers
Vampire Nights
Bloody Nights
Renegade Nights

The Divine Vampire Heirs
Blood Match
Blood Rebel
Blood Debt
Blood Feud
Blood Loss
Blood Vows
Blood Holiday

The Royale Vampire Heirs Series:
Rebel Vampires
Rebel Dhampir
Rebel Match
Rebel Heir
Rebel Fight

Academy of Vampire Heirs Series:
Dhampirs 101
Blood Sources 102
Coven Bonds 103
Personal Donors 104
Blood Wars 105

SERIES IN THE MATES OF MAGAELORUM WORLD

The Pack Mates of Lunar Crest:
The She-Wolf Games
The Wolf-Mate Trials
The Omega Hunt
The Witch Chase

Fated Mate of the Dragon Clans
Caged by Her Dragons
Freed by Her Dragons
Saved by Her Dragons

SEVEN SINNERS WORLD

The Seven Sinners of Hell's Kingdom:
Her Personal Demons
Her Deadly Angels
Her Darkest Devils
Her Sinful Saints
Her Twisted Sinners

ABOUT GINNA MORAN

GINNA MORAN IS the USA Today Bestselling author of over seventy novels including the popular The Pack Mates of Lunar Crest and The Seven Sinners of Hell's Kingdom reverse harem novels.

She always carried a fascination for all things paranormal and wrote her first unpublished manuscript at age eighteen. Her love of the supernatural grew stronger through her adult life, and she now spends her days with different creatures of the night. Whether it's vampires, werewolves, dragons, fae, angels, demons, or mermaids, Ginna loves creating and living in worlds from her dreams.

Aside from Ginna's professional life, she enjoys binge watching TV, crafting and design, playing pretend with her daughter, and cuddling with her dog. Some of her favorite things include chocolate, mermaids, anything that glitters, learning new things, cheesy jokes, and organizing her book-shelf.

Ginna is currently hard at work on her next novel and the one after, and the one after that.